THE ALLARDS

BOOK ONE
THE NEW WORLD

Wilmont R. Kreis

Second Edition

1

INTRODUCTION TO THE SECOND EDITION

This is a story. More precisely it is two stories. Most of it is true, or should I say based on records thought to be true. Some of it is fiction and some of it based on speculation of what *may* have happened.

First it is a story of my mother's ancestors. Second is the story of the people of which they were a part, their amazing journey from the old world to the new and the two new nations they would eventually help create.

When I initially wrote Book One, it was entirely for members of my immediate family. I had no idea others would be interested. But they were, and I have written this second edition to improve the rhetoric and make it more readable for the general public. The story has not changed at all. How could it? It actually happened.

PROLOGUE

During the first four centuries A.D., the area of northwest France now known as Normandie was occupied by a Celtic tribe known as the Gauls. Starting in the late 5th century, Normandie was invaded by the Franks, a fiercely independent tribe from now western Germany. The eventual population was an inbreeding of the two groups. In the ninth century the area was again invaded, this time by the Vikings, and again a mixture of the groups resulted.

The descendants of these three fierce, strong cultures are called Normands and they remain in Normandie today. In 1066 under Guillaume, the Duke of Normandie, the Normands conquered England and their genes have remained in its monarchs to this day. In the 17th century, the Normands were instrumental in the settling of the New World. It is this Normand stock that produced the Allards.

Five men named Allard came to the new world, but only one left a large, lasting progeny. Today there are many of his descendants in Canada and the United States. The name Allor is also now commonly used in the United States.

My mother was born Gladys* Genevieve Allard in 1917. This is the story of her family who experienced the early voyages from Europe to found the New World. They

8

witnessed the building of America. They were in Detroit at the signing of the Declaration of Independence and stayed to the present day. Taking my inspiration from Alex Haley, I have decided to tell their story. At the end I hope to have *Les racines canadienne française* or the French-Canadian roots. Realizing this will be a rather long story, it will be told in segments.

At the end I have listed the important fabrications for accuracy, however all these people did exist and the major events are all accurate. This is for the most part the true story of her ancestors. I hope not only to tell the names and vital statistics of these people, but also who they were and why they did what they did, perhaps giving some insight into who we are and why.

As many of the people in the story have the same first name, each of my mother's actual ancestors has an asterisk* after their Christian name to help distinguish them from the many other Pierres, Maries, etc.

THE ALLARDS
BOOK ONE
THE NEW WORLD

MAIN CHARACTERS

Organized by groups, some people appear in more than one group. Ancestors are noted with asterisk.

François* Allard: First immigrant Allard ancestor.

Jeanne* Anguille: His wife, *Fille du Roi.*

Father André Anguille: Jeanne*'s brother, a priest.

Came to Canada with François*

Marguerite Bourgeoys: Patron Saint of Canada, organized the *Filles du Roi* program and accompanied the group that came at the time of François*.

Jean* Poitevin dit Laviolette : Came to Canada with François* and became his neighbor.

Guillaume* Renaud : Soldier with the Carignan Regiment, came to Canada with François* and became his neighbor.

Mathurine* Gouard : Came to Canada as a *Fille du Roi* with François*. They fell in love and he gave her half of a wampum he received from an Indian.

Came to Canada with Jeanne*

Anne Gasnier-Bourdon: Wealthy widow who sponsored the *Filles du Roi* and accompanied Jeanne* to Canada. She helped arrange Jeanne*'s marriage with François*.

Madeleine de Roybon: Wealthy girl sent to Canada by her father as a *Fille du Roi* to escape her scandalous behavior. She came with Jeanne* and they became close friends. She continued her lifestyle and became the mistress of LaSalle.

Neighbors of Jeanne* and François*

Guillaume* Renaud : Soldier with the Carignan Regiment, came to Canada with François*.

Anne* Ardouin-Badeau : Early settler of Québec. A widow, she hired François* when he arrived in Québec.

Pierre* Tremblay: Early immigrant from Perche. Worked as a lumberjack in the off-season.

Noel* Langlois: Early settler of Québec and prominent citizen who befriended François*.

Noel* Morin: Early settler and carriage maker.

Helene* Desportes: His wife.

The Indians

<u>Henri:</u> Algonquin brave, worked for Anne* Ardouin, he became a good friend of François*.

<u>Angélique:</u> His wife.

<u>Philippe:</u> His son who accompanied François* to his farm.

<u>Marie:</u> His wife.

<u>Anuk:</u> Henri's brother who lived in the wilderness.

PART ONE

FRANÇOIS*

Chapter 1

Saint Joan of Arc Church, St. Clair Shores, Michigan - The
Present Day:

Limping as briskly as he could away from the church
and toward the rectory, Harvey Allor realized today was
going to be a scorcher. Channel Four said it might hit
ninety by noon. Entering the rectory, only slightly cooler,
he found Father Socia seated at his desk intent on his
computer screen.

"You wanted to see me, Father?"

Socia looked up, "Yes, Harvey, There's a contractor
uncovering the northeast corner of the church foundation
today, trying to see why it's cracking. Keep an eye on them,
would you?" and with a wink added, "Don't let them knock
the whole building down."

"Sure thing, Father," Harvey replied as he turned to
leave.

The priest watch the older man limp out of the door.
Harvey Allor had come to work at the parish a short while
before Father Socia had arrived. Allor had come to the
church in ruins after years of drinking following the death
of his wife. Here he had turned his life around and was now
indispensable; he knew every inch and every quirk of the
buildings.

The truck labeled "Maison Excavating" sat at the
corner of the church, and old Ben Maison sat in his usual
perch on the front bumper with his trademark cigar butt in
the corner of his mouth. Standing shoulder deep in a hole at

the corner of the building was Ben's oldest son, Leonard, scraping dirt from the foundation with a spade.

"How's it goin', men?" Harvey asked leaning over the hole.

Ben replied, "Looks like the new foundation is separating from the old. Seems this foundation was put smack on top of the old one. We'll hav'ta shore it up with a new footing."

Hearing a metal on metal clang Leonard disappeared into the hole. As he arose he shouted, "Hey, Harvey, I think I found your old lunch box." He handed an old metal box up to his father. Taking it to the back of the truck Ben managed to pry open the lid.

"Well, what the hell do you make of this," as he produced a bag made from animal hide and decorated with beads.

Harvey took the box, "I better show this to the Father." And he limped off.

The priest removed the old sack. In it he found an intricately carved wooden amulet adorned with small beads made from shells. It was actually two identical pieces fit precisely together. Next to it was a very old metal medallion on a leather strap. He remarked, "These look like Indian artifacts. I'm going to the Archdiocese this afternoon and I'll see if they have anything to say about it."

A few days later he received a call. "Father Socia, this is Jim Trombley from the Burton Historical Collection. The Archbishop asked me to look at your box. Where exactly did you find this?"

Socia replied, "It was buried at the bottom of the foundation of the original church which was built about 1920. The current church was built over it in the early sixties. What do you make of it?"

"I need to study it a little more, but the sack and the wooden object would be Indian. They are from different cultures and neither from around here. I would guess the sack is Iroquois from the Lake Champlain region of New York State. The wooden object is Algonquin, but not Chippewa. It's more eastern, probably *Abenaki,* from eastern Québec. The most remarkable thing, however, is the medallion. It's a European religious medal, but would seem to date from well before Columbus!"

Chapter 2

<u>Rouen, Normandie, France - 1431:</u>

With his face in his hands, Jean* Allard sat on the steps of the church of Saint-Maclou. He was even more set by despair than usual. Looking considerably older than his years, his hair was already turning grey. The truth be known, he was not yet twenty-two, although he was not certain of his actual age. His life had been that of war. The war between France and England had raged in his homeland since before the birth of his grandfather.

As a boy he had lived on land worked by his peasant father. Both of Jean*'s older brothers had been taken off to war and died in battle. His sister had been carried off and both his parents succumbed to the plague, leaving Jean* alone at the age of ten. He had never known a good year for farming; if the weather was good the crops were still ruined by marauding soldiers.

Arising, he wandered across the square and into the shoemaker's shop. "They did it, Guillaume, the godless bastards did it." He was speaking to an older man working at his bench. The man was his Uncle Guillaume, the younger brother of Jean*'s late mother. Guillaume took Jean* in and had made him an apprentice at his shoemaking trade. "She was no witch. She was hardly a woman, more a girl in truth; but she led the King's forces to victory at Orleans and returned the King to his throne." Slumping into an old wooden chair, "For this they give her to the devil Cauchon, and when she won't confess, he has her burned.

17

Chapter 3

Rouen, Normandie, France - September 1665:

The countryside of Normandie had not changed much in the 399 years since Guillaume the Conqueror marched across it to sail to England. In fact, it has not changed much even today. Rolling green farmland with interspersed fields of bright yellow and pale gold, each farm bounded by trees and hedgerows. Each small town on the rise of the hill as it was originally built for protection. Each hilltop crowned with the spire of a small stone church, each spire topped with a cross.

The sight François* loved most in autumn was that of the wheat fields. On a sunny day as today, the fields seemed to be the color of true gold. Or so he thought. The only gold François* had seen was the crown of the blessed virgin in the cathedral at Rouen, and actually that was paint. However, he was sure this was the color, made more spectacular by the bright green of the grass and the apple orchards. The trees were now filled with ripe apples ready for harvest and the fabrication of the wonderful *Cidre Normand* and the more wonderful strong Calvados.

This morning, François* was on his way to Rouen on an errand for his father. He had hitched a ride with his friend, Pierre, taking his cart full of produce from his family's farm to the market. Pierre liked the company and the help unloading, and François* was grateful for the ride. François* studied the fields of sheep starting their winter coats, and the fields of typical brown and white, and black and white Normand cows. François* preferred the classic *tete noir* or black faced cows with a totally white body and black head, but no matter, because François* would never have a cow, or a wheat field for that matter.

As bright and wonderful as the rolling Normand countryside was today, François*'s prospects were bleak. His father, Jacques* Allard was a shoemaker, a good trade; but François*'s brother, Jacques, was eldest, had learned the trade and was assuming his father's duties. There was certainly only room for one shoemaker in their small town of Blacqueville, 10 miles to the northwest of Rouen. This was not important to François* as he did not care for the shoe trade, he wanted to be a farmer. He had worked for Pierre's father since he could hold a farming tool.

His friend Pierre would take over his father's farm. Admittedly it was not his father's land or farm. It belonged like all the farms in Blacqueville to Monsieur Longchamps, *le sieur de Blacqueville*. Pierre's family worked the land and paid a high tax to Monsieur Longchamps who then paid the Duke of Normandie who then paid the archbishop of Rouen and the King. But Pierre's father was the managing tenant because his father and grandfather had been the managing tenants before him.

The only hope for François* was to continue to work as a *journalier* or day laborer for Pierre's father. François* loved farming and was very good at it. He was bigger and stronger than most of the men, and smarter too. Pierre's father often looked to him for advice, but alas, his future was no better than that of a black face cow.

The men (they were hardly boys, François* was 26 and Pierre one year his junior) arrived at the market and unloaded the goods. François* left to do his father's business. Passing the enormous cathedral of Notre-Dame de Rouen with its high gothic spires and large stained glass windows, he peeked in at the gold crown on the virgin. A few paces down the street stood the church of Saint-Maclou, also an impressive gothic edifice in its own right but not like the cathederal. François* wondered as he often did, why there was a need for a grand church for the rich and another for the poor.

After completing his business, he returned to the market. François* studied the statue on the eastern edge of the market place. It was a monument to a peasant girl from the east of France who had been burned at the stake in this market place in 1431. The girl was known as Jeanne d'Arc and she would some day become the patron saint of France.

His attention was quickly drawn to a group of young men listening to a well-dressed gentleman outside the local tavern. He was an older man, and a persuasive speaker. He was an agent of Robert Giffard, a surgeon from the region of Perche, a day's ride south of Rouen. Some years before, Giffard had abandoned his practice to become a recruiter for his friend Samuel Champlain and the *Compagnie des Indes* to recruit colonists to New France. He was particularly interested in young, strong, committed men.

The speaker was explaining that the men could sign a contract to be transported across the Atlantic to the Colony of Québec where they would agree to work for room and board for three years. At the end of this time they could return to France or remain in Québec as they wished. François* had heard of Québec from the men in the taverns in Rouen. He had heard that many of those who went to Québec returned with stories of a cold and savage country. The speaker told him Québec held opportunities not available in France for those strong enough to meet the challenge.

After the market, François* convinced Pierre to come see the gentleman, but Pierre had thoughts of the farm he was to manage and François*'s cousin, Monique, whom he planned to marry. François*, on the other hand, had few prospects. The youngest of three children, his older brother Jacques was already taking over their father's shoemaking business, and his sister, Marie had recently married. His mother had died and his father was helping Jacques in the shop. The lure of adventure and opportunity was more than he could ignore. François* signed the document provided and agreed to sail for New France in the spring.

On the way out of town, François* asked Pierre to stop at the cemetery of Saint-Maclou near the main town square. Before her death, his mother had asked the children to stop here when they came to Rouen and say a prayer for her mother who had come to Rouen many years earlier to help nurse the victims of a plague that devastated the area. She also fell ill and was buried here in a mass grave.

The cemetery was in a courtyard surrounded by the charnel house, where bones from exhumed graves were stored to make way for newer bodies to be buried. The walls of the building were intricately carved with macabre scenes of death. In the center of the yard stood a sole monument to the victims of this and other plagues. As he looked up he could see the spires of the two great churches, Saint-Maclou and the giant cathedral of Notre-Dame de Rouen.

François* removed his hat, crossed himself and said a brief prayer for a grandmother he never knew; but his thoughts were on the other side of the world, and the tale he had heard today of a wild and savage country where a man such as himself could have his own land.

Chapter 4

<u>Blacqueville, Normandie, France - The Next Day:</u>

Jacques* Allard was tired. His eyes and back were getting weaker and he could only work at his shoemaker's bench for a few hours a day. Jacques* was now in his sixties, his wife, Jacqueline* Frerot, had died two years before. He saw his oldest boy, also Jacques, only when he went to the shop as the boy was married and had his own family. Jacques*'s only daughter, Marie, was newly married and only young François* was left at home.

That morning, when François* entered the shop, the old man knew that something was on his mind. François* recounted the story of the man in Rouen and the contract. The old man's heart sank, but he knew that there was little for the young man in Blacqueville and remembered his own younger brother who died in a farming accident while working as a *journalier*. King Louis XIV had begun to turn his lodge at Versailles into a palace, which promised to keep the French tax burden high. So the old man reluctantly gave his blessing.

As he watched his son's jubilant face, he remembered his own father. François* had his unusual eyes. It was only striking once one noticed them. They were different. The left eye was dark brown like most of the Normands, but the right was light green. Jacques*'s father had told him his grandfather had had such eyes as well. When François* was baptized, the curé told Jacques* Alexander the Great was said to have such eyes. Jacques* was certain his own father, always an adventurer, would approve of François*'s plan.

As François* exited his father's shop, the day seemed as bright to the young man as it seemed dim to his father. Across from the few shops and tavern on his side of the street was the church of Notre-Dame de Blacqueville where the Allards had been baptized, married and buried. François* had been baptized in 1639, and now at the age of 26 he was more than ready to go. The cemetery in back held many Allards including his mother whose wooden cross was still bright and easily read.

Plunging into a working frenzy during the next six months, François* turned no job down, trying to earn as much as he could to start his new life. That winter was very cold and there was more snow than anyone could remember, but François* felt it would only help harden him for the frozen world ahead.

In the spring of 1666 the time for François*'s departure had arrived, he gathered his few belongings and the few francs he had saved and said his farewells. His father took a medallion from around his neck and gave it to François*, "They say the first Allard in Blacqueville came at the time of Jeanne d'Arc wearing this medal. I was planning to give it to Jacques, but you will need its luck more than he." François* felt a slight tingle as the medallion touched his skin. As François* kissed his old father's cheek and turned away to leave, they both knew he would not see France, or the family again.

Chapter 5

Dieppe, Normandie, France - June 1, 1666:

Walking across the rolling hillsides and through the small villages, François* made the 50 mile journey in three days. He passed numerous farms and many herds of his favorite *tete noir* cows. He had never been anywhere but Rouen and the villages between it and Blacqueville. He kept the sun on his right in the morning and his left in the afternoon. The next town was always identifiable by the next visible church spire, usually on a small hill.

To save money he slept in the fields at night which was never difficult in June. On the third day, he climbed an unusually high hill, and there he saw the masts. A few paces further, for the first time in his life, he saw the ocean! He thought he was prepared for this sight but it was grander than he could have ever imagined. If anything rivaled a golden wheat field, it was this. A cautious man may have been daunted at this point by the prospect of the traverse, but François* had nothing but enthusiasm as he began his descent to Dieppe.

On the road into Dieppe he was almost run over by several carts, laden with fish and rushing south as fast as the horses could gallop. He asked an old man at the entry to town what they were.

"Going off to the markets in Paris, the sooner they arrive, the richer they get."

Dieppe takes its name from the Viking word for deep. The harbor was not large, but to François*, it was enormous. Four sailing vessels lay at anchor, the largest at least 200 feet long. There were many fishing vessels of all sizes, and everywhere there was activity as he had never seen it.

The fishermen emptied their boats of nets with an amazing array of all manner of fish and sea creatures François* had never seen. They were surrounded by shouting crowds, checking their catches and bargaining to purchase them. François* walked to the end of the harbor to see the ocean. He had heard of water with no land in sight, but it was more than he had dreamed.

There was a fresh westerly breeze and wonderful white caps on each wave. A large triple-masted boat made its way toward the harbor with all sails open as it moved majestically through the waves. As it made land the sails began to be furled and the boat slowed. Three smaller boats with many oarsmen went to greet it.

The town of Dieppe faced the harbor. It had a row of buildings each as high as four stories. The buildings virtually ringed the harbor. François* had been instructed to go to the *Terre Sauvage* Inn, and he was pleased when he found it so easily. Upon entering he collided with a man younger and shorter than himself and decidedly intoxicated. François* excused himself and the man continued out. The ground floor was a typical harbor tavern and quite busy this afternoon. He enquired about the *Compagnie des Indes,* and the innkeeper told him the recruiter would be there in the morning.

"Will you be needing a bed, then?" he asked. François* said he would and was surprised at the low cost of a room and a meal. Francois gave the man his name and went off to see the town. The bedlam of the harbor continued. François* noticed a few men his age in military uniform, but what really caught his eye was a well dressed lady being followed by at least twenty young girls in country dresses of rough gray cloth.

Sitting down on a small bench, he was joined by an older man. "Off to the new world, I'd wager."

"Indeed," François* replied.

"You have the look. I was there some years ago myself."

"Why did you return?" François* queried.

"Sign from the Lord," he responded. "The work is hard, I'll tell you that, but the land is a thing of beauty. The winters, well, I won't tell you, wouldn't believe me any way. Have to see it yourself."

"What was the sign?"

"*Peaux rouges*"

"The what?"

"The red man, the Indians. Now they're not all bad, most of them are what they call Algonquin, good ones, even speak some French. Help with the beaver trade and the farms. No, it's the Iroquois, come from the East. Savage, evil, murderous bastards.

"I signed on for my three years working for a man and his family. Had a big farm. I was almost done with my three when one night they came. I was out in the woods, but when I came back, the house was in flames. They were all dead, cut up, hair cut off, even the little ones. I knew after that day that I could never stay."

A young man in uniform broke in, "You won't have to worry much longer friend."

"How's that?" François* asked.

"We're being sent to end it, the Carignan Regiment. We're going to fight under Marquis de Tracy and end the Iroquois problems once and for all."

The older man replied, "Well, I wish you well, son, but be careful, they're a mean lot and you can't see them or hear them until they're right upon you."

François* asked, "What about the beaver."

The older man replied, "Beaver is what started it all. See that gentleman in the tall hat? That's a beaver hat. Beaver's a critter that lives in the streams. The good Indians trap them and trade the pelts with the French *voyageurs*. The *voyageurs* comb the pelts and make the hats. Real popular in the big cities. I hear in Paris they can't get enough to sell. Big money in it."

As the older man arose to leave, François* had one last question, "How will I know which Indians are the Iroquois?"

The old man gave him a sinister look and replied, "Oh, you will know, my friend, you will know."

François* arose and made his way back to the *Terre Sauvage* Inn. The innkeeper sat him at a table with the young man who had almost run him over earlier in the day.

The younger man extended his hand, "Jean* Poitevin at your service. Going to the New World, are we?" François* indicated that indeed he was, and a conversation ensued. Poitevin was from Dampierre-sur-Boutonne in the Poitou region near Larochelle. He had come by boat from Larochelle a week earlier and was also to join the *Compagnie des Indes* the next day.

They were joined by three men in uniform including the young soldier François* had encountered at the harbor. "Guillaume* Renaud of the Carignan Regiment, Company Colonelle, going to fight the Iroquois." He was a bright lad, a few years younger than François* and from the town of Saint-Jouin-sur-mer 20 miles south of Dieppe.

They were joined by another man named Lemieux from La Rochelle. He too was bound for the colonies and a lively conversation ensued. Dinner arrived and François* realized why the price was low. It was a greasy soup and a roll with a mug of the worst cider he had ever tasted. After dinner the older man from the harbor happened by and placed a large bottle of Calvados on the table.
"Something to fortify you bucks for your voyage." François* and Renaud, being from Normandie, had grown up with the potent liqueur and knew how to drink it and how not to drink it. The burning liquid was said to "put a hole" in one's stomach to aid with digestion after a large, fat-laden Normand meal.

The two Normand lads sipped it sparingly whereas the others drank freely. Eventually it was time to retire. The innkeeper escorted them to a room and again the reason for the economy was evident as there were six men in a small room with one bed. François* and Poitevin decided the floor would be better than sharing the bed and set in for the night.

That morning François* rose early. The room smelled worse than Pierre's father's barn. He gathered his meager belongings and went down to the tavern. The other men not as knowledgeable in the ways of Calvados would come down later and in a decidedly less jovial mood. Breakfast was a hard roll and a cup of a dark brown substance accused by the innkeeper as being coffee. François* was told the agent would arrive soon so he waited outside where the activity of the harbor was even more intense than yesterday. Eventually, the same man he had met in Rouen entered carrying a chest of documents. He was accompanied by a well-dressed man in his forties.

Back in the Inn, the two men sat behind a table set up as a desk, and thirty men of various ages sat or stood in front. The younger man introduced himself as André Leblanc. He would be their representative on the voyage. "I am delighted to introduce our guest, Monsieur Nicolas Juchereau, Sieur de Saint-Denis. He will be accompanying us to Québec." François* later discovered that Monsieur Juchereau was a prominent fur merchant and one of the richest men in Québec. His father, Jean Juchereau, had help found the *Compagnie des Indes* that recruited settlers and *Compagnie des 100 Associés* that managed Québec in the name of the King.

Leblanc continued, "If the winds remain favorable, we will board tomorrow before dawn. You will be assigned quarters and may remain above deck for the departure.

While at sea you are under the absolute authority of Captain Pelletier. Other rules will be discussed on board tomorrow. Upon our arrival in Québec, you will be selected by employers. You will work for these people for three years; you will be compensated by room and board.

"You will be indentured for this time. That is to say, you may not quit or leave. You may only marry under special circumstances and with the permission of your employer. You may be transferred to another employer if deemed necessary. At the end of three years, you may apply with us for passage back to France or for residency in Québec. I assure you the work will be difficult, but I can further assure you that the rewards, if you are faithful to your work, will be greater than any available in France."

Later in the afternoon, some of the men had gathered down by the harbor to swap tales they had heard about monsters, winter, and Indians. François*'s friend from yesterday happened by, and François* said, "Here's a man who can tell us about it, he's been there." The older man sat down and began to hold court.

"What's the difference between Canada and Québec?" someone asked.

"Canada's the whole place. It's an Indian word that Cartier learned when he landed over 100 years ago. No one has seen it all, some say it goes all the way to China. Québec is where the government is. It's a big area too, but it's also the name of the town."

"What are the towns like?" another shouted.

The man replied, "Most towns are nothing more than a cabin for trading. Québec's the city, but it's not a city like

33

Rouen, more like one of our villages. No, it's the country that's different… Woods so thick it's like night inside at noon, water so clear you can see the bottom at 100 feet and it tastes the way God meant water to taste. There's so many fish you can catch a week of meals in an hour; and the animals, the woods are full. And not just rabbits and the like, but big deer, mountain lions, and bears as big as a house. So many turkeys you can hardly walk without tripping on them."

"How about the Indians?" another asked.

"The Algonquin are good. I had two friends who run off with them and never came back."

"Why would they want to live in the woods?" asked one of the boys from the city.

"Indians got their ways in the woods; they know them, understand them. They're wild but they have a real society about them. And they say the Indian women like to work hard and are real warm at night."

After a short laugh, another asked, "How about the bad Indians?"

He replied, "Iroquois are real savages, worse then the bears and mountain lions. They'll skin and cook you while you're alive, eat you while you're still screaming. I heard a man tell how they cut out a man's heart while it was still beating." With this story the men began to drift off.

That evening the group for dinner was larger and the celebration more lively, even François* had more Calvados than he should. Before dawn they were up and making their way to the harbor regretting the revelry of the evening. Jean* Poitevin stopped at the roadside and picked a few spring flowers. He said, "My mother always said that violets bring luck".

Chapter 6

<u>The English Channel, June 6, 1666 - First Day at Sea:</u>

They met Monsieur Leblanc in front of the ship *l'Aigle d'Or* or Golden Eagle. It was one of the largest in the harbor and François* was pleased. The roll was called and only 29 were present. "Where's Lemieux?" asked Leblanc.

Poitevin replied, "I believe he may have run off after our discussion of Indians."

"Just as well," said Leblanc as he led the men below to a corner in the front of the hold where they were assigned a section of floor. The only light was through the openings for the canons with which they shared their quarters. "You men may go above for now, but stay out of the way and obey the seamen. We will meet again after we're well under way."

Once above, François* and Jean* were amazed at the activity. All manner of tools and machinery were loaded. François* began to realize that all things modern would have to make this long journey from France. There were other men like Monsieur Juchereau in fine dress with large chests of goods. They were housed on the main deck. Twenty men in uniform including their friend Guillaume* Renaud boarded and were stationed in the hold but in a more spacious location toward the center.

With amazement they saw six horses lifted aboard on slings one by one. A man nearby told them, "That's a more important cargo than us. There were no horses in Canada two years ago and these six are going to double the number in all of Québec."

Then the most amazing part of the cargo, the well-dressed lady he had seen in the harbor followed by 24 young ladies in gray country dress each carrying a small chest. "This can make our stay below more interesting," said Jean*. François* remained silent. He then spied his old friend from the harbor waving at them from the dock.

"What are you about?" shouted Jean*.

"I'm how you get out of the harbor," returned the man, lifting up a large oar. "My new job."

Soon the men saw three long skiffs each with 30 men including their old friend and each man with a long oar. As they took lines from the ship and started to row, to the amazement of the men, *l'Aigle d'Or* began to move. It turned and slowly gained speed. Soon the seamen began to unfurl the sails and the boat proceeded at a surprising speed as it left the skiffs and headed to sea.

l'Aigle d'Or was a fine, sturdy craft: 110 feet in length it held 10 cannon, 5 per side. It had three large masts now with canvas sails being unfurled by the seamen as the boat took on an impressive speed. There were three decks, the first elevated and crowded with ropes with men managing them. The back deck was highest and held the helmsman behind his large wheel. The cabins below it had real windows, and were reserved for the officers and wealthy passengers.

The central, largest, and lowest deck where François* and Jean* stood with many other passengers was the busiest area, full of lines and other implements that were a mystery to François*. As they glided into the English Channel, their soldier friend, Guillaume* Renaud came by and pointed to the coast of France. "There is my home, St. Jouin de-le-mer, above the cliffs". François* could see high gray cliffs. "North of that are the famous cliffs of Etretat reaching out into the sea, with giant holes worn by many years of waves. They look like an elephant, drinking from the sea."

François* could not envision this and he also wasn't certain what an elephant looked like. At this time Monsieur Leblanc appeared and ordered the men to come below. As usual, Jean* was slow to respond. "You with the flowers, *Laviolette,* come along." Below decks he continued, "Dinner will be here each night at sunset. Be on time or go hungry. Breakfast is at dawn. Keep your area clean and clear. Each morning a man will be assigned to empty and clean the toilet buckets. No fighting, gambling, or drinking other than what is served. You will be allowed above deck twice a day, weather permitting. Every third day you will be able to bathe above deck. Are there questions?"

Jean* responded, "Who are the ladies?"
The answer, "They are of no concern to you, and the captain has assured me if any of you bother them in any way you will be invited to walk the plank. Also if you have valuables, guard them well." François* had little to lose,

his few coins were always close on him and his few clothes were of little value. He was also among the tallest and strongest men in the group and it was unlikely that he would be troubled by the others.

Then the question no one had asked, "How many days to Québec?"

"It depends mainly on the weather, usually about two months, I've made it in just over 3 weeks. Three years ago *le Neptune* took 117 days." The silence was deafening as reality set in.

Dinner was a grease soup and hard roll with a dark beverage described as wine but falling somewhat short of the mark. The close quarters and the fact that the six horses were in makeshift stalls across the hold made François* think that the room at the *Terre Sauvage* was rather luxurious, but with the excitement of the day and the gentle rocking of the boat, the men were soon asleep.

Chapter 7

<u>The English Channel - June 7, 1666 - Day Two at Sea:</u>

As directed, the group arose at dawn. Having drawn the first toilet bucket duty, François* carried the buckets two at a time to an opening where they could be spilled into the sea, then lowered down on a rope to be rinsed. The unpleasant task took about an hour. Fortunately a stable-hand provided this service for the six horses.

Breakfast was dinner without the soup, a hard roll and cup of water. Some of the men passed on breakfast as their stomachs were not accustomed to the roll of the sea. Fortunately François* found he was not prone to *mal-de-mer* or seasickness, probably for all the years working in the waves of the wheat fields.

Later that day, he and Jean* Poitevin were allowed above, and the sight of the sea was refreshing to say the least. The air had an aroma that surprised François* with its smell, salty and fishy, but at the same time as clean as any air he had breathed. The fresh westerly breeze continued to require the boat to sail at angles to the wind and consequently at angles to the direct route of their destination. "It's called tacking," explained a seaman, "The boat cannot sail into the wind directly, but we can adjust the sails so we can sail closer to it. We'd rather have the wind at our back but that's not common on this side of the voyage. On the way back to France it's quicker as the wind is often behind us."

"Lots of good it will do us", complained Jean*. The coast of Dieppe had disappeared, but now they could begin to see the western tip of Normandie at Cherbourg.

The seaman continued, "Tomorrow or the next day we may see the tip of Bretagne or the tip of England depending on the wind and the direction we sail. After that it's only blue for many days. But look! There's a sight you won't get everyday!" A school of porpoises swam along jumping ahead of the bow. "It's a good sign, means a few days of good weather."

François* was heartened by the beauty and comfort of the sea. Having adjusted to the motion, he came to love the sight of the sea with its fresh white caps and clear spring sky. Suddenly Monsieur Leblanc appeared and called, "Allard, time to go below, bring *Laviolette* with you." It appeared that the nickname was going to stick.

Dinner was the same and every bit as awful as the previous evening. A man named Dery had a fiddle, and one named Deschamps had a concertina. They played into the evening, and the tight quarters began to seem a bit friendlier. Monsieur Leblanc came down the spiral staircase leading from above deck into the hold. Addressing the group, "You may have lost track of days, but tomorrow is Sunday and Captain Pelletier has invited everyone above at dawn for a short service before breakfast."

Chapter 8

The English Channel - Sunday June 8, 1666 - Day Three at Sea:

It was the first time all passengers and crew had met together. Along with the 29 men with François*, the 20 soldiers, 24 young ladies, two small families, crew, officers and a few gentlemen passengers, they numbered just over 120. Captain Pelletier spoke, "I had hoped to be accompanied by a *curé* so we could have a mass each Sunday, but he was taken gravely ill and could not accompany us. We are, however, fortunate to have Sister Marquerite Bourgeoys who is directing a group of young ladies. She has agreed to lead us in prayer. We shall try to do so each Sunday, weather permitting. Sister."

The older lady in religious dress stepped forward, "*Merci*, Captain Pelletier."
As she moved forward, she stumbled and the book she carried slid across the deck toward the edge. François* leaped forward, also sliding and grasped the book just as it began to plunge toward the sea. In the process he put a gash in his forehead. He returned it to the nun who replied, "Thank you, young man, but I fear you have been damaged."
Applying a handkerchief to his wound, François* replied, "It's nothing, sister, please continue."

They did continue with prayers and a hymn. They were then dismissed for breakfast. Stopping François*, Sister Bourgeoys said, "Please young man, you must allow me to attend to your wound." François* began to protest, but this was certainly not someone who took no for an answer. She led him down the spiral stairs and to the rear of the boat and the forbidden stronghold of the young women.

Seating him on a barrel, she had him remove his bloody shirt and gave it to a young girl instructing her to rinse the blood from it. She then washed his head with salt water and then applied a brown salve that burned like fire. The giggles from the shadows of the ladies' quarters turned François*'s face as red as his blood.

"What is your name, young man?"

"Allard, François*Allard, Sister."

"And where is your home?"

"Blacqueville, near Rouen, Sister."

"Ah, the Normand men are always most polite, the young Normande ladies as well. The book you saved is most valuable, not just for its prayers and hymns, but I keep the papers pertinent to my work in it as well. I fear it would have been a catastrophe had it gone into the sea." She continued, "My work is with the convent in Québec. I sponsor these young women to come to our great new land and help our young settlers such as yourself raise great new families. Most of my work is in Ville-Marie, although most of these girls will be staying in Québec or Trois Rivieres."

She handed him his shirt. "This is still damp but we've removed the blood, it will dry, and thank you once more."

"It was nothing, Sister, and you should not have troubled yourself."

"Nonsense, now go back to your friends."

43

When François* returned to the front of the hold, the others looked at him with mouths gaping. "Well, Allard, that's the luckiest cut forehead you'll have."

Jean* broke in, "What was it like, François*? Did you see the girls? Who are they?"

"I saw nothing. The Sister cleaned my wound is all. I can tell you that that end of the boat smells some better than this end."

Dery broke in, "They don't have horses at that end."

A man named Moreau replied, "The horses make it smell better, besides we have *Laviolette* as well," referring to Jean* Poitevin's new nickname.

"But who are they?" asked Petite, a young man from the country.

Moreau replied, "Leblanc told me they're *Filles du Roi.*"

"What is that?" questioned the youth.

"Single women recruited for the King and sent to Québec to be wives for the settlers," answered Moreau.

"Maybe we should look them over so we can have first pick," said Petite.

"Dream on, *mon vieux,* you will not marry anyone for three years, and these women don't want you, they want men with established farms."

Dery broke in, "I hear some are from Paris, and some have been *putain.* I have also heard that some from Larochelle are Huguenots and our *curé* told us that if you make love to them, they'll cut off your manhood."

At this point Monsieur Leblanc appeared, "Well lads, I see you've identified the ladies. I must tell you that these are virtuous girls from good families and they have no interest in you or your manhood, Monsieur Dery."

"Is it true some are Huguenots, sir."

"I don't know, but they won't let them sail unless they have renounced it. Now let's get above, it's your day to bathe."

The men disrobed on deck and were provided with buckets of seawater and a lye soap that seemed to remove one's skin with the dirt. The salt rinse took some getting used to, but it was better than nothing. Another young man had another query, "What do you mean by Huguenot."

Moreau responded, "Did they teach you nothing in the country? Huguenots are Calvinists, Protestants, non-believers. They let them live in the south around Larochelle. In Rouen we banish them to the galleys or put them in jail."

François* remained silent. His mother had told him of Huguenots. She said they had been massacred in the last century, but Good King Henri IV had signed the Edict of Nantes giving rights to Protestants. Henri's son, Louis XIII, however, had repealed it and since then, they had been treated poorly in many areas of France. François*'s mother had said the Lord would not make them if they were no good and they should be tolerated. However, she had warned François* not to say this publicly.

Chapter 9

The Atlantic Ocean - June 20, 1666 - Day 14 at Sea:

Standing at the rail, François* and Jean* watched the sea. The voyage had been tolerable, almost tranquil. A steady wind and two days of light rain helped the ship obtain fresh water and allowed the men to remove the salt by standing in the downpour. The western sky was becoming dark and François* thought this would probably bring more rain. He relished the thought of another rinse.

Appearing on the back deck referred to as the bridge, Captain Pelletier called to the head seaman, Monsieur Denoyer, also called the first mate, "Prepare to reef the sails and batten the hatches, I fear we are in for a blow."

One of the sailors came by and told the men to return to the hold. "Can't we at least stay out to rinse?" François* asked.

"You may get a chance to rinse right overboard if you stay here. You lads have yet to see a storm."

As they descended the spiral staircase, François* reflected that he had seen many storms and did not see how there would be a problem with a boat as big and sturdy as *l'Aigle d'Or*. Once below the seaman instructed them, "See all your things are securely tied down, I must see to the cannons."

"Why do you need the cannons," asked François*.

"They must be lashed down well, the last thing we need in a storm is a loose cannon."

A few minutes later they heard the first roll of thunder, then rain on the deck. François* wished he could sneak out to rinse when the boat started to roll more than previously. The stable hand came over and asked François* and some others to help him secure the six horses. "You others empty all the toilet buckets while you can but don't take time to rinse them."

The stable hand had covered the heads of the horses, François* knew this trick from the farm. "If they fall they'll break a leg," shouted the stable man over the rising sound of the storm. They put each horse in a sling and tied it to the ceiling so that they could not fall, then they lashed them to the bulkhead to keep them from moving sideways. "Thanks lads, now go and secure yourselves."

Back in their section, Dery asked François*, "Allard, why don't you go ask the Sister if she needs us to help secure the women?" François* thought it might not be bad if a Huguenot woman would remove Dery's manhood. The sound of the wind was now frightening. The Captain had turned the boat to the wind to ride out the storm but the rolling was much worse and not as predictable as it had been. The direction of the roll would change and throw everything off balance.

François* spoke up, "We have storms like this on the farm, they don't last long."

Several hours later, François* began to regret his words. The sound was deafening, and with each roll the boat seemed as it would overturn. There was never much to eat on the boat, but François* was certain he had lost everything he had ever consumed. Even the most seaworthy of the lads was writhing with nausea from the dreaded *mal-de-mer*.

François* was now so disoriented he was unsure of his position in the hold, but suddenly he grabbed Jean* and shouted, "Thank God! Do you hear it Jean*?"
"Hear what?"
"The wind."
"Of course I hear it, I've heard nothing else for hours."
"No, *LaViolette,* listen! It's dying."

Indeed the wind died as quickly as it had started but the end of the roll took a few hours. As soon as it was calm enough for the men to stand, jubilation prevailed. They all thanked God and congratulated one another for surviving. They helped the stable hand release the poor horses and clean up the terrible mess in the hold.

Monsieur Denoyer came down, "I'm sorry we were not able to show you men a proper storm, but perhaps this little blow has livened up your day."
"Little blow!" returned Moreau, "It was almost the dooms-day itself."
"Let me assure you, Moreau, there's much worse from whence that one came, at least this one was enough to give us some more fresh water."
"Just trying to scare us," said Moreau after the mate had returned to the deck.

After the sea had calmed, dinner was served with its usual lack of grandeur. A surprised François* found he was again hungry. Afterwards they were allowed on deck. The roll remained impressive, but it was now steady and the breeze had shifted to southeasterly allowing the boat to sail with the wind. The sunset was spectacular. One of the seamen told them, "It's always the best after a blow. I think it is God's reward for braving the storm."

Chapter 10

<u>The Atlantic Ocean - The Evening of July 10, 1666 - Day 33 at Sea:</u>

The day was fair. The weather had been good for several days. There had been some rain, but generally good winds and a few small storms. One of the seamen had told François* if the weather held they could make land in two more weeks. François* and Jean stood by the rail. "Tonight is as peaceful as we've seen," said François*. "I feel that the rest of the voyage will be calm."

<u>The Atlantic Ocean - July 11, 1666 - Day 34 at Sea:</u>

The morning was glorious. François*, Moreau, and Petite surveyed the sea, not a cloud, bright sun, hardly a breeze. "A little lack of motion is just what I need," said Moreau. "I'm going to enjoy it before that dratted wind picks up at midday."

In the early afternoon the men noted the wind had not arrived as it had each previous day. In fact there was no breeze, and the day was quite hot. "If it gets much warmer, I'm up for a swim," joked Moreau. The men had been cautioned swimming in these waters was an invitation to dinner with the sharks.

After dinner there was still no breeze. The sails hung limp. The heat had abated as the sun sank, but it was extremely hot below. One of the seamen happened by and

François question him on the weather. "It's best not to say the word out loud." He replied, "Bad luck."

"What word?"

The sailor bade him to bend down, "I must whisper it in your ear." François bent forward and the man whispered almost beyond hearing, "Becalmed."

The Atlantic Ocean, - July 13, 1666 - Day 36 at Sea:

L'Aigle d'Or had not moved 100 meters in the past three days. The water barrels were locked and water strictly rationed. The captain had allowed the passengers to remain on deck, even the women who were cordoned off in a small area on the bridge. The stable hand had opened all hatches in hopes of preserving the precious horses. The heat was intense and below it was unbearable.

The Atlantic Ocean - July 14, 1666 - Day 37 at Sea:

The sun rose to an eerie sky, the horizon was entirely pink. The first mate addressed Captain Pelletier, "We shall be out of water by midday, Sir."

The captain replied, "Stop all rations until further notice." As he finished he heard the faintest noise in the distance. "Do you hear it, mister?"

" Hear what, sir?"

"Listen closely, lad."

They then heard the unmistakable sound of distant thunder. "God Almighty be praised," Pelletier murmured, "God be praised. Monsieur Denoyer, call the men and the passengers."

After he had the attention of all, he began. "Ladies and gentlemen, I believe God is about to answer our prayers, but he may do so rather violently. I believe we are in for a change in weather. You may remain on the deck until we feel the breeze, at that time you must all make haste to your quarters. I realize it is quite warm below but it will cool and time will be of the essence.

"Monsieur Denoyer, take four of Monsieur Leblanc's men to help secure the horses, and take three of your men to secure the cargo and cannons. The rest of the crew is to begin to reef the sails and secure the decks, that is all."

François* was chosen for horse detail. He could scarcely believe the heat in the hold. The horses were very lethargic and easier to secure this time. He then helped with the cannons. As they finished he felt a blessed breeze come down the hatch, and the passengers began to descend.

Jean* was among the first down, and he gave François* a bag of water. "This is your ration, drink it slowly so it will stay down. The captain said this is the end until we collect rain, but it will be soon, François*, this storm is coming very fast." With that there was a bolt of lightening that seemed to hit the ship with an instant clap of thunder. The wind and the rain began and the boat began to toss.

The motion of the boat made the previous storms seem like a waltz. People were thrown about if they lost hold. Petite cried out, "The cannon is moving!" He jumped to grab the rope as it broke and the cannon slid across the room. It collided on the other side but the collision was padded. Unfortunately it was padded with Petite. The men threw lines around the cannon and were able to secure it. François* tended to Petite who was bleeding through his mouth and couldn't speak.

François* went to the back of the hold with difficulty often crawling. "Sister!" he cried. Marquerite Bourgeoys poked her head through a canvas drape. "One of the men has been hurt badly by a rolling cannon, please come." After struggling to the front of the hold, the nun examined the youth. "I fear he needs my help as a religious more than that of a nurse." She murmured a prayer and opened his shirt, beside his entirely collapsed chest she noticed a small odd bare cross. "Huguenot!" She exclaimed quietly. She removed the cross and said to François* "Tell no one of this. We are all God's people. Wrap him in a blanket and secure the body, his soul has already left us."

One of the seamen appeared and shouted, "I require the two strongest men!" François* and Moreau went with him. "We must man the pumps, seawater is coming through the hatches and the cannon windows." They descended into the cargo hold, waist deep in water when they found the pump made to work by two large levers like a teeter-totter, François* and Moreau grabbed the handles and pumped for their lives.

Later two other men appeared, and they took turns resting and pumping. The work made the storm pass more quickly for François*. When the wind began to abate, François* was shocked to discover he had worked for ten hours. Eventually the hold was dry and the men returned to their quarters. The area looked as if a giant had overturned it.

Soon the passengers were allowed above deck. The chaos was being cleared. Sails were torn, and apparently two crewmen had been lost overboard. The Captain appeared. "There is now new water and plenty of it. Please drink some and move on. I'm asking you all to return to your quarters and make them as tidy as possible. We will try to eat soon. Tomorrow we should finally have good sailing."

The following morning, the passengers and crew assembled on deck for a service for the three souls lost during the storm. The Captain and Sister Bourgeoys said prayers. At the end, the body of Petite, wrapped in a shroud, was buried in the sea. The weather was fair and the winds were fresh and the boat was again on its way to Canada.

Chapter 11

François* and Jean* sat with a few of the other men and Monsieur Leblanc. A glorious day, the ship jumped forward with each wave, coming closer to the New World. Surveying the horizon with his long glass, the watch officer suddenly called down, "Summon the Captain at once!" Captain Pelletier arrived with Monsieur Denoyer, the first officer. They looked in turn through the glass and then summoned the crew.

From their position on the deck, François* and the others could overhear the orders. "Men, we are being followed by a larger ship which will soon over take us. This close to land we must suspect pirates. Get the passengers to their stations, man and load the cannon and prepare for battle procedure. Tell Sister Bourgeoys to follow the plan for hiding the women."

The men were hurried below, and once back at their berths, they questioned Monsieur Leblanc about the situation. Replying, "Along the costal waters of the Americas there are pirates of two sorts. Most are called privateers; they sail under the protection of a European nation and are allowed to raid the boats of other nations. Here we are most likely to encounter English privateers. They may sack the ship and take our cargo, but they will likely not harm the passengers.

"The most feared are the renegade pirates who owe allegiance to no one and will take the ship and what personnel they desire, kill the rest and sail off with the ship and all its cargo. It is likely that this much faster ship on the horizon will overtake us in less than a day's time."

The day passed slowly and the men paced nervously with no news. In the early afternoon, Monsieur Denoyer came below, "Half of the men are to take all their belongings and come with me." He led them to the forbidden rear of the hold to the women's area. "Spread out your belongings as though you have been in this spot for the entire voyage. If any strange men come, act as though you do not understand their language, even if they speak French."

François* being in this group was amazed that there was no sign of the girls and no sign that they had ever been here. He asked Denoyer, "Where are the girls?"

Denoyer replied, "They have never been here and do not say otherwise even if it means your death!"

Two hours later a great commotion arose on the deck. A seaman came hurrying down the stairway, "Good news! The boat is French, none other than Captain François Guyon and *le Faucon Noir*. Without asking permission, the men cheered and rushed to the deck. They could see the larger boat still at some distance. Leblanc said, "Guyon is himself, a famous French privateer. We won't be troubled as long as he's in the area."

l'Aigle d'Or lay to and dropped its sails to wait for the other boat. It arrived about an hour later and the long boat was lowered. The captain and some of the other men rowed to the larger boat. A short while later, the skiff returned and they called for a few of the stronger men. As usual, François* and Moreau were selected with two others and entered the smaller craft.

They boarded the deck of *le Faucon Noir* noticing ship was considerably larger than *l'Aigle d'Or* with many more cannon. It flew a strange flag with a black bird of prey and did not show the French flag, as did *l'Aigle d'Or*. On board, Captain Pelletier stood with a large, fierce looking man in a large hat, apparently Captain François Guyon, the famous French privateer. "Men, very good news. Captain Guyon informs me we are only ten days from land; furthermore, he will accompany us to the St. Laurent River. Best of all, he has just relieved an English ship bound for New York Harbor from the islands of America of some goods and is making a gift to us. You men are to load these barrels into the skiff."

François* and the others loaded the goods, and the group returned with the captain to *l'Aigle d'Or*. The two boats made sail continuing their westward journey together. That evening, the normal meal was concluded with a collection of fruits the men had never seen. They were glorious. Jean* exclaimed, "I believe we have all died and are now in heaven itself!" There was also a strange new drink, smoother and sweeter, but no less powerful than Calvados. It was called rum.

Dery and Deschamps played, and the men sang into the night. François* sneaked a look into the rear of the hold. The girls had returned as though they had never left. The passengers all slept well this night.

Chapter 12

<u>The Atlantic Ocean - July 21, 1666 - Day 44 at Sea:</u>

As François* was just finishing his usual gourmet breakfast in the hold, Monsieur Leblanc appeared and called him aside. "It appears Sister Bourgeoys has an urgent need of you," and he led François* to the rear of the hold where the nun awaited them.

"Monsieur Allard, I require a strong honest man of discretion and prudence. You seem to be the best choice on board, may I count on you totally?"

"Yes, Sister."

"One of our young ladies is gravely ill. I fear it could be cholera, and I must quarantine her from the others. Captain Pelletier has provided a room on the main deck. I will stay and nurse her when I can,. However my duties with the others will demand most of my attention. I am asking to you to stay with the young lady and help care for her and to protect her from the other men. Do you have any questions?"

"No, Sister."

"Very well, first of all we must carry her above," and they moved into the shrouded quarters where the young ladies who stood off to the side, somewhat frightened but obviously interested in François*. The young lady in question lay on a small mattress on the floor. She was thin, about 18 years old, and appeared quite ill but still quite lovely.

"Mathurine*, this is Monsieur Allard, he is going to help me care for you." François* gathered her up in his arms and carried her up the spiral stairs. She was very light but François* was surprised how much effort he made in carrying her after sitting on the ship for one and one-half months. They proceeded into the cabin on the main deck and into a small room with a bed.

"One of the officers has been kind enough to give us his room, now Monsieur Allard could you go and fetch a bucket of water, soap and towels?" François* did as he was told, and when he returned, the nun had undressed the young girl. She said, "I realize this is not the job for a man, but I cannot risk exposure to the other girls, and I believe you are a man of character. Now we must bathe this lady to get her fever down." After finishing the task and tucking the girl into her bed, the Sister arose, "I must return to the others. I leave her in your safety. If I am required, send the watch man to summon me."

In the dark of night with only the moon light through the small window, François* watched the young woman breathing with difficulty and fighting for her life. He was filled with confusing emotions of fear, pride and admittedly a little lust, but mainly with excitement and the knowledge that he was approaching his true destiny.

Three days later, the girl's fever broke. Sister Bourgeoys' attitude turned hopeful in her regard. François* had sat in the room almost continuously for the entire time, he only slept during the brief visits by the nun. He had learned that the young lady was Mathurine* Gouard, that she was from Paris and about 18 years old. This morning the Sister had told François* to spend the morning on deck to get much needed fresh air.

François* noticed the air had become much cooler in the past three days, and saw white, floating objects in the sea. He inquired of one of his seaman friends who replied, "Ice, even in summer we see some this far north." Just at this moment an unbelievable monster appeared off the port bow, a fish truly as large as the ship! *"Baleine,"* the seaman said using the French term for the whale, "we'll see them often well into the *Fleuve Saint-Laurent*, or St. Lawrence River."

When François* returned to the room, Mathurine* was sitting up for the first time with her dark brown eyes wide open. "It appears that our patient has made a miraculous recovery, Monsieur," exclaimed the nun, "Mathurine* this is Monsieur François* Allard. Monsieur Allard gallantly volunteered to guard and tend you in your illness. François*, (this was the first time the sister had addressed him by his first name) it seems, praise be to the lord, our young lady did not have cholera and is indeed well on the mend. I believe she should stay here one or two more day to make certain there is no risk of contamination, then we will move back to our old quarters."

François* was relieved at the news with the exception of the part about moving back down below. He and Mathurine* spent the next day in conversation about their past lives and their futures. She was from the parish of Saint-Sulpice in Paris. Her mother had died when Mathurine* was a small child, and was raised by her father who ran an inn. He had died three years ago, and she was taken to a convent where she had lived until the present time and was given some rudimentary education. She had planned to search for work in Paris this year, but the

Mother Superior had recommended her for the *Filles du Roi* program, and now here she was. François* explained his circumstances and his dream of some day having his own farm and his own family.

The Atlantic Ocean - July 28, 1666 - Day 51 at Sea:

The day to move below had arrived. Sister Bourgeoys asked François* to take Mathurine* for a walk on the deck to see if her legs would hold. He was happy to do it with only one fear. It was realized when he saw Jean*, Moreau and some of the others on deck. He knew he would be the butt of all the jokes at dinner tonight. As they stood at the rail, François* felt a large drop on his head. One might have thought it a large raindrop, but as an old farm boy, François* knew what it was.

"Glory to Jesus!" he exclaimed as he looked up. Indeed it was as he suspected, a bird! "Look, Mathurine*, a bird, like the story of Noah, we must be nearing land!"

As Mathurine* looked into François*'s smiling face, she noticed his eyes, "François*, you have two different eyes!"

"A gift from my grandfather," he replied.

That evening François* was the highlight of the hold, the man of the hour and the butt of all jokes. The men talked well into the night excited by the news of the bird and the announcement that they should see land within the next three days.

Chapter 13

<u>The Gulf of Saint-Laurent - August 2, 1966 - Day 57 at Sea:</u>

The call came up about ten o'clock in the morning *"LA TERRE VOICI!!!"* The men rushed to the rail and indeed there it was, a green bump on the horizon, enlarging as they went. *le Faucon Noir* fired a cannon shot, raised the rest of her sails, and sped off ahead. The birds became numerous. Jean* turned to Monsieur Leblanc, "When are we to land at Québec?"

"Laviolette, I think perhaps your mother did find you in a violet patch. This is the Saint-Laurent, Québec is yet hundreds of miles upstream." Jean*'s spirits sank. "But cheer up lad, this is the fun part of the journey. Tomorrow we will land for a day or two to clean the ship and become reacquainted with the land. There will be no more rough seas and in four days time the water we sail in will become fresh. We are however still a week or more from the city."

By the end of the day they could truly see land, the green hills, higher than anything François* had ever seen. However, there seemed to be fewer trees than he had expected. François* inquired into the lack of trees. Monsieur Leblanc explained, "What you see now is *Terre-Neuve* or the new-found-land. It is in fact a giant island, first seen by an explorer named Cabot over 150 years ago. The rock soil and the salt sea along with the cold weather make it what is called tundra, trees don't grow well. Neither do people. There are only a few fishing camps here. We will stop further in on a smaller island where we will have less to fear from the Indians and wild animals."

"But the trees," François* interjected, "I yearn for trees."

"Believe me, my friend, by tomorrow, you will never again have the need to yearn for trees."

As predicted, the water was much calmer as they sailed south of Newfoundland through the Cabot Strait. The water was still quite wide and occasionally all sight of land was lost. The whales became a major event. Whales of all sorts, not as large as the one François* saw in the ocean, but white whales, gray and even black whales of all shapes and some over 50 feet in length.

As they sailed closer to land, François* was mesmerized. Indeed the trees were thicker and grander than he could imagine. There was land everywhere as far as the eye could see, and no sign of people or civilization. He remembered the words of his friend in Dieppe, "So big no one knows how big it is." *Compagnie des Indes* could forget about transporting François* Allard back to France, this was the place for him!

Leblanc explained, "The land to our south is called *Acadie.* The first French settlers lived here, today there are only a few fishing posts."

Chapter 14

Monsieur Leblanc addressed the men, "The ship will anchor here for a day or two, and we will be taken ashore on the long boat. It is a large island with two large lakes. You can easily get lost. Stay in sight of the ship. There is generally no trouble from animals or Indians, but one cannot be certain. Do not go off alone. When the cannon is fired, return to the beach. When the boat departs, we will not wait for anyone who has not abided in this order. We will have opportunity to rest, eat well, exercise and wash. Gentlemen, you are about to set foot on Canada."

During the day, the long boat ferried all the groups: settlers, women, soldiers, and crew to land. Each group had an area where tents were erected. The weather was cool but excellent. François* was surprised that he began to feel nauseated, and many of the men vomited. Leblanc told them, "You must again be accustomed to the lack of motion below your feet, just as there is a _mal-de-mer,_ after a long voyage there is a _mal-de-terre._ The malady was short lived, and François* began to feel the exhilaration of land under his feet. However, he was surprised at how weak his legs had become and hoped it would be very temporary.

Once they were settled, Leblanc came with Guillaume* Renaud and summoned François*. He then addressed the men; "Sister Bourgeoys is taking the women to the fresh water lake to bathe. She has instructed me to post Monsieur Allard and Monsieur Renaud on the other side of the hill. Monsieur Allard will be instructed to keep all men away from the lake. Monsieur Renaud will be instructed to shoot anyone who is not discouraged by Monsieur Allard." (Leblanc truly understood Frenchmen.)

Once the women had completed their bathing, the men were turned loose on the lake. The water was frigid, but it was fresh and clean. François* felt as though he was scrubbing the long journey out of both his body and soul. That night there was a large fire at the camp and the women were allowed to speak with the men. Dery and Deschamps played and everyone sang.

The next morning Leblanc came again with Renaud and another soldier. He summoned François* and Moreau, "You two men are to accompany these soldiers into the woods to get some game for the remainder of the voyage." Now ready for anything, the two men grabbed their hats and were off.

The woods were incredibly thick and the going was slow. Fortunately, Renaud had a military compass. The smell of pine was overwhelming. There were small streams running to the lake, and birds and squirrels were everywhere. After a short while the men heard something moving. What appeared to be a small horse came into view, and François* realized it was a deer. It looked much like a French deer. François* had never seen one in the wild but he did see the heads once on the walls of the Longchamps hunting lodge when he had been hired to haul firewood. Renaud fired and wounded it but it started off and the men gave chase. François* tripped on a log and fell flat on his face.

When he arose, the others were already out of his sight but he heard someone in back of him. He turned to look, and was startled at what he saw. It was a dark man with long black hair, tied back with a leather strap with a feather. He was naked from the waist up and had a type of trousers made of animal skin. He pointed at François* and in a guttural voice said *"Français?"*

Startled by the use of French, François* replied, *"Oui."*

The strange man pointed to himself and grunted, *"Abenaki."* Then he hooked his index fingers together and said, *"Amis"*. François* guessed this was a hopeful gesture. The man motioned to his rear where François* saw a dark-skinned boy of about 12 years with his leg pinned under a fallen tree. The man motioned to lift the tree, and with François*'s help, they were able to free the lad.

It appeared the boy's leg was broken. The man took a length of leather strap and cut a branch from the tree to fashion a splint. François* helped him apply it to the lad's leg. He had done this with animals before but never on another person. After satisfactorily splinting the limb, the boy was able to walk with difficulty. The man removed a leather strap from around his neck and placed it on François*. He pointed to himself then to François*, *"Très bons amis, merci."*

At this, François* instinctively removed his father's medallion and gave it to the man. Then, as if by magic they were gone without a trace, and he remembered the words of his old friend in Dieppe, "You can't see or hear them until they are right upon you."

He did, however, hear a terrible commotion from in front. It was the hunting party attempting to drag two large deer. "Well, look at who has decided to return to work. Been thinking of your *Parisienne?*" said Moreau. On the way back to camp François* recounted the tale.

François* told it again in camp. Leblanc explained, "Your Indian was an *Abenaki*, an Algonquin tribe in the east, friends with the French and many of them know some French words. If he'd been Iroquois, you would be without your hair. Let me see your souvenir." It was a small wood carving in a leather cord along with a few beads that seemed to have been fashioned from shells. It was made to be easily separated into two identical pieces. "It's called wampum, and it brings good luck. You must have impressed this man for him to give you something so finely made. Wear it, maybe it will work."

That evening they had roasted venison which was by far, the best thing François* had ever tasted. They had the rest of Captain Guyon's fruit and rum and sang into the night. François* sat by Mathurine* who reported, "Soon I'll be off with a husband and a new life. I will miss you, Monsieur Allard."
François* replied, "Please call me François*, and perhaps you could wait for me?"
She sighed, "Dear François*, I could wish for nothing better; but you have three years of service, and I must marry a man with land. Remember, I am a poor orphan girl from Paris, and have only the King's meager dowry.

Furthermore, I'm a city girl and not likely to be much use on a farm at least for a while. Besides I'm to go on to Ville-Marie with Sister Bourgeoys to stay at *la Maison Saint-Ange* until my marriage. We will likely never see each other after tonight."

They walked back toward the girls' tents. When they were in the shadows Mathurine* said, "Let us say goodbye here," and she stood on her toes to kiss him, not on the cheek like his sister but on the mouth as he had never kissed a woman before. "Goodbye François* Allard, and thank you. I know that the Lord has a great life awaiting you."

François* removed his Indian necklace and separated it into the two parts. Giving her one, "Take this and remember me. Perhaps it will bring us both good fortune." Mathurine* then turned and ran into the tent. François* returned to the men's tents more certain than ever that he would never make a sea voyage back to France.

Flueve Saint-Laurent, St. Lawrence River - August 6, 1666:

The ship was quickly loaded at dawn and made sail. The captain said they would anchor at night as the river would become too narrow to navigate in the dark. Leblanc had been correct as this was the best part of the voyage. The men were allowed above deck all day, with the exception of the two hours the ladies used for their walk. François* was more amazed each day at this grand country.

The shore was alternately sand beach or granite cliff, always with majestic stands of pine and hardwood.

François* thought there were more trees in 100 arpents of Canadian land than in all of Normandie. Occasionally there would be a small cabin or post, sometimes a "town" of two or three cabins. There were rivers everywhere running to the Saint-Laurent often with waterfalls.

Soon the bank on the north began to rise, and soon there were mountains a few miles from the shore, much higher than François* had seen or ever imagined, even a few with small vestiges of snow on top. "They are called the Laurentian Mountains," explained Leblanc. "Filled with all manner of wild game, mountain lion, wolf, bear, deer, wild boar, wild goat, an animal called caribou, and the *élan*, or moose, as large as three horses."

"What of the beaver?" asked François*.
"Many of the beaver have been taken from here, the best trapping is farther upstream near Ville-Marie and the Mount Royal."
"Mount Royal?" questioned François*.
"When Cartier landed in Ville-Marie he noted the small mountain on the island and claimed it was a '*Mont Royale*'. Now people often refer to the Ville-Marie as Montréal. The real beaver trade is now there.

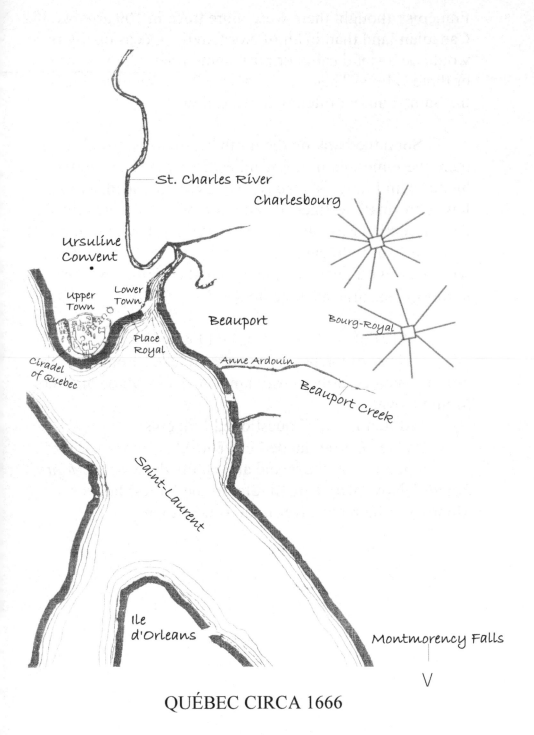

QUÉBEC CIRCA 1666

Chapter 15

<u>Québec City - August 11, 1666:</u>

L'Aigle d'Or weighed anchor and set sail at dawn. There were now more farms located sporadically along the shore and becoming more common every few miles. They came to a fork in the river which was actually a large island called *l'Ile d'Orleans*. It was ringed by sporadic farms as were the opposite shores on the mainland. The north coast was particularly beautiful with large farm meadows and a small wood church. Leblanc noted, "It is said that when Champlain first saw this coast he exclaimed, '*Quel beau pré!*'" meaning beautiful meadow. "And now it's known as the Beaupre Coast and the church is that of Sainte-Anne de Beaupre."

Near the western tip of the island on the north shore was a sight even more impressive than that of the whale. The mountain rose rapidly from the shore, nearly straight up; and from its top, almost in the clouds, came a rush of water that was beyond belief. The waterfall fell 300 feet to the river with a deafening roar. Leblanc explained, "This is Montmorency Falls, named by Samuel Champlain for the Duke of Montmorency."

Around the bend was the long awaited sight. The City of Québec set on the north side of the river in a *détroit* or narrow strait. High above on a granite cliff was the most unapproachable of fortifications, the grand *Citadelle*. The town was in two tiers, the lower town flat at the level of the harbor and the upper town high on the cliff above.

The harbor was teaming with activity today, particularly with people who had come to greet the ship and see its cargo and passengers. This was François*'s first close view of the canoe. He had seen a few of these truly Canadian craft in the Saint-Laurent but always from a distance. There must have been one hundred canoes in all, from the small two person to the large thirty-man canoe. They were all made of wood; actually, he had heard, they were made from tree bark. Some were brown, some were white and some were painted colors. Some contained Indians, some Frenchmen and some both. The Indian canoes were highly decorated with painting and carving. He was most amazed by how fast and effortlessly they moved and maneuvered.

"I have heard that canoe builder is the highest paid trade in Québec," said Leblanc who was standing by and watching François*'s fascination.

The ship was drawn along the harbor wall by skiffs and the men were happy to see that they would be able to walk ashore as they had boarded in Dieppe what seemed a lifetime ago. Appearing on the bridge, Captain Pelletier announced, "Ladies and gentlemen, we will disembark and proceed to the church on the east side of the harbor for a *Grace Dieu*. Afterwards each group will proceed with their representative. The men with *Compagnie des Indes* will go with Monsieur Leblanc, the ladies will follow Sister Bourgeoys up to the upper town and the Ursuline Convent. An officer of their regimen will meet the soldiers."

The open area at the harbor called Place Royal was a cleared stone-paved square about 1000 feet long and 300 feet wide stretching back to the sheer granite cliff on the south and the eastern sides. The western side was flat and ran into a meadow. The shops and other buildings of the lower town were built right up to the cliffs which served as their back walls.

As the passengers unloaded, the horses ended their journey being lowered down in slings. They didn't look as good as they had two months before, but François* knew that they would soon recover. The local men seemed even more interested in them than in the ladies.

The church of *Notre-Dame des Victoires* was built into the rock on the eastern cliff. It was larger and more grand than François* had expected. The bottom portion was of stone with a superstructure of wood. The interior was as ornate as French churches. The ceiling was hung with boat models, many of boats that had been lost at sea. François* had seen this custom in the church at Dieppe.

After thanking God for their safe voyage and praying for the souls of the three men who had died, they were dismissed. The men followed Monsieur Leblanc to the center of the square. The army marched up the steep walk that led to the upper town and eventually to the *Citadelle*, and the women followed them up toward the Convent. François* had heard that they would be housed there temporarily, and in a day or two, half of the girls, including Mathurine* would board small boats and be taken to either *Trois-Riviéres,* or *Ville-Marie* (later to be named Montréal). The girls remaining would be introduced to the eligible men of Québec in a few days.

The men were soon surrounded by a number of settlers. Leblanc was joined by a few men including one in official dress. "Gentlemen," Leblanc began, "in a few minutes the citizens of Québec who have applied for your services will have the opportunity to speak with you and at the end of the day you will each have your new job, but first it is my great honor to introduce his Excellency Jean Talon, Governor of Québec."

Talon eyed the twenty-nine men in front of him, some robust like François*, some quite young, some rather old. "Men, life here can be hard, but if you have industry, the rewards can be greater than anything in France. Let me be the first to wish you *bonne chance* and welcome you to New France, Québec, and a new life. Gentlemen, allow me to welcome you, on the part of all her people, to Canada!"

With that, the combination job fair and slave market began. Before François* had a chance to be approached, Leblanc who was standing with Talon and a lady in her fifties in rather rough dress summoned him. "Monsieur Allard, may I introduce Madame Anne* Ardouin."

François* removed his hat and with a slight bow replied, *"Enchanté"*.

Madame Ardouin spoke, "Monsieur, you have been recommended by both Monsieur Leblanc and Sister Bourgeoys as a man of strength and character. These are not people to make such a statement lightly. As a result, I wish to offer you employment at my farm down the river. What do you say?"

Not knowing that he had any say, François* replied, *"Oui Madame*, of course, *merci."*

"Good, then it is settled. As long as we are in town we will go purchase some provisions. Follow me." And with that François* stepped into the next phase of his life. As they withdrew, Leblanc grabbed his arm, "Congratulations, Monsieur, this is a grand opportunity, *bonne chance,* François*."

François* hurried to keep up with Anne*, his sea legs were no match for her legs today. They entered a store up against the cliff. *"Bon Jour Madame,"* said the shopkeeper.

"Bon jour, Monsieur, do you have my order, Monsieur Robert?"

"But of course, I will have two boys aid you."

"I will only require one today, Monsieur Robert. May I introduce my new man, François* Allard, fresh off the boat from France."

"Welcome, Monsieur" said Monsieur Robert as he held out his hand. François* shook it as two boys appeared with a number of packages. They carried them down to the edge of the harbor wall where a number of canoes were tied.

"Mine is the red rail," Anne* announced motioning to a canoe of brown bark with a red railing. It was larger than most and appeared that it would hold as many as eight men. "Do you know canoes, Monsieur?"

"I'm afraid not, Madame."

"Stay low as you enter. Step in the center and hold both rails, kneel on the floor and sit on your feet with your back on a cross bar. Remember, stay low."

François* was surprised at the instability. He instinctively stood up to get his balance and heard a loud splash. It was him. As he surfaced, he was pleased that the canoe remained upright. He had drawn a small crowd who were having a laugh at his expense. As he pulled himself up on the wall, Anne* declared to the on-lookers, "At least we know this one has no Indian blood," and the merriment continued.

"Let's try it this way," she said; and she hopped in the back and was seated without so much as a ripple. "Now you get in the front, and remember, stay low."

François* made it in this time although he caused considerably more motion than Anne* had. "Now we'll have the boy hand us our goods. Put them at the bottom and in the center or toward the back." They loaded quickly and she pushed off with her paddle. "Watch me a bit and then do the same. Take a few strokes on one side and then change to the other side. "I'm in back so I do the steering."

François* paddled as hard and fast as he could and realized he was making about one tenth as much progress as Anne*. He was amazed at the canoe, its speed was unbelievable. It maneuvered like a fish and took the large waves as easily as the small ones. They were headed north-northeast from the harbor. The city came out as a peninsula into the river. The Saint-Laurent continued along the southern side of the city, and there was a bay going into a smaller river on the north side which Anne* called the River Saint-Charles. They crossed this bay to the north shore of the Saint-Laurent. There were farmhouses regularly located along this coast.

"I'm only 2 miles from the city, very convenient," said Anne*. As they passed a large parcel of land occupied by a large building, she said. "The Jesuits live here, real

handy, they can come right down if we sin." François*
thought he noted a tone of sarcasm in her voice. "Well,
there it is." François* was elated, it was the best farm on
the coast. A large frontage of land was cleared as far back
as he could see. The borders were wooded, and there was a
large stream on the eastern side. The meadow rolled up
from the river to a large prosperous house with
outbuildings.

Anne* glided the canoe up on the sandy beach with
no effort. Exiting the canoe, she said, "You take the front,
I'll get the rear." They carried it up onto the meadow and
set it down by a stand of trees where two other canoes set
turned over. François* was again impressed that Anne*
moved the heavier rear of the craft more easily than he
moved the front. They removed the packages and turned
this canoe over under the trees. "Harder to see them here,
they're less likely to be 'borrowed'."

A young girl about 14 years came running down the
slope from the house followed by a large black and white
dog. As she approached, Anne said, "This is Charlotte, my
house girl. Charlotte, our new man, Monsieur Allard."
Leaning to pat the dog, she continued, "And this is Fleur."
The girl bowed slightly and said, *"Bienvenu,
Monsieur."* They picked up the provisions and took them to
the house.
When they were inside, Anne* said, "Charlotte will
put things up and I'll give you a tour. We'll eat early
tonight so you can get some rest. We have work tomorrow,
and I remember the first night we had off the boat. We slept
as though we were dead."

Anne took a long rifle from the corner, "Doesn't hurt to be prepared out here." Fleur followed them out, "In truth, Fleur is better than the gun," she said as they exited. In the front stood a large porch with a grand view of the river, the city to the right and the *Ile d'Orleans* to the left. Anne motioned to the left side of the property, "That's Beauport Creek, goes up a few miles to the mountains, full of trout, it's the north border of my property."

Behind the house was another large porch. She continued, "Charlotte came to me a few years ago, she's *métis*."

"What is that?"

"Mixed blood." Her father was a *voyageur* and her mother Algonquin. Neither group wants her much. Seems people are like that whether it's your country, religion or your race. She's a good girl and a good worker."

In back there was a large *potager* or vegetable garden. Then several rows of grape vines. "We are from Larochelle. My husband, Jacques* Badeau, rest his soul, loved to make wine. I still do but it's not as fine as his."

Next was a large orchard of apple and pear trees, "I hope being Normand you can show the Indians how to make real cider."

François* replied, "If I have the right equipment, I can even make Calvados."

"Monsieur, you're looking better all the time."

Next were two outbuildings: a barn with a fenced area and a smaller shed. In the barn was the best surprise. A cow, four pigs, two goats, chickens and geese. "I hope we'll have some families here come spring," said Anne* "I bred the cow this summer and I think it's taking." There was a wagon in the barn, "The cow can pull it", she claimed, "I hope next year we can get a horse."

François* interrupted, "Where is the road?"

"Down by the beach, it's passable if it's not too wet. There are a few trails up to the mountains. As you have seen, the canoe is usually the best way to go around here."

Next they came to a large field of an unusual looking crop. François* questioned, "Is this maize? I've heard of it but never seen it"

"This is it all right, best thing about Canada. You can make all sorts of food from it, everything from bread to whiskey, and the stalks will feed the animals all winter."

Next they saw a great field of gold. "I know this one well," said François*.

Anne* replied, "Wheat grows better here than in France. The next fields are hay and clover, then trees. We'll start harvesting more trees this winter. Well here comes trouble."

François* was startled to see an Indian man and boy approaching. He looked to see if Anne would raise the rifle, but she shouted, "You two just get up from your nap?"

In surprisingly passable French, the man replied, "We just 'napped' half the hay field this afternoon."

Anne said, "Monsieur Allard, this is Henri, and the boy is his son Philippe. His wife Angélique is probably down in the hayfield doing the real work. Tomorrow Henri will show you what's to be done." The men shook hands. Anne continued, "Henri and Angélique came to work with us when my husband was alive. If it had not been for them, I don't know if I would have survived when he died."

Henri replied, "No one could kill this woman. She's tougher than Iroquois."

As they returned toward the house, François* asked, "Aren't those strange names for Indians?"

"Those are their Christian names, they've been baptized. Makes it much easier for them to live in close to society. They're good people. You will learn a great deal from them." As they approached the barn, Anne* said, "There's a room in the loft for you, I'll show you after dinner."

François* asked, "Where do the Indians sleep?"

"They have a small camp in the woods. They don't abide with the indoors."

François* asked, "What do they do in winter?"

"They still prefer the outdoors. If you think I'm tough, Monsieur Allard, you haven't seen anything."

Dinner that night was chicken in a stew with vegetables and dumplings, and real bread. There was a wonderful fruity red wine from the local grapes and apple dumpling for dessert. Anne* and Charlotte told stories of Québec, but François*'s head was swimming from excitement and fatigue. "It's been a great while since I've eaten anything this wonderful, Madame."

Anne replied, "We are blessed with good food on this farm, and a good cook in Charlotte." Rising, she said, "I will now show you your quarters", and they walked out to the barn. In the loft was a small room with a straw mattress and strange animal skins. "You'll need these later as the nights get cool. *Bonne nuit,* and I will see you at dawn." As he lay down on the soft deerskin, he realized Leblanc was correct. He was a very lucky man.

Chapter 16

At dawn François* was awakened by the sound of the rooster and the sunlight coming through his small window. He had indeed slept as though he had been dead. He could remember no dreams and felt rested and wonderful. He noticed a ladder leading to a door in the ceiling and went up, he found himself on the roof of the barn with a spectacular view.

The day was sunny and warm with a slight breeze from the south. He could see Québec and the fortress of the *Citadelle* to his right and the *l'Ile d'Orleans* on the left. A small sailing vessel was making its way to the harbor. He could see over Anne*'s fields to the north all the way to the endless forest which rose into the Laurentian Mountains almost 3000 feet high. He came down and ran off to the farmhouse.

Charlotte had breakfast ready, eggs, bacon, real bread, fresh milk and real coffee!
"I trust you slept well, Monsieur," she said.
"Very well, thank you Mademoiselle, but please call me François*."
"Then you must call me Charlotte."
"Is Madame Ardouin up this early?" he asked.
"Madame has been up and eaten and asks that you join her at the barn after your breakfast." Fearing being late his first day, François* excused himself and ran to the barn.

Anne, Henri, Philippe and Angélique had harnessed the cow to the cart and were loading it with tools. François* exclaimed, out of breath, "Forgive me, am I late?"

Anne* replied, "You are and we do forgive you. I will have been in this country twenty years next summer and I still remember how I was after that awful voyage. We've had time to milk the cow and goat, and feed the animals, but we have saved work for you."

They went off to the hay field. About one-third of the hay had been cut and raked into stacks. Anne* said, "Today we'll finish this and haul the hay to the barn." The field was quite large by French standards. She continued, "We have hundreds of acres of land on this farm and much more if we want to go back from the river. About one-third is cleared. We will clear more when the harvest is done in the autumn."

François* and Henri cut the hay with large sickles, while Philippe and the women raked it into stacks. Then they started loading the cart so Philippe could drive it to the barn. In the late morning Anne* said, "I have business back at the house. I believe you folks can finish. Henri, if Monsieur Allard does not work out, you may scalp him." And with a wink, she headed back to the house.

At noon Angélique produced great jugs of water and yellow bread that was very sweet and very delicious. "This is made from the maize," she explained. François* had forgotten how good fresh water could taste and felt that he had already eaten more since last night than he did on the entire voyage.

By mid-afternoon the sun was baking the workers, and François* was glad that water was so plentiful. Henri put down his sickle and asked, "You hot?"

François* looked at him and trying to look strong said, "A little."

Henri replied, "There is an Indian cure for hot, follow me." And François* followed the three Indians over the east side of the field to a path in the woods leading to the Beauport Creek. At this point in the creek there was a dam of sticks forming a small but beautiful lake ringed by the thick forest. Henri exclaimed, "Here is cure." And he stripped off his clothes and plunged into the water. To François*'s amazement, Angélique and Philippe did the same.

François* recalled his mother saying, "When you are in Rome, you do as the Romans." So he removed his clothes and with a face as red as the Indians, he jumped in.

The water was cold and clear, and gloriously refreshing. The Indians crawled out onto the bank and François* did as well. Noting his embarrassment, Angélique came up to him, completely naked, and said, "Indians wear clothes to stay warm, not to be foolish." And they all had a good laugh.

Henri then noticed the wampum around François*'s neck, "Algonquin, and Abenaki," he said. François* explained how he came to possess it, and Henri replied, "You impressed this man much, this will protect you and bring you luck."

After a while they returned to the water. As François* went in, he collided with a furry animal as large as a dog, smacking the water with its flat tail, the animal disappeared. François* jumped out of the water as the others laughed. Henri shouted, "So now you know the beaver." And François* jumped back in.

Just as he jumped in he heard someone on the path and Anne* appeared. François* thought, "This is where I get sent back to France."

Anne* surveyed the group and said, "I thought this is where I would find you hiding." And as quick as could be, and to the amazement of François*, she removed her clothes and jumped in with the others. After they had finished the swim and dressed, Anne* said to François*, "The Indians have some wonderful ways. However it is best not to speak of this in town."

That evening Charlotte had prepared duck with an applesauce. The side dishes and dessert were just as unusual and delicious as in the previous evening. After dinner, Anne* and François* retired to the front porch where they could sit and watch the sun set behind the Citadelle. Anne produced two pipes, lit them and offered one to François*. "This is Indian tobacco, very strong but good after a hard day." After a short pause, she asked, "Do you know of Huguenots?"

"A bit, there were none in Blacqueville."

"In Québec," she continued, "there are many who were Huguenot in France. They fled to avoid persecution, but everyone in Québec is now Catholic.

"You should know that I was born Huguenot in a small town near Larochelle. The Protestants had a better life after the Edict of Nantes by good King Henri IV, but after the changes by his son, Louis XIII and his mother Marie de Medici, the persecution became worse. My family was forced to convert. I married Jacques* Badeau in Larochelle in 1631 at the Church of Sainte-Marguerite. He had a good trade as a master butcher and we had a comfortable life.

"All Huguenot who came to Québec have converted. It did not seem so important here where the winter is more powerful than the Pope. Monseigneur Laval, the Archbishop of Québec seems to be a good man, certainly not a Cardinal Richelieu," and with that she seemed to choke on her pipe and spit on the ground. François* wasn't certain if this was symbolic or not, but decided not to ask.

She continued, "I don't know if God is Catholic, Protestant or Indian. I don't know if he truly cares, but I am certain that he lives here in Québec for this is truly God's country. I would not trade one day of my hard life here for my entire privileged life in France.

"Four of our children were born in France; François our oldest is now a notary in Québec, next came Madeleine who died in France, next Jeanne* who is now married with five children, finally Jean who is to marry next month. He works a trade as a rifle maker. After the death of Madeleine, my husband became despondent. Then he heard of Québec and we set sail with the three children.

"When we landed in 1647 there were very few French in Canada and only a few farms. My husband had the opportunity to buy this farm in what we now call Beauport. As you can see, there is some advantage to being first. We worked the land and he worked as a butcher. We had hoped to raise cattle here and exploit the beef. Our last child Suzanne was born here as one of the first Québec natives. She was married this summer. My husband died in 1658 and I have worked the land with the children and the Indians. Now that we have you, we can again begin to expand. I hope you will meet my family Sunday."

Chapter 17

The next morning François* was on time for breakfast. Anne* asked, "Do you know *pain perdu?*" François* indicated that he had eaten a type of fried bread in France. She continued, "This may be some different." Charlotte dipped large slices of the wonderful local bread in a mixture of milk, egg, sugar and spices and fried it in a small amount of lard. Softer than the toasted bread in France, it was covered with the most incredible syrup. It was like nothing François* had tasted, sharp and sweet and not like anything in France.

"Maple syrup," said Charlotte, "We get it from the trees in the winter. It can make sugar, candy, liquor, many things."

François* again thanked God for bringing him to where a substance like this grew on trees. Anne* said, "Monday we will start to bring in the wheat, next it will be the apples, grapes, and nuts. The maize will be last, but today I have asked Henri to take you out to get fish." When they finished, they went out, and Henri was sitting waiting.

Carrying a small deerskin pack and a bow with a quiver of arrows, Henri motioned for François* to follow. They worked their way up the creek. Henri moved like a butterfly, without a sound. François*, on the other hand, sounded like a bull crashing through the woods. Henri stopped and said, "Must be more quiet or all fish will be scared off to France." He showed François* how to move and step quietly and how not to damage the foliage and leave a trail.

After a two-hour hike they stopped in a beautiful setting. The creek came from a higher point forming a short gentle falls into a large pond which continued on as the creek toward the Saint-Laurent. Henri pointed to a pile of sticks blocking the stream partially and causing the pond. "Your friend beaver makes a house here to make pond. Then he chews down the trees." The trees in the pond had been cut at the level of the water line. "Makes home for trout too."

Henri set out his pack, pulled out a coil of string and attached a hook made of bone with small feathers attached, smearing the feathers with grease and tying a piece of wood to the very end of the line. "String from grape-vine, bone from sturgeon. He lives in big river. We will see him some other day. Feather from jay-bird, grease from bear. Trout not too smart."

He threw the line silently and skillfully to the pond just below the falls. It hit with barely a sound. He let it sit, then gave it a gentle tug, waited and tugged again. When the wood disappeared, he gave a long pull on the line. A large fish broke water. Henri said, "Not too smart," as he pulled the fish to the shore. It was a beautifully colored trout of at least 18 inches. He put a second thicker line through its gill and lowered it into the water. "He stay fresh like this. Now you try."

François* threw the line, but it only went halfway across the pond. After a few tries he hit the right spot, gave small tugs and a fish hit! He pulled hard and the line went slack. Henri said, "This fish more smart," and laughed. On the next attempt François* succeeded. His fish was not as large as Henri's but respectable.

By noon, Henri said they had as many fish as they needed. He indicated François* should continue to practice, and he would walk up the slope to look for game. Henri disappeared without a sound. François* continued to fish concentrating hard on his technique. He took off his shirt as the day was getting hot. About an hour later he heard a slight sound in the brush and looked up expecting Henri, but it was someone else.

An Indian appeared in back of him, dressed in deerskin but different than Henri. His face was fiercely painted, and he seemed to project evil. With a large knife in his hand he approached François* slowly, looking like the devil himself. Trembling, François* remembered his old friend in Dieppe explaining how to recognize Iroquois, "You will know, my friend, believe me, you will know."

François* didn't know whether to yell or run, for he had no weapon. He stood up and faced the man who studied him before turning to flee into the woods. François* turned and saw Henri in the brush behind him with his bow drawn. "Henri, thank God, you returned!"

Henri replied, "He never saw me. He saw your wampum. I told you it would protect you. He lucky, too, he was about to taste my arrow. Look! You lucky, too, he leave pack." And Henri stooped to pick it up. He looked inside, "Even more lucky, Iroquois tobacco, valued by French and Algonquin. Keep this to trade." And he handed the sack to François*.

The men gathered their fish, strung them so they could be carried and started for home. Halfway back they came to a small clearing. Henri motioned for François* to stop. In one motion, Henri pulled an arrow to his bow and let it fly landing squarely in a large turkey at the side of the clearing. The bird fell without a sound. Henri retrieved his arrow and strapped the bird onto the fish. "Miss Anne* like turkey."

On arriving home, Henri delivered the day's catch to Angélique who proceeded to clean them. Henri turned to François*, "Indian catch food, woman clean and cook." And with that, Angélique threw a small fish and hit him on the back of the head. He continued, "Come, we go."

François* asked him about the bow. Henri replied, "I teach you." François* indicated he would prefer a rifle, but Henri replied, "French gun not so good, too much noise, scare game, hurts ears. Takes too much time; bow is better." They stopped by a very wide oak tree and he took his knife to carve off a six-inch square of bark. They backed up about 50 feet. "You watch." And Henri drew out an arrow from the quiver on his back, took aim and sent it squarely into the center of the bare spot on the tree.

He added, "Can be fast too." He fired three arrows in rapid succession all on target. "Now you." He handed the bow to François* who was surprised at the tightness of the string and the strength required to pull it back. Henri retrieved the arrows from the tree selecting one with bright red cardinal feathers. "Easy to find if you miss tree." François* felt that although he may miss the target, he could certainly hit this giant tree.

He pulled and took aim; the arrow landed ten feet in front of the tree. Henri retrieved it and returned it to François*. "This time, pull on string." François* gave it all his pull and let it fly, this time missing the tree by five feet. Henri said, "Now we go find arrow. Miss target bad, lose arrow worse." The arrow had not gone far and was stuck in a smaller maple tree. "Ah, you aim for wrong tree." And laughing he removed the arrow. He gently licked the tip and handed it to François*. "Taste." François* touched his tongue to the tip and was surprised at the tangy taste, bitter but something like the syrup at breakfast. "Sap run this winter and we make syrup."

François* persisted with the practice and actually hit the tree a few times and even the target twice. The men returned to Henri's camp and there was a large cloud of smoke. Angélique had cleaned the trout, started a smoky fire and placed the fish on an arrangement of pine branches and animal skin. Henri explained, "Fire from hickory tree to smoke fish, then they last long time." There were several more trout on the ground, "These for dinner, rest for ice cave."

François* questioned him about the ice cave, and Henri took a sack with most of the remaining fish and motioned for François* to follow. Over toward the barn was a small pile of brush. Henri moved it aside and uncovered a rough door on the ground. He pulled it open and François* was hit by a blast of cold air. Inside were a large number of sacks. Henri explained, "Ice cut from big river in winter, put in hold and keep cold all summer."

They lowered the fish, replaced the cover and returned to the camp.

The Indian camp was quite simple. There was a lean-to of branches, which would accommodate the three Indians in tight quarters. There were many skins of various sorts, and several fire areas. Henri produced another bow and some arrows. He showed François* how to string the bow and how to adjust the tension. "Leave loose to start, easy for practice. Make target on the side of barn, you can hit that and not lose arrows, but careful you don't hit cow. Miss Anne* get mad."

As François* returned to the barn, he pondered on Henri's French. He had noticed he rarely used articles and almost always spoke in present tense. He would later learn that this is characteristic of the Algonquin language. He also noticed that Henri's French was better when he spoke to Anne*.

At dinner that night, they ate the fresh trout and it was again delicious. François* had eaten trout from the ponds around Blacqueville, but nothing as rich and red as this. There was another unusual and wonderful sauce and the usual accompanying vegetables, potatoes, bread, and dessert. Anne* said, "Tomorrow is Sunday. I don't always go into Québec for mass, but it will be good to show you around. Charlotte has fixed some of Jacques* old clothes so that they will fit you. You can wear that."

"Henri told me that you met an Iroquois today. I didn't know any of those rascals were around. I've been told that the army is going to try to run them all back to

New England. I'll have Henri show you a place to hide if they come in a bunch." She took an old rifle from the corner with a sack of powder and balls. "This is one of the first rifles made by my son, Jean. I suppose you should have it. Keep it at your place and take it if you have to go off the farm without Henri. He'll show you where you can practice, just don't shoot the cow."

That night he wondered if his brain could hold all the new things he had seen and would see, but he soon drifted off to sleep and dreamed of saving Mathurine* from the Iroquois.

Chapter 18

<u>Québec - Sunday, August 14, 1666:</u>

After breakfast, Anne*, Charlotte, and François* went down to the canoes. They selected a smaller one, boarded and headed for town. Charlotte took the front and Anne* again took the rear leaving François* in the center. Anne* said, "I'll have Henri show you how to steer so you can take this job."

Soon they landed among several other canoes at the wall of Place Royal. The square was filled with churchgoers. As the bell tolled, people entered the church of Notre-Dame on the north side of the square. Holding about 200 people, the church was almost full. The congregation filled the main section with the well-dressed men and ladies toward the front. The nuns of the Ursuline Convent and many young girls were in the side areas at the front. François* recognized some of the girls from the ship but did not see Mathurine* who he feared had already left for Montréal.

The priest came to the altar for the sermon. Anne* leaned over and told François*, "Archbishop Laval himself." The sermon was about life in the wilderness and the problems of Christians in a savage world, not a great deal different from the sermons in Blacqueville. After mass, the congregation went out to the square to socialize.

Anne* took François* by the arm and said, "Let us go and show you off, Monsieur." They first encountered a well-dressed gentleman with two ladies. Anne* started,

"*Bon jour mes amis,*" and they all responded in unison, "*Bon jour Veuve Badeau,*" referring to her widowed status.

Anne* returned, "Allow me to present my new hand, Monsieur François* Allard newly come from Normandie. François* allow me to introduce Monsieur Jean Bourdon, prosecutor of Québec and his wife, Lady Anne Gasnier, and Madame Peltrie who works with the girls at the convent."

They all responded and Madame Peltrie exclaimed, "Why Sister Bourgeoys was just extolling the heroics of Monsieur Allard at dinner this week. Welcome, young man. She told me to expect good things from you."

Monsieur Bourdon added, "When Sister Bourgeoys compliments a young man, I certainly take interest. Welcome to Québec, lad."

François* shyly responded when Anne* exclaimed, "Excuse us, I see my son," And off they went to a different group. Anne* led François* up and addressing a well-dressed man slightly older than François*, "François, my dear, let me introduce my new man, François* Allard. François*, my son the notary François Badeau."

The man held out his hand and said, "Welcome, sir, I know my mother welcomes the assistance. Allow me to introduce Monsieur Noel* Langlois and the Marquis de Tracy."

Anne* added, "Monsieur Langlois is one of Québec's first settlers and pillar of our community. Monsieur de Tracy, I hear, has been sent to quell the Iroquois." They all gave their pleasantries and Anne* added further, "*Monsieur le Marquis* may be interested to know that François* ran an Iroquois off our land only yesterday."

The Marquis replied, "Good for you. How did you accomplish such a feat sir?"

François* replied, "I can't say, sir, perhaps I still smelled like the hold of a boat."

The men all laughed and Langlois said, "At any rate they are usually not frightened off and it is best to be wary."

Anne* then broke in, "Oh, there is Monsieur and Madame Morin. Don't forget dinner today, François, dear." And taking François* Allard along, she greeted the older couple. "Noel* and Helene*, permit me to introduce Monsieur François* Allard. François* is from Normandie."

"As am I," replied the gentleman, "from the region of Perche."

Anne continued, "Madame Morin is a mid-wife. She helped me with the birth of our youngest, Suzanne, and served as her godmother. If I am not mistaken, Madame is the first person of French descent born in the New World."

"That is correct," replied Monsieur Morin, "and we hope you can help provide us with many more, Monsieur Allard. Welcome to Québec,"

With that Anne* whisked François* off to the canoe. Once there she said to him, "The more you know these people and they know who you are, the easier things will be."

After they stowed the canoe at the farm, François* looked across the bay to the city. Anne* asked, "Is something troubling you, lad?"

François* replied, "Here I am, a poor country boy, three days off the boat, with only the shirt on my back. No, with a borrowed shirt on my back, and I've just been greeted by the royalty of the nation."

Anne* replied, "There is little royalty here. It is truly the land of opportunity where you will be judged on what you do more than on who you are. Here the country needs you more than you need the country. In many ways it is 'the New World'." And they headed up to the house.

François* asked Anne*, "Why did the Indians not come to mass?"

"They go when they like, but they usually go to the Jesuit mission church nearby. Most Indian sacraments take place there."

Upon arriving at the house, there was a flurry of activity to get ready for Sunday dinner. The Indians came up and all pitched in. Tables were moved outside and Charlotte began the creation of the meal. Soon there was a canoe off the beach; two men, a young lady and an Indian came up to the house. François* recognized François Badeau from town.

Anne* greeted them and introduced François*. "This is my son, Jean, his fiancé, Marguerite Chalifou, and his friend, Anké. As I told you, Jean is a gunsmith and lives in Québec, he and Marguerite are to be married at the end of the harvest. Marguerite's grandparents came from Larochelle at the same time as Jacques* and I. Jean and Anké have been friends from birth. François you have met is our boring notary." They all laughed and shook hands.

François* had been told all contracts legal and religious in Québec were done by notaries. They were very important men in Québec as advocates or attorneys had been outlawed in the province.

Just as they were settled, another canoe arrived. A young couple with children came running up the yard. Anne* greeted them more warmly than the others. "François*, this is my daughter, Jeanne* and her husband Pierre* Parent. Pierre's parents came from Saintes, near Larochelle, one year after Jacques* and I, and his father is also a master butcher. Here are my angels!" as she was surrounded by the children. "This is Marie* age 10, Jacques age 8, Pierre age 5, Andre age 4, and our newest angel, Jean-François 6 months. They live close-by on the Beauport coast."

As another canoe arrived and three Indians came up, "And here are Jean, Marie, and Joseph who work with them."

As a young couple appeared out of the woods into the yard, Anne* said, "And here is the rest, my youngest daughter Suzanne just married this summer to Jean de Rainville who arrived from Normandie three summers ago."

Suzanne explained, "We live close by on the coast and thought we would walk up the beach on this beautiful day."

Just as the party had settled in, a figure in black came strolling up the yard. Jean and Jeanne* shouted in unison, "Germain!" and ran down and hugged the figure who appeared to be a priest. As they approached the house with arms intertwined, Jeanne shouted, "Mother, you should have told us!"

Anne* walked down and hugged the man before adding, "And ruin the surprise, never. Welcome Father."

The young man replied, "Not until next week, Madame."

Then Anne* turned to François* and said, "François* Allard, allow me to present soon-to-be Father Germain Morin. Germain, Jean and Jeanne were inseparable childhood friends. He is to be ordained this week as the first priest born in Québec. You met his parents, Noel* and Helene* Desportes-Morin in town this morning."

"Make yourself at home, Germain, but realize that curé or not, I'll not change and in my home, I am in charge."

"Madame, I would not dream of anything else."

The group descended on a dinner fit for Louis XIV. It included the turkey shot yesterday, ham, fresh trout, and a new treat for François*, the maize, coated with butter and eaten directly off the cob. In addition there were all kinds of side dishes, wine, and for dessert something François* had heard of from Paris but never seen or expected in Québec. Balls of a creamy ice cold substance with hot maple syrup. "*Glace*, or iced cream," said Anne*. "Charlotte makes it with the ice from the ice cave. Very labor intense, but fit for this wonderful occasion."

After dinner was over, everyone settled in to a conversation of "the good old days," although to François* it was strange to apply anything old to this new world. However the conversation was broken when Henri appeared with a strange stick with a small narrow net. François Badeau spoke up, "Henri, are you still trying to win at *La Crosse*?"

Almost immediately, the group was mobilized. A number of these sticks appeared and the rules were made. Jeanne* said, "Henri and François Badeau will be captains and choose players in turn." The teams were soon chosen including the children. François* Allard was on Henri's team. The object was to move the ball by running or passing and trying to put the ball in the goal of the opposing team (a sheet tied between two sticks). Anne* was designated the *arbiter* or referee.

François* was amazed by the speed of the game and the skill of the players, with the obvious exception of himself. He was also impressed with the strength of the players, especially when he collided with the petite Suzanne who knocked him on his back. The game reached a designated score, and the team of François Badeau had won.

Then Henri spoke up, "How about traditional sides? Indians versus French." After some groaning, the sides were drawn and the game commenced. François* was more amazed by the skill of the Indians who floated through the game as Henri ran through the forest. Soon the game was over with the Indians winning 21 against 2. The group returned to the tables where Charlotte had brought a large jug of cold cider. It was refreshing but François* announced to Anne*, "Perhaps there is something in Québec on which I can improve."

Germain Morin said, "I am overwhelmed by heat,"
Jeanne* replied, "In the old days we would go for a swim in a Beauport Creek pond." The group went silent.

Morin replied, "I don't know if the Archbishop would approve."

Anne* replied, "Perhaps if he had played the game, he would see it otherwise."

The group had a laugh, but it was clear that they would forego the swim. Eventually goodbyes were said and everyone headed home. Charlotte, Anne* and Angélique began to clean up. Anne* said to François*, "I'd be getting to bed if I were you. Tomorrow we take on the wheat."

That night in his bed François* reflected on the last few unbelievable days. Québec had been more than his wildest dreams. Even the encounter with the Iroquois was beginning to take on the appearance of fun.

Chapter 19

The following day work began in earnest on the wheat field. Larger than the hay field, this would take a week or two, but it was work François* truly understood. François* and Henri would cut the wheat, Philippe, Angélique and Anne* would gather it in bundles, separate the grain and place it in bags. Periodically a load would be taken to the barn where the grain was stored and the chaff placed with the hay to feed the animals.

Halfway through the project, Henri announced, "Time to start plow." When François* questioned the urgency, Anne* explained, "Here we can plant a second crop of 'Indian Wheat'. We will plow and ready the field, then plant before the snow and it will be ready to harvest in the spring."

What a wonderful country, thought François*.

The following day there was a break. "The entire family has been invited to the ordination of Germain Morin," Anne* announced to François*, "and they've asked you attend as well." So François* again donned Jacques* refitted clothes, as Anne* and he took the small canoe to town.

The ordination was in the upper town at the church of the seminary. The upper town was ringed by a wood fortification. They walked the steep walk from the lower town that Mathurine* had taken on the day of the arrival from France. They entered a gate and came to a pleasant grassy square ringed by houses even nicer than Anne*'s.

She explained the government officials and rich merchants who did not also farm lived here.

Next to the seminary was the foundation of a new building. Anne* explained this was to be the new Cathedral of Québec. Three other men were to be ordained, but Anne* told François* they had been born in France like him*. The real show was for Germain. In his sermon, Monsiegneur Laval said today marked the true beginning of a Church that belonged to New France.

After the ceremony, Anne* walked François* through the upper town. He was impressed at how modern and prosperous it appeared. Where shops in the lower town were roughly built and occupied by rough sorts of people, the upper town shops were clean and prosperous, and the merchants were well dressed. The town hall and the small *Hotel Dieu* or hospital were small wood structures. The largest building was the Ursuline Monastery set inland from the others.

They passed the impressive *Citadelle*, set high on the Cliff, with a 360-degree view of the river up and down stream. Highly fortified, the walls housed cannon. Anne* explained that the granite cliff on which it perched was called *Cap Diamant* by Cartier as it had the shape of a diamond. There was a large beautiful farm just outside which belonged to Abraham Martin, an old Scottish sea captain and one of the first settlers. He was married to a sister of Noel* Langlois and the locals had nicknamed his magnificent meadows "The Plains of Abraham".

They continued inland to a large prosperous farm, the home of the Morin family where a dinner was to be held. Again it was an outdoor affair with a large group including nuns, priests, citizens in country dress and citizens in elegant dress. They were greeted by Noel* Morin and his wife Helene* whom François* had met on Sunday. They were talking to a young man dressed in deerskin. Noel* said, "Ah, Monsieur Allard, allow me to present Monsieur Louis Jolliet. Louis, I believe you know Madame Anne* Ardouin." They exchanged pleasantries, and Anne* left with Helene* to see the other ladies.

Morin continued, "When I first came to Québec, I worked for Monsieur Jolliet's father. Now Louis is leaving us to explore the wilderness."

Jolliet added, "I entered the seminary with Germain, but it was not for me. We sit on the edge of the world's great wilderness, and I hope to discover some of it."

Noel* took François* by the arm and led him away. "I came from a small town in Normandie, just as you. My father was a carriage maker, but I had an older brother and few prospects. I left in 1632 with Champlain himself. I worked for Monsieur Jolliet's father and began a carriage shop which you can see across the way. We have also managed to acquire this fine farm.

"I married my wife in 1640. Her family had also come from Normandie, but before 1620. Her mother is the sister of Noel* Langlois, the ship builder who is over there. They were among the first settlers. My wife first married Guillaume Hebert, whose father Louis Hebert was the very first settler to come to Québec. Guillaume died in 1639 when Helene* was 19 years old. We were married the following year. It was a fine affair, Madame Champlain was Helene*'s matron of honor.

"The reason I'm telling you this, François*, may I call you François*?"

Shocked by the question, François* responded, "Of course."

"The reason is I was a poor lad with few prospects, and today I am one of the wealthiest men in all Québec. This is a great land, my lad, and if you work hard, great things will come of you; but enough of this, let us join the others."

They were greeted by two other older men. François* recognized Noel* Langlois. The other man was quite old with a great white beard. Morin said, "François*, let me present Captain Abraham Martin. It was Captain Martin himself who piloted the boat that brought me to this great place. He is married to Monsieur Langlois's other sister and he and Monsieur Langlois now build boats rather than sail them."

When François* and Anne* went back to the canoe, she pointed out the shipbuilding factory at the end of the harbor. On the way back, François* again wondered at this place where he was socializing with the most powerful men in the land.

Fourteen days later the wheat was in and the field was plowed. Enough grain was set aside for next year's crop, and Henri, François* and Anne* loaded the sacks into the large canoe setting off down stream toward the mill at

Montmorency Falls. The trip downstream was quick. They pulled the canoe ashore and Anne* proceeded up to do business while the men hauled the sacks up to the second mill. Henri told François* that the lower mill was a lumber mill. They would return here later in the winter with wood from the trees they would clear.

Anne* met them at the mill with a burley gentleman, "Monsieur Leroi and I have agreed on our price. You boys will wait here for our share of the flour." Here, as in France, the mill kept some flour to be sold in town. This was the "price". Some would be given to the seigneur as tax, and Anne* would keep the rest. If she eventually chose to grow more, money would also change hands.

While they waited, Henri and François* hiked up to the top of the falls. The power of the water was overwhelming. The view over the *Ile d'Orleans* into the valley of the Saint-Laurent was equally spectacular. Henri said to François*, "Must get you deerskin boots." François* objected as his were new and of fine quality, having been made by his father just before his departure. Henri responded, "Not so fine for winter." They continued down the hill, collected Anne* and the flour, and headed home.

Beauport, Québec - September 1666:

The harvests continued, first with the grapes. Half of them were made into preserves by Charlotte, and the other half crushed in a homemade press and set aside to ferment. Then the apples were picked. The best were stored for the winter along with potatoes and other storable staples in a dug-out cellar beneath the house. A few were placed in the

107

hiding cellar, which Henri had recently revealed to François*. It was a cave large enough for the entire group, cleverly covered so not to be discovered and stocked with provisions for a few days. "For Iroquois raid," said Henri matter-of-factly. The remaining apples were preserved or crushed and set a side to ferment into cider. François* was happy to provide some expertise into the making of the cider.

One day Henri brought François* to his camp. Fleur the dog followed. François* was surprised to see three wild looking dogs lying about the camp. Fleur seemed to know the others. François* inquired into the beasts and Henri replied, "Indian dogs, part wolf, use in winter." Angélique then asked to see François*'s boots, so he gave them to her and she made a pattern of the soles with charcoal. Then she turned to him and said, "Now pants and shirt." François* balked at first but seeing that she was determined handed them over. She completed inspecting them and gave them back.

Henri said, "Women come to kill pig today. Good day for men to find sturgeon." He picked up his bow and a small sack and motioned for François* to follow. Angélique and Philippe followed as well. At the house, Anne* and Charlotte had gathered by the barn with a few other women including Anne*'s two daughters.

She explained, "The women go from farm to farm to slaughter the pigs. Each farm selects one or two depending on their needs. The pig is killed and gutted, the skin is cured by the Indian women, and the blood is saved for pudding. The meat is cut, salted, wrapped in cloth and hung in the chimney to smoke over the winter. The remains are cut to small pieces, mixed with spices, stuffed into the intestines, twisted in small sections and hung to smoke as sausage. If all the women do a job, it goes quickly."

At the river, Henri selected the large canoe. He, François* and Philippe took off. François* was surprised they had taken the large craft. Out on the river they saw a large raft with three Indians and a canoe; they approached the raft and Henri spoke Algonquin. He then introduced them with Indian names, like Anké the friend of the Badeaus. François* could not see much difference between the Christian Indians and the others.

The men pulled up a large sunken net which was filled with a large number and variety of fish. They gave a few small ones to Henri, who threw them in the canoe, and they headed to the center of the river. Henri stopped and brought out his sack. He had tackle such as he had used for the trout but much heavier. The hook was large, metal and barbed. He set up two tackles each with a stone on the end so that it would sink and baited each hook with a small fish, "Sturgeon more smart than trout."

He told Philippe, "You paddle, I show François*." The boy made slow progress with the canoe while Henri let the line sink. He showed François* how to play it off the bottom. Once François* had the idea, Henri paddled and Philippe handled the second line. Philippe told François* to lock his leg under the canoe support.

They paddled about without much action. François* asked Henri why his French was better when he spoke to Anne. Replying in almost perfect French, "I believe that the day will come when the Indian must adopt French ways to live. For now it is better not to be too French, or the Indian will not be trusted by his own people."

Just at this moment, François* felt a great pull on his line. He thought he had snagged the ground but realized that it was too strong for that. The canoe changed directions and began going east on its own and with a good deal of speed. He realized why Philippe had told him to put his leg under the support. Henri laughed and said, "Now we get free ride, you hold on, he get tired."

The fish pulled for what seemed forever. They were almost to the church of Sainte-Anne de Beaupre a few miles down stream when the boat slowed. Henri instructed François* to gradually pull up the line. Eventually an enormous gray form rolled on the water surface. François* thought of the whale. As it got close to the boat, Henri nodded to Philippe who stood up with the bow and landed an arrow squarely in the fish's head. Blood spilled out and the fish went limp. They brought it to the side of the boat. And after distributing their weight evenly, pulled it aboard.

François* now knew why they had brought the large canoe. The fish was unbelievable. It was almost as long as he was and seemed to be armor plated. Henri put another fish on François*'s line and threw it back and began to paddle slowly west, "See if we can get ride home," he said with his typical laugh.

A few minutes later it was Philippe's turn. He handled the fish more easily than François*, and indeed, they were pulled almost back to the farm. When the fish surfaced, Henri handed the bow to François* and said, "Big chance." François* aimed carefully and just missed. Henri grunted. He aimed again and hit it squarely. Henri grunted again and motioned to Philippe, "Now get arrow." Quickly and without a motion on the canoe, Philippe removed his shirt and dove into the water. He returned in a few seconds with the errant arrow. François* was most impressed at how he reentered the canoe without any motion.

They retrieved the second fish, which to François*'s surprise was somewhat larger than the first. They noticed the three Indians who had given them the bait working over the side of their canoe. Henri said, "Night line, good to see." And they proceeded over and watched. The men were pulling a line over one side of the canoe and letting it back in over the other, periodically they would remove a fish, re-bait the hook and continue. They took many fish and François* counted at least five sturgeon.

Henri said, "Night line have many hooks, stay in water, Indian check it morning and night. Get many fish but hard work and no fun. These boys sell fish in Québec." Back at the farm, the pig slaughter was over. They showed the fish to Anne* before giving them to Angélique.
Anne* said to Henri, "The maize will not be ready for several days. Why don't you take François* hunting? Also Henri, I have been thinking, do you think we can get two glass windows at the *rendez-vous* this year?"
Henri thought for a minute, "Windows rare, need something good to trade, or much money. I will try." And with that he, Philippe and the sturgeon were off.
Anne* looked at François*, "Perhaps a short swim in the river would be good for you before dinner, Monsieur."

111

She reached to the table she had been cleaning from the pig slaughter and threw him a piece of lye soap. "Even though I have been killing pigs, I don't know if I can abide with the smell of sturgeon tonight."

Realizing he was soaked in fish, François* went to the river and jumped in fully dressed. Although the weather had begun to turn cool, he was surprised at how very cold the river was. He soaped his clothes and then himself and headed to the barn where he hung up today's clothes, put on his other set and proceeded to dinner.

Dinner was fresh sturgeon which François* found remarkably sweet. He asked Anne* about the windows and the *rendez-vous*. She replied, "I have the one glass window in the front; I would like to add more where we have only open windows with shutters. It would allow more light in the winter. The *rendez-vous* is a gathering in the fall of each year in the backcountry. It is for trappers and Indians. They raise hell and trade. Many things can be had there. As you can imagine, glass is very dear here. Perhaps you can go with Henri; but beware, many young French men have been seduced into a life in the wilderness. I want both of you back."

She thought for a while and continued, "When we came to Québec, there were very few families. Most of the settlers were Frenchmen. The King believed they would breed with the Indian women and raise French families. However, Indian women nurse their children for years and it is uncommon for an Indian woman to have more than three children. Indeed many like Angélique only have one. Their society does not feel the need to grow as ours does.

112

"In addition, many Frenchmen found that the wilderness and the Indian ways were actually easier than life in Québec, particularly in the winter. It was also more fun and exciting. As a result, the government regulates travel and business in the backcountry, and the King has began to recruit young girls to come and marry the settlers. Already some of our men have been thusly wed, perhaps you will be as well."

Chapter 20

François* met Henri at his camp at dawn. He had brought his bow, arrows, rifle, powder and bullets. Henri looked at the rifle, "Good, if paddle break, we can use this." Angélique demanded François*'s clothes. He removed them, and she presented him with a set of deerskin clothes like Henri's, including deerskin boots. As he put them on, she inspected them. Satisfied, she took his old things saying, "I clean these." After careful inspection, "Maybe I burn them instead," and laughing Henri's laugh, she disappeared.

Henri called Philippe, and the three went to the river bank. Fleur the dog followed, but Henri sent her back, "She think we go for duck," and they selected the canoe François* had not seen used. It would easily hold all three and much more gear than Henri had brought. It was very light but looked very rugged. Henri said, "Stream canoe." They pushed into the bay and went up the bay to the Saint-Charles River.

The forest was ablaze in color. Among the dark green evergreens stood endless patches of yellow, orange, and an unbelievable bright red. Autumn in Normandie was beautiful, but it paled compared to this.

They continued up the river which was wider than François* had anticipated. Moving quickly in spite of the counter current, François* was now making very worthwhile effort paddling. In the mid-afternoon they had gone about sixty miles. They beached at a clearing and got out. Without breaking stride, Henri gripped the front and said, "Portage."

Carrying the canoe over a trail for about two hours, they came to a spectacular lake ringed with pine punctuated with the yellow and red deciduous trees. They set the canoe on the beach, and Henri said, "Now rest." As they sat on the beach, Henri broke out some maize bread and pemmican, a dried meat prized by the Indians as it was light weight and never spoiled. François* asked if they had water, and Henri looked at him as though he had two heads. François* realized his error and put his face in the lake for a drink.

François* asked why the trail was so well maintained, and Henri replied, "Indian road. Indian always use same path. Path stay good, hard to follow trail of just one man. Sometimes good to use, other times bad. Now we go. Rest over." They started across the lake heading due north toward the mountains. The lake was calm but the water was not as clear as François* would have expected. Henri explained that it was due to the type of rock and soil in the basin. Ringed with forest, the south shore was beach while the north side had many large granite boulders, blue, gray, green and a bright pink, as well as cliffs up to 20 feet high as the landscape became more mountainous.

Steering the canoe up to the side of a cliff and stopping, "Time to get dinner." He pulled out three small fishing lines from his pouch and a small sac with small white worms. "Maggots. Never fail." He put a maggot on each hook and the men lowered them into the water. Within two minutes there were three fish about two pounds each in the bottom of the canoe. "Pickerel. Never fail." Shortly the men were up to their ankles in fish. They stowed their lines and headed to a flat rock on the shore. Beaching the canoe, they took it far enough inland as to not be seen.

They unloaded the fish on the flat rock, and Henri said, "Problem now, no woman. Must clean fish." He pulled out his knife and showed François* how to gut, filet and skin the fish in three strokes. François* tried with his French knife, but the result was less grand. Henri gave him his knife and a few pointers and he began to get the hang of it. Taking François*'s knife, Henri rubbed it with a small stone and returned it. "Try now." To his amazement it was every bit as good as Henri's. Later he showed François* how to sharpen it.

In a short while, François* and Philippe had cleaned all the fish. "Almost as good as woman," Henri said, surveying the filets. After collecting dry wood, Philippe showed François* how to start a fire by spinning a straight stick on a flat one surrounded with dry leaves. Once the fire was going, they placed a number of fish on a spit and let them cook over the flames. Henri took the rest and put them between two layers of heavy leaves with salt and wrapped them in a skin.

The fish were excellent. Having their fill, they totally extinguished the fire and laid on their deerskins to sleep. At dawn they bathed in the lake, ate maize bread and fish, and set off. They went a short way down the coast of the lake to a stream head. The stream was full of rapids so they portaged up the west bank to above the rapids and put into the stream heading north toward a pass in the mountains.

The current was strong, and the men had to paddle hard to make their way. They soon came to a falls. "Portage here." They carried the canoe uphill for some time. François* could hear the thunder of the water to their right. They put in above the rapids that lay above the falls. After another vigorous paddle they came to a second falls, and the second portage. François* sensed the falling temperature as they climbed.

After the third portage, they followed the stream into a beautiful mountain lake. Henri said, "This lake of mountain valley floor." They continued to a landing point on the bank. "Rest here." The sight was breathtaking, the mountains ringed the lake and the wilderness extended forever.

François* asked if the current was always so strong. Henri laughed, "Here easy in autumn. In spring with big water from snow, current is strong." Then he continued, "Camp here tonight. Tomorrow, leave canoe, and hunt on foot." They carried the canoe inland and turned it over after taking their belongings.

François* asked, "Aren't you afraid it will be taken?"

Henri pointed to two symbols carved in the bow. "This French sign of Miss Anne*, this Indian sign of Henri. This canoe protected by both French and Indian. Also there is honor in high country."

They made their camp, started a small fire and cooked more fish. After dinner they smoked pipes and François* asked, "What are we to hunt tomorrow?"

Henri replied, "Good meat and good skins. Deer, caribou, maybe black bear and wolf." Then he looked up and said, "Snow tonight, good for hunt."

When they awoke, they were covered with five inches of snow with more falling. "Good news," said Henri. "Easy tracking, even Frenchman can do it." They ate the rest of the fish, assembled their packs and began hiking up. With every turn François* was dumbstruck by the beauty and enormity of the wilderness. Occasionally they would come to a cliff edge with an overview of forest that stretched into eternity.

After about an hour, Philippe, who was leading, held up his hand. They stopped and he pointed to the snow, "Deer," he said and pointed to the right.

They continued to go up and François* asked, "Why don't we follow them?"

Henri replied, "Must get downwind. Upwind deer smell me at one mile. Smell you at four miles." And with his faithful laugh, they proceeded.

They continued half a mile up, then half a mile right, and half a mile right again. They came to a bluff above a clearing, and down below were six deer. Henri turned and said, "Big chance François*." François* took aim at the largest buck. The arrow struck it square in the chest; It looked up as the others fled. Henri said quietly, "Again." And François* drew a second arrow and hit the great deer again. This time he stumbled and fell to the ground.

The men descended on it. François* felt a bit of sorrow as he saw the gasping beast. Henri knelt down and said, "Goodbye, great friend," and with his knife he opened the underside of the deer and a great gush of blood and entrails flowed to the ground. Henri reached in and cut out its heart and gave it to François* saying, "Here eat." François* looked aghast. Henri continued, "Indian tradition for first kill. Honors you but also honors soul of deer." And François* took a bite of the warm bloody mass.

After this, Henri and Philippe painted the deer's blood on François*'s face. "You real hunter now." Then Henri and Philippe carefully cleaned the insides and tied the deer to a large stick so it could be carried.

Two hours later, they happened on a second herd and Philippe shot one. They cleaned and tied it without the ceremony. Henri said, "Enough to carry, now back to camp." And the men made their way slowly back to the canoe.

Henri took the deer to a flat rock where he and Philippe carefully removed the hides, washed them in the lake and hung them from the trees. They then butchered the animals into more manageable portions, rubbed them with a salt and herb mixture that Henri carried and tied them in bundles and suspended them high in the trees. "Not dinner for bear," said Henri. They cooked some of the deer meat for dinner, it was delicious.

After dinner, François* lamented at killing the animal to eat it. Henri laughed, "You not so special. When you die, worm eats you."

The next morning they set out in the other direction. Not far out of camp they literally walked into a giant deer-like animal, but black and as big as three deer. "Moose," said Henri, "dumber than trout, not good eating." And they walked around the creature who continued grazing as if they were not even there. Some time later, in a small clearing below, they saw a black bear and two cubs. Henri said, "Good skin, not so good to eat, babies need mother, and I smell caribou."

A short while later they saw a magnificent animal below them, almost as big as the moose, and almost as black, but this one appeared spirited and not sluggish. "This for me," said Henri as he aimed his bow and with surgical precision, the arrow struck the caribou. It grunted and fell to the ground. They climbed down, gutted the animal and Henri said, "This enough to carry." And they headed back.

They skinned and cleaned the animal as before. Tonight they had caribou which was surprisingly different from the deer, more tender and sweeter. François* could see why Henri waited for this.

The weather was turning colder. François* was pleasantly surprised at how warm and dry his new deerskin clothes were, especially the boots. That night the moon was full, and there were wolf cries throughout the night. François* was frightened at first but later he began to feel as though this was all becoming part of him and he part of it.

The following morning Henri said, "Today last hunt, find something very good." And off they went; they passed another black bear and two moose. In the early afternoon they came upon a small group of caribou. Henri pulled out his bow as did the others. He knelt silently. As he started to rise there was a sound behind them. François* turned and there was a bear, but not a bear like the others. This one was brown and as big as Anne*'s barn. It stood on its hind legs and seemed to be twice as tall as François*.

Henri quickly fired an arrow into its chest with no effect whatsoever. He hit it with two more and François* and Philippe added two more. The bear let out a roar that must have been heard in Québec. Henri tried to get to his neck with his knife, but the bear threw him ten feet into a tree where he fell limp. Philippe approached it and the bear leveled him with one casual swat of its paw. It came at François* who could feel the heat and smell the stench of its breath. Paralyzed with fear, he suddenly remembered what he had been hauling around at the expense of Henri's teasing. He pulled the rifle off his back, and hoping he had loaded it properly, took aim. He pulled the trigger. There was an explosion of blood. The bear came forward, reached for François* and fell forward lifelessly.

He had hit it squarely in the face. Henri and Philippe were regaining their bearings and Henri gave an enormous laugh. "François* Allard, you will be great hero now!" And he continued to laugh.

Feeling quite brave François* said, "Well, I guess I did save our lives."
Henri continued to laugh, "That not it. Greatest honor for Indian is to be killed in battle with brown bear. You have just shot Miss Anne*'s windows."

François* was confused. Henri continued, "Great brown bear hide like this be biggest prize at *rendez-vous*. We get whatever we like for this."

As there was no way they could carry this creature, Henri carefully skinned it and took as much meat as they could carry. Back at the camp he completed the storing of their treasure and they had bear for dinner. François* found it greasy and rather foul, but he was beyond complaining.

The following morning they packed the canoe and began to retrace their voyage. In spite of the extra weight, the trip was less work and the downstream runs were quick and effortless. The portages were heavier but being downhill they were easier than before. They reached the big lake in the afternoon and made camp once more. In the morning they brought the canoe across the lake to the rapids they had portaged earlier in the week.

Henri got out and surveyed the situation. He returned to the canoe, "Now some fun." And they pushed the canoe into the stream. The pace was amazing, Henri in the back and Philippe in the front threaded the craft around the rocks and through the white water. At two points they came to small falls and became airborne going over them. In a short, frightening, and exhilarating time, they arrived at the Saint-Laurent.

There was even a little trace of snow here, but the weather had turned decidedly colder. Some trees were now bare, and the primary remaining color was brown-orange among the green pines. The trip down stream was easy, and in a short while they were unloading their gear at the farm.

122

Anne*, Charlotte and Fleur came down to greet them. They showed them the treasures. Anne* was amazed at the bearskin and the story. She said, "Jean will be pleased to hear that his first rifle still functions well."

Henri and Philippe took the packs to their camp where Angélique would finish tanning the hides and curing the meat. François* went to the barn to ready for dinner. During the usual grand dinner, Anne* said, "While you boys were killing bear, we harvested the chestnuts and walnuts. With the cold weather I think the maize is dry enough to harvest, we will try to begin tomorrow."

After breakfast they gathered in the cornfield. The weather was cold and a few inches of snow had fallen overnight. François* had heard of maize which now existed in many areas of Europe. The Indians gave maize to Columbus who returned it to Europe, but it was not yet grown around Blacqueville. Anne* explained they would first walk among the rows with large sacks and pick the ears. She showed François* how to determine which ears were suitable for grain. After this the women would strip the grain and the men would cut the stalks.

It was laborious work. The kernels were dry and could now be stripped of the cob intact with an odd tool. They were rock hard unlike the soft sweet kernels they had eaten off the cob in the summer. The kernels were stored in sacs and could be kept in the barn and used as a high quality feed for the animals, but most would be taken to the mill to be made into maize flour for cornbread and other delicacies.

Henri took the ears too soft to strip and squeezed them in the apple press and put them in containers to ferment. Cutting the stalks was more difficult than the other grains as they were as thick and strong as a young tree. They had to be individually cut with a large knife-type instrument, and then carted to the barn where they were composted into a pile to rot into animal feed.

The morning after the maize was in, Henri announced, "Leave tomorrow for *rendez-vous*." François* was excited at the prospect of another wilderness tour.

Chapter 21

That morning there had been more snow. François*
was careful to walk as Henri had showed him always in the
same path to keep the snow packed down. He was delighted
at how his deerskin boots worked for warmth and traction
in the snow. François*, Philippe, and Henri carried their
supplies down to the canoe, including the precious brown
bear and other skins as well as several trinkets and old tools
that Anne* and Henri had assembled for purposes of
trading. François* brought his sack of Iroquois tobacco.
When they returned for the last load at the Indian camp,
Henri said, "Dogs might be handy, and he gave a subtle
whistle and all three Indian dogs trotted along."

At the beach there was a small amount of ice, the
trees were rapidly becoming bare and the water was filled
with brown and yellow leaves. They pushed off and headed
west in the main river, crossing in front of the city and the
Citadelle and the rocky face of *Cap Diamant.* This was
François*'s first view of the area southwest of the city.
There were regularly spaced farms along both shores, but
within a few miles, it turned to wilderness.

A large flock of birds flew over in a southerly
direction. Henri motioned to stop and made a great
squawking noise. The birds circled and a large flock of
black ducks landed close to the boat. Henri and Philippe
took their bows and shot six in a few seconds. The rest flew
off, and the dogs jumped out and retrieved the ducks.
François* was dismayed that even the dogs could leave the
canoe more quietly than he. When they returned, the men

removed the arrows and Henri said, "Black duck stupid, but taste good." And they continued on.

Fifty miles later they again encountered civilization with periodic farms. A short while later they came to a small town. "*Trois Rivieres*" said Henri, named for the confluence of three rivers. They followed the branch to the north. Henri saw a man walking the bank and hollered," Boucher!" Landing on shore, Henri greeted the Frenchman. Dressed in deerskin, he appeared about twenty years François*'s senior and very rugged.

Henri introduced him as Pierre Boucher. "I suppose you boys are for the *rendez-vous.* " Henri indicated they were, and the man continued. "Well, I suppose I'll see you there." And addressing François*, "Stay very close to Henri, lad, this is a rough group." They said their farewells and were on their way.

They took another fork to the west and came to a lake. On the side of the lake was a long beach with at least one hundred over-turned canoes with supplies under them. They landed and similarly overturned their canoe and left their supplies underneath. "Aren't you afraid of theft?" François* asked remembering Boucher's warning.
Henri replied, "Only crime at *rendez-vous* is stealing, but never canoes. It is safe." They started inland and the dogs followed immediately behind Henri.

Inside a nearby clearing was a mass of humanity and activity. There were perhaps 200 people, French, Indian, men and women. François* noted that all the women seemed to be Indian. There were tents, lean-tos and fires large and small. Men were eating, drinking, singing Indian and French songs. They played strange games and there were a few fights.

Henri made the rounds talking to most everyone, asking what they had brought to trade and introducing François*. It seemed Henri knew almost everyone. He had a particularly warm discussion with an Indian man in a small camp of Indians. They spoke Algonquin, and he introduced him to François* as Anuk. After they moved on, he said to François*, "Anuk is my brother, not Christian." François* noted that when Henri spoke French around other Indians, he used particularly poor grammar.

François* noticed a man in black religious dress, sitting under a tree and writing in a journal. François* sat down and introduced himself. The man replied, "I am brother Robert from the Jesuit missionary in *Trois Rivieres*. I am writing for the 'Relations'." François* appeared puzzled and the man continued. "The Relations of the Jesuits, a journal of the workings of the Jesuit order in New France. It has been kept since the beginning in 1610. It is published periodically in France and is a big seller in the cities. I am writing a description of this *rendez-vous*."

As the night progressed, the crowd became more rowdy. There was much drinking. Henri cautioned François* against it, "Some whiskey here bad, also good to keep clear head at *rendez-vous*". He brought out three of the ducks and cleaned them and put them on a stick at the fire of his brother's camp where he said they would spend the night. Again roasted duck was better than anything similar in Normandie.

Pierre Boucher came down and sat to speak with François*. "From where do you come, lad?" François* indicated, "Blacqueville near Rouen."

"I was born in Mortagne in the Perche region. Many people have come from there to Québec. My parents brought me when I was quite young. My father was a carpenter and worked for the Jesuits. The Jesuits educated me in both French and Algonquin. They suggested that I study the priesthood, but the life in the wilderness seemed too exciting for me to be a priest."

"I have become an interpreter and have been quite fortunate; I am now Governor of *Trois Rivieres*. As was common in the early days, I married an Algonquin woman. We had one son, that man over there. His name is Jacques, and he is *métis* but well accepted in French society because of my position. My Indian wife died after two years, and I married a French woman. We have seven children and hope to have many more. The Indian ways are interesting, in many ways a more Christian-like society than our own. However I fear it will not always be. Even as we speak, the Marquis de Tracy is leading his men against the Iroquois. Rather than reason, we would prefer to murder each other. Well, Monsieur Allard, I will leave you to experience the festivities."

As Boucher left, an inebriated Frenchman stumbled into Philippe and fell down. He arose quickly and hit Philippe square in the face, bloodying his nose. Philippe arose and stood. The man cursed and pulled a long knife. François* began to rise but he felt Henri's hand on his shoulder cautioning him to stay down. Philippe drew his knife and the men faced off. Philippe was all of 14 years and a head shorter than the other man, but he maintained an icy calm. The man lunged and Philippe stepped aside. The man plunged again and cut Philippe's cheek before falling again. He grabbed Philippe in a hold and the men fell to the ground. Philippe was quickly on top of the older man and held the man's arm behind his back and his own knife to the man's throat.

Giving the man a second to worry, he slid his knife slowly across the man's throat making a faint cut only enough to draw blood. With this he stood back and the man stumbled to his feet amid the laughter of all the men around. The man stumbled away still cursing. Philippe returned to his father's side. Henri looked straight ahead and murmured almost unheard, "Good." As subtle as it was, François* could see how meaningful that "Good" was to the man and his boy.

That night they slept in the Indian camp of Henri's brother. It was becoming as cold as François* had experienced, and he was chilled even beneath his deerskin. Henri made a motion to his dogs and then to François* and Philippe. And each dog crawled under the deerskin of one of the three. François* was amazed at how warm this made him. Henri said, "I tell you dog good in winter."

The camp awoke early. François* noticed that a number of the men had used Indian women instead of dogs for warmth. Some of the men had gone to the lake and broken through the ice to wash away the excesses of last night. After breakfast, they began to set up their wares around each camp. Then everyone started making the rounds. Henri made a motion to one of the dogs who climbed on top of the bearskin.

The men made a quick tour of the camp. At the far end Henri stopped and talked to a group of Indians that looked somewhat different. François* had learned a little Algonquin, but he could not understand any of this conversation. After they left François* asked what Henri had been speaking, and Henri replied, "Iroquois." François* stopped dead in his tracks. Henri continued. "These good Iroquois, come from far west of here in the endless lakes. Tribe called Huron. Friend of Algonquin and French. The Huron hate Iroquois of New York more than anyone."

Henri told François* that he should go and see what he could get for his tobacco. Henri said, "Iroquois tobacco very valuable. You can trade here for Indian woman."

François* replied, "I don't think it is right to take a woman for one night."

Henri replied, "For Iroquois tobacco some men give you woman for life." And he laughed his typical laugh.

François* indeed found great interest in his tobacco and struck a deal with an old French trader for a number of items he wanted. The old man took the sack and emptied it into a container and returned the bag. He said, "Son, I can see you're an honest man and also a friend of Henri. I won't cheat you. Your sack is worth as much as anything here. If you carry this sack, it means you took it from an Iroquois, makes men want to steer clear of trouble with you."

Back at the camp, Henri and Philippe had traded for a number of goods, including three large windows. "Miss Anne* be very happy." After dinner that night, there was more drinking, fighting and revelry than the night before. François* and Henri smoked a pipe and talked. François* asked, "Where do these people get windows?"

Henri replied, "Along border with New England, always fighting. Iroquois and English raid Canada; Algonquin and French raid New England. Burn house, take windows. Then trade."

François* replied, "Then these windows could have come from anyone's house."

Henri said, "Man always say, 'come from other side', but no one know for sure. At least they not burn windows."

Later François* asked about Henri's brother and what the relationship was between the Christian and non-Christian Indians. Henri replied, "French God, Indian God, who knows. Sometimes I think same guy. Priest don't go with woman. This can't be what God want. Sometimes I think French not too smart."

Later in the evening an odd little Indian man, deformed with very short legs and arms and dressed in a robe full of feathers and baubles came dancing around. The Indians seemed to give him great deference. "Medicine man," said Henri, "Like doctor and priest at same time. Great man in Indian tribe." François* recalled a similarly shaped little man in Rouen who did odd jobs around the cathedral. However the people of Rouen always treated him with scorn. Maybe Henri was right about the French.

That night as he crawled into his skin with the dog to keep him warm, he thought of his friends from the ship and wondered how they had fared. It had been only six months since they had left France, but in a way it seemed like a lifetime.

The next morning they loaded and took the trip back to Beauport. It was fast and easy because of the downstream current. Anne* was ecstatic with the windows. She said, "You boys are back just in time. We will start to clear trees tomorrow." This was a job François* did not look forward to. They had two axes, and Henri and Philippe had hatchets. Anne* had said that they should clear two acres, but François* didn't see how they could cut more than one tree per day.

At breakfast the next morning, François* enquired into the logistics of such a task. Anne* replied, "I have a little help coming." When they went out, there was a new canoe on the beach. Two enormous men made their way up to the house carrying two long metal saws. Anne* said, "François* this is Monsieur Pierre* Tremblay and Gabriel. They come from Chateau Richer just east of here where Monsieur Tremblay has a farm, but he and Gabriel work as *bucherons* or lumberjacks in the winter. They have brought two *longscies* to help us."

Both men were taller and wider than François*, and when they shook hands, Tremblay's was almost too large for François* to grasp. Gabriel was Indian and only grunted. Henri, Philippe and Angélique had come down and were carrying other small saws and tools from Tremblay's canoe. They loaded the cart, hitched the cow and went to the northern extent of the cleared land.

The process was very automated. Tremblay and Gabriel took the largest *longscie,* or long saw, and working each end, cut a tree, always making it fall exactly to the south. Henri and François* used a smaller long saw to cut the tree into moveable sections and Philippe removed the branches and moved them to the edges of the field. Angélique would hook the cow to a section of tree and haul it to the beach. The coating of snow made the trees slide easily. At the end of the day, they had cut and hauled over twenty large trees.

François* inquired, "What of the stumps?" They explained that they would be left in place for now and this season they would plow and plant around them. Next fall the stumps would be easier to pull out. Somehow François* felt little excitement for this pending task.

Tremblay and Gabriel were to stay at the farm for the duration of the job. They ate at the farmhouse and slept in the barn with François*. Gabriel was a man of few words, in fact he never spoke except to say, "here, there, yes, no", or swear. Pierre* Tremblay never stopped talking.

That night after dinner he told François*, "I came to Québec in 1647 from Randonnay in Perche. Like you I worked three years. After that I had trouble holding work. I did everything, worked the docks, fished, lumberjack, farm hand. Finally in 1657 I found a woman and we have a farm. Have four children now and hope for many more. Gabriel and I cut trees in the winter. Make good money but we

unfortunately find ourselves drinking a good deal of it."
And with a hardy laugh, he took a swallow of maize
whiskey from his ever-present jug.

The job lasted five weeks. At the end they had split
the smaller logs for burning and had amassed a wall of
wood that looked as it would last ten years. There was an
enormous stack of trees at the beach and they began to tie
them together and row them the short distance to
Montmorency Falls and the mill where they were cut into
boards. Some were returned to Anne* and some kept as
payment for the mill. Some turned into cash. Some of the
cash paid Pierre* and Gabriel who went off to their next
job.

Chapter 22

<u>Beauport Québec - November 1666:</u>

Early November, the weather was generally quite cold although there was the occasional warm day. They had managed to install the new windows with the help of the new boards. The wind was frequently ferocious out of the north. A foot of snow had fallen, and ice was forming on the river in spite of the current. Anne* told François*, "Tomorrow you, Henri and I will make a trip into Québec with the large canoe for supplies. For a while after, we will have to go by land, and ford the Charles River which is difficult for transporting goods."

The next morning they departed for town. The journey was more difficult than usual due to the ice flows in the river and along the bank. When they arrived at Place Royal, there was a commotion in the square. Anne* made inquiries and replied, "It seems that Marquis de Tracy and his Carignan Regiment have routed the Iroquois at their winter camp by Lake Champlain in New York. They returned victorious only yesterday."

While François* waited for Anne*, he caught sight of his old friend Jean* Poitevin. He hollered, "Laviolette!" and Jean* came running over. They greeted each other enthusiastically and exchanged as much information as was possible in a short time. Jean* had been contracted to Mathurin Moreau who had a farm inland from Anne*'s. "It's in Boug Royal, at Charlesbourg," he said, "a new area just opening to farming, we've had our first crop this year and are clearing more land." A man called Jean* and he said, "I must run, François*, how wonderful to see you. I'm sure we will meet frequently after the winter."

As he watched his old shipmate run off he saw another familiar figure seated on a wall. It was Guillaume* Renaud, sitting alone in his uniform. François* went over and said, "Well, if it is not the returned Indian slayer."

Looking up with bleary eyes, Renaud appeared to have aged ten years. "Oh, François*, how nice to see you."

"You don't seem like the returning hero," returned François*.

"François*, it was horrible, the most horrible thing you can imagine. François*, we slaughtered them, the men, the women, the children. Then we burned the whole village. You could here their screams into the night. François* I don't know how God can forgive us. They may have been savages, but we should be better." He put his head in his hands and sobbed. "My duty is over next month, I cannot rejoin. I don't know if I shall return to Normandie, or perhaps stay here and start a new life. I just know I can never again be a soldier."

François* sat with him silently for a while, until Henri whistled when Anne* was ready to haul packages. He got up putting his hand on his friend's shoulder. "My advice is to remain. I am certain that you can again find God in this country. Good luck, my friend."

The return trip was just as difficult. Arriving in Beauport, Anne* said, "Put the canoes up high tonight, boys. It is unlikely we will use them again before spring."

Chapter 23

Québec - Christmas 1666:

Work was now tending the animals, managing the snow, and repairs. Daylight was short so there were not as many hours to work. The animals were doing well. It appeared that the cow, a goat, two sheep, and two pigs were pregnant. Spring would be extra busy. Winter had descended. Snow was waist high, but where the paths were used it was passable. The cold was truly unbelievable. Angélique had given François* two sets of deerskin gloves, one pair so he could use his fingers and another pair to go over the glove, a mitten, for use when fingers weren't necessary.

Ann gave him a woolen scarf and hat. All skin had to be covered at all times for in a very few moments it would freeze. François* noted that his urine would actually freeze before it hit the ground. Realizing what could happen to exposed skin, Henri cautioned him he should always urinate in a protected place.

Anne* had François* cut a pine tree and bring it indoors where they decorated it with candles and ribbons. This had been a custom in France but never with such a large tree. As Christmas day drew near, Charlotte was hard at work preparing for the great feast. Anne* hoped that at least some of the family could come.

The most astounding occurrence was that the river had frozen across, so people were able to cross it. Henri came to get François* one morning and said, "Time to make winter cart." The men went to the barn and removed the wheels from the cart. They then attached a set of long boards to the axle. They hitched the cow and took it out. François* was amazed at how effortlessly it slid and how fast it could go even with the cow. Henri said, "Now you ride to town."

Christmas morning was beautiful and clear. They hitched the cow, and Anne* and François* made their way to Québec for mass. The square was full of people and a large crowd of carts on boards, pulled by all manner of animal, cows, goats, mules, and even a few of the newly arrived horses. After mass they saw many of their friends. All the Badeau children were in attendance and planning to come for dinner. Taking three of Jeanne*'s children, Anne* whisked François* to the farm to prepare.

Dinner was spectacular and went into the night. Even the Indians came inside to partake. After dinner gifts were exchanged. François* was surprised to be included and received an Indian hatchet, or tomahawk, from Henri, new arrows from Philippe and a hat of raccoon fur with ear covers from Angélique. This would be much warmer than his wool hat. Anne* gave him a large new knife such as the one Henri used, but this one made with French steel.

François* surprised the group when he had gifts to distribute as well. He had obtained them by trading his Iroquois tobacco. He had a French pipe for Henri, hair ribbons for Angélique and Charlotte and a small broach for

Anne*; but the most interesting was a French firebox for Philippe. This was a metal box that would hold a combustible such as oil or alcohol. When it was struck with its metal cover, the spark would ignite it. Henri grumbled that an Indian would not need such foolishness, but the boy was obviously delighted.

The Indians departed soon afterwards, as they did not care for being indoors. The entire group stayed over that night and at breakfast, François* gave thanks for being allowed into this wonderful family. After breakfast, Henri appeared with a stick in his hand. "Warm day, time for a real game." The group donned their heavy outdoor clothes and went out.

A crack had formed in the ice as it did periodically, and water covered the ice and snow and refroze, creating a large smooth ice surface. The game was basically lacrosse, but they slid rather than ran and the ball was a heavy disc pushed with the sticks. Henri said, "Winter lacrosse, called *ah-kee*."

The holiday passed, and things returned to normal. There were two enormous snowstorms back to back, and in places the snow was drifted up to the roof. Anne* said. "Noel* Langlois tells of the first days of the colony when they lived in "long houses" which were copied from the Iroquois. They were open inside with only the outside walls, and as there were no fireplaces, a large fire burned in the center, vented through a hole in the roof. When the snow was deep like this, the men had constantly to clear the opening so the fire would burn. If they did not, the house would be buried.

Chapter 24

The Laurentian Mountains - January 1667;

Caution: The story of the old trapper is very graphic but taken from an allegedly true account.

A few days later, Henri appeared, "Time to get new meat." François* questioned how they could possibly travel to hunt in this snow. Henri said, "Come see." They made their way down the path to the Indian camp and François* saw a small sleigh, lightweight and close to the ground. The three Indian dogs were hitched to it. Henri told him to get his things. When François* returned, he and Philippe sat in the sled and Henri stood on the back and beckoned the dogs.

The sleigh lurched forward, and they sped through the woods faster than a man could run in summer, heading straight north until they reached the foothills of the Laurentians. "Camp here," Henri said, and they set up a lean-to and fire pit. The following morning they took the sleigh in another mile. Henri bade François*, "Get out here." As François* climbed out the sleigh, he went up to his shoulders in the snow. Henri and Philippe laughed uproariously. "You forget Indian slipper," he said as he produced strange pairs of what appeared to be giant shoe soles. The three men strapped them on, and François* was astounded at how easily he could navigate the deep snow.

They spent the day in the foothills. Animals had come down for the winter, and they shot several turkey and large white rabbits. After they had returned to the camp, they heard a sound in the brush, and an old man in deerskin came into the clearing. He held up his hand in a friendly gesture and said, "If you don't mind sharing your fire, I have good meat to share."

He joined them and pulled out three colorful birds. "Can't usually get pheasant this late but I got lucky." After dinner he lit his pipe and started to talk. "My name's Marin, at least that's what it is now. I came from France in 1620, worked as a *voyageur* for some time. Eventually I became a *coureur de bois*. That is to say I didn't work with government permission. Now I just trap and hunt and fish for myself. Usually live alone sometimes with the Algonquin."

As the conversation went on, François* mentioned the Iroquois, "I saw a soldier friend of mine a while ago who claimed the army massacred them ruthlessly."
Marin replied, "Nothing could be evil enough for those devils. Let me tell you about them.

"About ten years ago we was trapping over to the east, me and three other French, a few Algonquin and a couple of Indian women. One was my woman at the time. She had a boy with her but he wasn't from me. We were setting up a camp such as this when two of the Indians fell dead with arrows. They was on us like flies. They tied our hands, put ropes on our necks and dragged us for two days back to the Iroquois village.

"The Iroquois live in real villages. They have long houses which are wood and about forty feet long, with a fire pit inside. First there was a lot of yelling. Then they formed what they call a 'gauntlet' which is all the Iroquois in two lines with clubs. They'd run us through one by one while they beat us with the clubs. Two of the men didn't get through alive. Then they stood us up and told us to sing, and we did. Then one took the boy and held a knife to his throat. When his mother protested, they slit his throat and let him fall dead.

"They took us into the long house which was all hung with dried plants and skins, where they stripped us naked, tied us up and then took a clamshell and real slow cut off one finger each." He held up his three-fingered hand. "The next day they came with torches and burned us." He removed his hat to show where his ear had been burned off. "The next day they took us all out, chose one of the men and skinned him alive in front of us. I still can't sleep for fear of dreaming of it."

François* interrupted, "What could they have wanted?"

"Didn't want nothin', just to see us suffer and die slow. That night, we was all tied up in the long house with a guard. My woman went over and tried to play nice to him. Stupid fellah cut her loose and started to have his way with her. She reached over and got a log from the fire and bashed his skull with it. Burned her hand real bad, tough woman.

"Well, we escaped and made it down river to an Algonquin camp and that was my finish with business, but I tell you nothing is bad enough for them devils."

After a long silence, François* said, "Well, thank God we have the French to protect us."

The old man replied, "Let me tell you about the French. Before the Iroquois thing we was in the far west by the inland seas, and we portaged across the great Niagara. Makes them Montmorency Falls look like a boy pissing on a rock. We made it up to the great lake of the Huron. The Huron are Iroquois too, but friendly. Too friendly, it seems. The French Jesuits had been there and started a mission. They brought them religion, but something else too, they brought them the pox. In a village of one thousand Huron, there was fifteen left living and one priest who had gone crazy praying over their souls. That's what the French have done."

On that note the men crawled under their skins. In the morning, the old trapper was gone.

Chapter 25

A few days later, after feeding the animals, Henri announced, "Time to cut ice." He took a long thin serrated blade and a heavy pole with a sharp strong metal tip. He, François* and Philippe took the cow, some rope and poles down to the beach. They went several yards offshore and started to chop a hole in the ice. This was difficult as the ice was now at least two feet thick.

Once they had reached water, they took the long blade and cut a square about 2 feet on all sides, built a tripod over the cube with the large poles, put a hook in the cube and used the cow and ropes to lift it out. Lowering it onto a sled, François* regarded their marvelous cow and wondered what her Normand cousins would think of life in the new world.

The work became easier as the hole in the river became larger. When they had enough ice, they hauled it to the ice hole, lowered the cubes into the hole along its periphery making a large hole now ringed with ice. They then used large sticks to brace the ice against the sides and leave the center open for the storage of food in the spring.

Two days later Henri announced, "Now best part of ice harvest." The three plodded out to the area where they had taken the ice. Since the ice was now only a few inches thick, Henri was easily able to cut a hole. He quickly produced their fishing lines with a block of spoiled pork fat and cut bait. The results were amazing. In one hour they had caught almost 100 fish, and by the afternoon they had a pile of fish that would require the sled to get them back. They had all manner of fish including some that François* had not yet seen. Henri explained that Angélique would gut the fish and freeze them in the snow. They would be thawed as needed, skinned and filleted and cooked. They would now have fish until spring.

Winter progressed slowly. François* was beginning to forget life without snow and ice. The cold was beyond anything he had imagined, yet it was not as bad as he had expected. The clothes and work made it tolerable, and there was a beauty and invigoration that he had never experienced. The entire world was clean.

His quarters in the barn were very comfortable. He had a large collection of skins, which enabled him to stay warm even on the coldest of nights. Bathing would have been an issue until Henri showed him the Indian way. In the Indian camp was a tent of heavy skins. Building a large fire inside Angélique would heat large stones. Water was then poured on the stones to make steam. Sitting in the tent, they could also wash with the hot water. Finally they would leave the tent, roll in the snow bank and return to dry and dress.

The first time François* was dumfounded, not to mention reluctant; but Angélique returned and took him out, pushed him in the snow and fell on top of him. The journey from very hot to very cold combined with this beautiful young, naked woman on him was almost more adventure than François* could endure. Angélique threw snow at him and laughed, "François* Allard, you are too worried about clothes. I think I need to find you Indian woman."

Saturday evenings, everyone including Anne* and Charlotte would come for the bath. As François* became more accustomed to it, he began to wonder if some of the Indian customs made more sense than those of the French. One day he questioned Henri about his attitude towards the "spirit" of the animals that they had killed. Pausing, Henri looked at François* and using much better French than usual, "The Indian believes that all animals including the man have spirits. If they are good and brave, when they die, their spirit remains with their people. The spirits of the dead Indians continue to hunt the spirits of the animals."

François* asked, "What of the cowardly?"
Henri replied, "Cowardly men do not have so privileged a place. If they become brave, it will change. I have never seen a cowardly animal so I don't know about that."
François* returned, "It seem like a naïve concept of Heaven."
Henri gave his laugh, "More naïve than sitting on a cloud? My friend, how could any heaven be better than this?" and he motioned to the surrounding countryside. François* had to admit to his friend's wisdom. He began to realize that the concept of the Indian as a savage was somewhat naïve.

Chapter 26

Beauport, Québec - March 1667:

François* smelled an acid odor from the Indian camp. On investigation he found Henri sitting at a large fire with an arrangement of containers and some tubes made from reeds. After studying it for a minute, François* realized what it was. Henri said, "Trappers buy maize whiskey, Henri makes good money."

After watching for a while François* said, "Henri, don't begin tomorrow until I arrive."

The following morning, François* arrived with two large containers. "Let's try your boiler with cider," he explained.

As the day progressed François* continued to taste and modify the device. Towards sunset, he exclaimed, "I think this is it", and gave Henri a taste.

Henri's face showed more expression than François* had seen, "Can use this to kill Iroquois."

François* took their last product and said, "You'll grow accustomed to it. I'm going to show this to Miss Anne*."

That night after dinner, François* produced his jug and poured some for Anne*. After tasting it she said, "We rarely had true Calvados in Larochelle, but I swear this is it." After her second taste she said, "Actually it is good. François* I think you have something here."

After some thought she launched a plan, "When Calvados comes from France, it is very rare and very dear. With more than half of our citizens being Normand, the market will be great. I will take some of yours to town tomorrow and get an idea of a fair price."

The following day, François* accompanied Anne* to Québec. François* ran errands while Anne* met with a few businessmen with an appreciation of liquor. As the old cow pulled the sleigh home, Anne* described her findings, "There is much enthusiasm. Morin and Langlois thought it is as good as the real thing. I have put out word that it is a project of ours. You and Henri can produce it in your spare time. Men will come to the farm and Henri will supply it but they must pay you. Some of these old coots have a problem with Indians and money and liquor. They don't mind with the maize but this is different. Henri will understand. As they are my apples, I will take fifty percent, you and Henri may keep the rest."

François* replied, "I'll share equally with Henri."
Anne* cautioned, "It would not be advisable. First of all, Henri would be insulted. I know that seems queer, but he has little use of money. In fact he gives most of his earnings from the maize to the mission. Give him ten percent; even there he will consider it too much. I believe it is you who had thoughts of buying a farm. Perhaps that will happen sooner than later."

François* questioned, "What will we charge?"
Anne replied, "Ah, that's the good part. Henri gets one-half livre for a jug of maize. Langlois said this would easily go for five livre per jug. Perhaps you should make

half-jugs as well and sell them for three. Morin predicts the only limitation is how much you can produce in such good quality."

François* was having difficulty staying upright, he worked the numbers slowly and realized that this was a great deal of money.

"One more thing," Anne* added. "Tell no one of your recipe. Say it is an old family secret and very complicated. It will keep out competition." So the enterprise was formed and François*'s finances as well as his prospects began to improve.

As March passed, the days became warmer, occasionally quite warm although the snow and ice caused life to remain cold. One morning, Charlotte looked out the farmhouse door and called, "Madame, look!"

Anne came to the door and saw a thin strip of blue down the center of the Saint-Laurent. As François* came in for breakfast, she exclaimed. "Look, Monsieur, we will soon have much work again." François* looked out and realized the ice was beginning to break and move. Although he had found a wonderful peace he had not expected in winter, the excitement of this was much like the excitement the day he saw land from *l'Aigle d'Or*.

Indeed over the next many days the ice began to move rapidly. Although it would again be necessary travel to Québec by land, the anticipation of spring was wonderful. Saturday there was a celebration in town. François* and Anne* went and the rest of the household: Henri, Philippe, Angélique and Charlotte came as well. Anne* explained, "The festival of the ice breaking is bigger than Christmas in Québec. Monsieur Morin asked we bring some jugs of your Calvados." Indeed this would be a wonderful occasion for François*.

The festival was like nothing François* had seen. Much of snow had melted, and the squares and roads were clear. Small spring flowers peeked through the grass, even grass still covered with snow. The day was relatively warm. There was music, dancing, tables of food and drink. Noel* Langlois had a table giving small drinks of François*'s Calvados. He asked François* to stay around so that people could meet the producer of this wonderful addition to the festival.

François* saw his old friends. Guillaume* Renaud had stayed in Québec and was working for the church. He planned to buy a farm and marry within the next year. "You were correct, François*, this is the place for me. I appreciate your friendship last fall."

Jean* Poitevin dit Laviolette was there and full of news of the growing new area in Charlesbourg. He too had hopes of a farm and a wife after his internment. François* even saw Deschamps and Dery, whom he remembered from the ship. They were, of course, playing their musical instruments.

After the festival, the group went to the home of Anne*'s eldest son, François Badeau, the notary. He had a fine house on the square of the upper town. Not married, he lived alone leaving considerable empty space. "Henri", he announced, "I do believe it's time for you to try to sleep indoors." After much discussion and good-natured kidding, the Indians agreed to stay on the floor near the door.

François* was given a small room with a real bed, the first he had felt in almost a year. In the morning, the Indians were camped under a tree in the garden. "Too hot," said Henri, and all had a good laugh. Charlotte made a wonderful breakfast before the group left for mass. The Indians attended but sat in the back. "Too hot in front", Henri joked.

After the post-mass socializing, mainly involving the wonderful new Calvados available in the wilderness, the group returned to the farm. As they went to the barn, Angélique stopped and smelled the air, *"La sève d'érable!"* she exclaimed with excitement, "The maple sap has started to run."

The next morning was a flurry of activity with all hands on deck. The Indians arrived with a large collection of buckets, sacks and large odd nails. Henri showed François* how to select the proper trees and the proper location on the tree to remove a small amount of bark, place the large nail in the tree, and hang a bucket from it. Soon the thick sap began to run in the bucket.

François* tasted it and made a terrible face. Henri laughed, "This sap, not syrup." As the containers filled, they were carried to the Indian camp where Angélique and Anne* had built a giant fire and were heating two large cauldrons. The sap was poured in and boiled down to a much smaller amount.

Anne* explained that timing was crucial to collect the best and most sap. The time of year could vary greatly due to the nature of the winter. Only certain maple trees gave the correct sap. The boiling would remove the water and much of the bitterness, and from the remaining material they would make syrup, molasses, sugar and sweet liquor, which was no substitute for Calvados. They took sticks of wood and packed snow around them and dipped them into the syrup. It made a wonderful cold and sweet treat.

The process took several days. When they were done, Anne* exclaimed, "This is God's reward for enduring winter."

Chapter 27

<u>Beauport Québec - Spring 1667</u>:

With spring came births. The farm gained three more pigs and four more goats. One evening as François* returned to the barn from dinner, he noticed the cow lying down in some distress. She had grown quite large in the past month. François* hurried back to the house to tell Anne* who came running. The outcome of this birth would be critical for the farm.

François* had some experience with delivering cows with Pierre's father in Normandie. The labor was longer than expected, but a head finally appeared and with some help from François* the new calf was delivered. Anne* noted, "It seems rather small."

François* returned to the mother and said, "I believe I understand why." And soon another head appeared. "I have only seen this once before with cows," he said, and the second appeared. This one delivered easily.

As Anne* surveyed the site "They say this runs in families. You know, I was a twin myself, although my sister was small and died soon after birth," and she crossed herself hastily. "And look, we have a new cow and now a bull as well."

François* delivered the afterbirth and stayed the night with the animals. In the morning, the cow was standing and nursing her new brood.

Next in line was Fleur. It was apparent, as she grew larger in the past two months that she, too, was in the family way. One morning at breakfast François* was greeted by a basket with eight black and white puppies. Anne* said, "From the look of them I think they are from one of Henri's Indian dogs."

Charlotte added, "Now there are more métis then just me."

Anne* told François*, "I'll keep two and I'm certain there will be takers for the rest. Part wolf and part border collie will make fine Québécois dogs. If you like, François*, you can have the first pick. It will be the first resident on your new farm."

Spring passed quickly, the last vestiges of ice left the river and the boat and canoe traffic reappeared. Winter wheat was harvested, and fields plowed and planted with the hay, summer wheat, and other crops according to the date. Henri explained that maize would be last as it did not tolerate any frost.

The berry harvest was very impressive. During the late months of spring, wild raspberries, black berries, boysenberries, mulberries, and strawberries, some wild and some from the garden were harvested. Something that François* had yet to see was the blueberry. These small plants grew directly from rocks and fruited in abundance. This was a wonderful and very new taste. They became part of bread, pancakes, preserves, tarts, and pies, another wonderful and unique thing of Canada.

Chapter 28

<u>Québec, The Fur Market - May 1667:</u>

After dinner one evening in May, Anne* asked François* to go with Henri to Québec for two days, "It is the annual fur market. I would like some things. I'll provide you a list. Take two jugs of your Calvados and give them to Jean-Michel at the lower town tavern. Tell him he may sell it to the voyageurs by the glass and if they inquire, tell them they can come and purchase it from you after the market ends. We will do quite well."

François* enquired into the nature of the market, and Anne* replied, "Each autumn the voyageurs go to the wilderness and spend the winter obtaining furs. As soon as the ice clears, they head back to civilization. It takes many days for some to return, so a time is set in May for the market where they will gather to sell. It is a wild time indeed. Henri will watch out for you."

The next afternoon Henri and François* tied the canoe at the lower town dock. The Place Royal was wild, filled with an assortment of the most foul and fearsome men François* had ever seen. It made the *rendez-vous* look like a tea at the Longchamps Estate. The actual market was to take place in the morning. Henri and François* made their way to the tavern. Passing through the square, they encountered four fistfights, three knife fights and one man bleeding to death on the cobblestones.

At the tavern Henri stayed outside, and François* entered. He spoke with the proprietor, Jean-Michel, who had been alerted some weeks ago by Anne*. He told François*, "I will take care of everything. You can take a tour about and see the action, but you might be better staying here after dark rather than in the square."

François* noticed that most of the men were relatively short although extremely strong. He was told that voyageurs preferred shorter men as they fit better into the canoes. The square was a veritable carnival of activity with all manner of contests of strength and sometimes stupidity. They saw knife-throwing contests and hatchet-throws, weight lifting, weight throwing, and wrestling. As darkness fell they made their way back to the tavern.

François* saw a man he knew named Michaud, who had bought a farm just this year in Charlesbourg. He was developing it himself but had yet to find a wife. "I tell you it is hard to start alone, and lonely as well. I have cleared one acre and built a small cabin. I'm living off game and doubt that I'll be ready to plant for one or two more years."

Just then, three rough men, visibly intoxicated, joined them. Dressed in deerskin, if not for their beards and hats they could be Indian. They congratulated François* on his Calvados. Two of them continued to drink heavily and the third who was more sober began a one-sided conversation with François*.

"We are part of a group of forty who have traded the north this year. We went as far as Montréal, then started north to the Ottawa country. Have you been to Montréal?" François* indicated he had not. The man continued, "Well, it's not so civilized as Québec. There's a market there as well, but the prices are better here, so it's worth the extra voyage for us. Montréal is an island in the river surrounded by rapids and can only be passed by portage. The rapids to the south are as long and rough as ever seen. It is said that when Cartier saw them, he thought they went to China. That is why that part is called *Lachine*."

François* thought of Mathurine* in that savage place. The man continued, "We made our way to the Ottawa River, then west to the great lake of the Huron which is almost as big as the ocean itself, but the freshest water you will ever see. Many of the Huron have died of the pox, and the beaver are not as plentiful as they once were, so we headed north across that great lake. We always make the best speed. We leave at dawn and paddle hard until sunset, only eat twice a day. I've been at it twenty years. I never miss a stroke in sixteen hours.

"At the end of the lake of the Huron is a river of rapids that takes one or two days to portage, called the River of Sainte-Marie. We portage straight through without stop and take all the packs. The way back is harder as each man carries two bales of pelts each eighty-pounds as well as his share of the canoe.

"At the end of the portage, we came to the big water, a lake so big it has no end. No one has been to the far side; the water is always cold and most places there is no bottom at all. In a storm the waves are as big as the mountains, but it is the most wild and wonderful place in the world, more game and fish than you can count and never a sight of man. The Algonquin call it *Gitcheegumee,* which means endless water.

"First Frenchman to see it was Etienne Brulé. Have you heard of him?" François* had, but he played dumb. "Brulé came to Canada when Champlain first came. No one knows from where. They say he was an orphan boy who stowed away. Anyway, he took to the woods real well, learned the Indian language and ways better that the Indians themselves. It was Brulé who first showed the big lakes to Champlain. Then one day he up and disappeared. They say he made the Huron mad, and they ate him.

"We went several days on the north side of the big lake, and found Algonquin to trade with. We had as many pelts as we could bring back in less than two months. Spent the rest of the time raising hell: hunting, fishing, having Indian women. I had three wives this summer, had them all at once every night. I don't know what you boys are thinking about building farms. The wilderness is the real life. Well, a few weeks ago we started back and here we are, but we'll head back there again this year."

François* asked the man if they ever trapped the beaver themselves. He replied, "No reason. Frenchman can't trap near as good as the Indian. When I started out, I was a *courier de bois,* did some of my own trapping, that's real work. The government started to frown on independents like me, so I quit and became a regular *voyageur.* Have to have a license, but it's easier and more

158

money. Now the Indian trap and skin the pelts and we trade for them."

François* asked what they traded and he replied, "Jewelry, tools, cloth, whatever they want. Some trade liquor but that's illegal," he said with a wink. "Some trade guns but that's real bad. Savages are bad enough with bows. We bring back the pelts and the Scotsmen that run the post pay us. We buy what we need for next year, drink up the rest and take off again. No use for the city when we got the wilderness waiting."

When François* asked where else he had been, he replied, "We used to go west past Montréal, then portage Lachine and take the Saint-Laurent to the end in a big lake called Ontario. You cross that and come to the Niagara. Now there's a sight a man should see before he dies, falls as high as a mountain and as wide too. You can walk the rocks in back and hide behind the water. If a man stood under, it would crush him to death.

"From there you go through another big lake to a long river that connects through a small shallow lake where there is a small trading post, and then to another fast river which brings you to the south end of the lake of the Huron. That used to be fine trading, but the beaver are no longer so many and the north country is better for us."

At this point the drink began to get the best of the man. François* excused himself and went to talk to Jean-Michel at the bar. Another rough, drunk trader came up behind him and said, "You the man with the Calvados?" François* indicated he had helped to make it. The man

continued, "Must have made a bunch of money tonight."
François* assured him that Jean-Michel and the tavern had
made the money and turned away.

At that point he felt the man fall against him, and
turning around he saw the man with his knife drawn, lying
dead on the floor, a knife in his back.

An onlooker exclaimed, "He was going to stab you!
But I didn't even see where the other knife came from." As
calmly as he could, François* placed the man's knife on the
bar and removed the knife from the man's back. He slipped
out as quietly as he could. As he went outside, he returned
Henri's knife to him.

Henri took it. "Miss Anne* tell me to watch your
back."

As they had arranged, the two men went to the gun
shop of Jean Badeau where they were to spend the night.
Jean, who lived above the shop, greeted them. They had a
light meal and retired for the night.

The following morning François* and Henri arose
early and headed back to the square where there was a bevy
of activity with the hung-over traders selling to the fur
merchants. François* had realized there were a few
Scotsmen in Québec, and he now saw they all worked as
bankers for the fur merchants. "No one can handle money
like the Scots." He was told.

He saw Jean Juchereau, the rich merchant who had
been aboard *l'Aigle d'Or*. François* was surprised that the
man remembered him and said hello. When the market

concluded, the *voyageurs* returned to the tavern and Henri and François* returned home.

Over the next few days there was a steady stream of men coming to purchase Calvados. They ran out and also sold the rest of Henri's maize whiskey. "We need to tend the apples well and make more next year." François* said as he saw his farm come closer.

Chapter 29

Beauport, Québec - Summer 1667:

As the weather turned warm, the days sped by.
François* was surprised that the days actually grew hot.
Anne* had added a new crop, tobacco, it was foreign to
François* as a farmer, but Henri had a grasp of it, and it
seemed like a simple crop. Peas were planted in large
amounts as they endured the early cold well. With a slab of
pork fat and special seasonings, Charlotte made a delicious
pea soup eaten at every dinner in the early summer. The
baby animals were all prospering particularly the prized
twin cows.

Summer was the social season for the Québécois.
Every Sunday there were picnics in the neighborhoods. As
the farmhouses were lined up along the waterways, travel to
the neighbors was quite simple. This also provided a greater
level of community protection. Gala affairs, the picnics
began after Sunday mass and lasted until after dark. There
was food and drink in great amounts, and wonderful sweet
treats such as berry pies and tarts. Lacrosse and other
games were played, races were run and other contests held.
There was always a spirited contest of the French against
the Algonquin; and as usual, the Indians prevailed, except
in some French games such as Boules. The classic French
discussions on every topic from politics to weather were
held. They became livelier as the day progressed and more
alcohol was consumed. Although they often ended in a
more physical struggle, everyone parted friends at the end
of the day making enthusiastic plans for the next Sunday.

Henri showed François* the art of Indian trapping. They would set lines of traps through the woods and check them each morning. Henri could trap rabbits, fox, and muskrat, a beaver-like animal prized for its pelt and strong tangy meat. They made trips to fish for trout in the stream and sturgeon and other fish in the river. Fresh fish were always plentiful. In fact, the Québec diet was so far superior to that in France, François* had almost forgotten what it was like to be hungry. He had certainly forgotten what it was to be bored.

One day the great news arrived: the first ship of the season was due from France. François* and Anne* took the canoe into Québec where most of the town had turned out for the event. The ship was about the size of *l'Aigle d'Or*. As the passengers disembarked, François* noted a group of about twenty workers, only a few soldiers, and fifteen young ladies led by a nun. The cargo included some farming machinery, a large weaver's loom, three cannon for the fort and ten horses including four large Perchon horses.

The ladies and the soldiers proceeded up the hill, and the selection of the indentured men began. Anne* told François*, "You can stay and watch, I have business with Monsieur Langlois." As she went off, François* was jointed by Jean* Poitevin and Guillaume* Renaud. Jean* said they had been able to put in a crop this season in Bourg Royal at Charlesbourg, and Renaud announced he hoped to win the approval of a *fille du Roi* and be married by winter.

Anne* returned and after greeting the men, said to François*, "Monsieur, could you come and assist me with

163

my new purchase?" François* followed her down to the ship where Noel* Langlois stood next to a wonderful white Perchon horse. Anne* said, "François*, meet our newest worker."

Langlois added, "Anne* asked me if I could possibly secure a horse for her this year, and now here she is. These are from my home town in Montagne-au-Perche."

Anne* added, "She was quite expensive, but I was aided by the profits from our Calvados enterprise. Monsieur Langlois tells me that the animals were taken off the boat at the *Iles de la Madeleine* to graze, and he has understood that our mare bred with one of the male Perchon at that time. So we may be in great luck."

Anne* returned home in the canoe and instructed François* to bring the horse by the land route and the beach. François*'s mind was filled with thoughts of the things they could now do with this wonderful beast. He had known Perchon horses in Normandie. Originally bred as riding horses for knights in full armor, they were now used as workhorses and could pull enormous loads.

This horse was typical Perchon, white with a fine brown speckle giving her a beige appearance. She was two feet taller than the other horses and almost twice their weight. She was energetic and in excellent spirits, especially after being a month at sea. François* reasoned the grazing on the island would have been beneficial, and reflecting on his own lonesome plight, lacking in female companionship, thought the breeding with another horse might have also raised her spirits.

When François* returned, Anne* reported, "We are going to need winter quarters for all our new animals. I have alerted the neighbors to come this Saturday and we shall try to raise a new barn with the lumber from last winter's trees."

Saturday morning all the neighbors arrived with tools. Anne* and Charlotte were busy putting out tables and preparing a hearty breakfast. Along with the close neighbors was also Rene* Reaume, a master carpenter who had come from Larochelle. He lived in Québec and had been working on the Cathedral. François* had encountered him in town. An interesting man, always with an opinion, and not afraid to express it with his fists, Anne* told François* that he had spent his share of nights in jail.

Reaume took charge of the project and everyone was assigned a task. The horse was invaluable in hauling lumber and helping to lift wood with ropes. François* was astounded at the progress. By lunchtime the superstructure was up and by dinner it was enough completed that Henri and François* could finish it during the week. Pierre* Parent, husband of Jeanne* Badeau, explained this group had built every barn in the area and had profited by the experience. After dinner there was drinking, games and music. Anne* invited everyone to a picnic after mass the next day.

Chapter 30

The great highlights of summer were ship arrivals, a total of five this summer. Each brought new workers and some new girls. All carried new items to ease the frontier life. François* attended the arrivals when he could, occasionally with Anne* and sometimes with Henri. One day he was with Anne*. When she returned from her errands, she handed François* an envelope. François*'s reading skills were poor but he understood this.

François Allard
Québec

Returning home, they sat on the porch while Anne* read the letter.

Blacqueville, Normandie
June 10, 1667

*Dear François**

The curé is aiding me with this letter. We pray you are alive and well. Each night at grace we ask God to protect you. It has been a good year in France, the crops are good and everyone remains in good health. Both Jacques and I have added children to our families, I have a new son and we have named him François.

Father continues to work, but his eyes are poor, however he and Jacques are doing well. Your friend Pierre is married, his father died suddenly last year, and Pierre now manages the farm. By the looks of his wife at mass, I believe they are expecting a birth.
If this letter finds you and a response is possible, it would be gladly received by all.

God bless and keep you,
Your sister, Marie

Anne* said, "I will help you write a response, but there will not be another mail until next summer." François* only gazed out at the river and the city of Québec beyond, lost in his thoughts.

Henri and François* finished the barn during the next two weeks. It would now house the three cows and the new horse with some room for expansion. Best of all, François* had new quarters in the loft with more space, better ventilation in the summer and a strong break against the winter winds.

The first night in his new quarters, François* was awakened by a sound and startled as the door to his loft opened. A young Indian woman came through. Slowly removing her deerskin dress, she quietly slipped into François*'s deer skin bed. In the morning she was gone, leaving François* wondering if he had been dreaming and whether he should feel guilty or elated.

When he went down, Henri was waiting. "You sleep well? Angélique send her sister for celebration of new barn." He laughed his typical laugh.

Two weeks later Anne* returned from town with bad news, "One of the girls from the last ship has become sick, and now a few others have followed. They have high fevers and a rash. They fear it is measles. Fortunately I survived the measles as a child, so I am to go to town to help nurse the sick at the hospital with two other ladies who have also survived the disease.

"The rest of you are to remain on the farm. There will be no travel into or out of Québec without permission. You should begin the harvest, and I will return when the outbreak is controlled. However, I have no idea when that will be." François* recalled the epidemics in France. He had heard how bad some could be. He had also heard in the 1640s, large segments of the Indian population had succumbed to measles and smallpox.

The following day, François* and the Indians began to cut the hay. The work was much easier with the horse. François* marveled that he was now in his second year in Québec. He wondered if the old cow was happy for the relief or upset at the loss of her prize position.

The lack of activity on the river, the harbor and around the city left an eerie quiet. They finished the hay and cut the new tobacco hanging it to dry and be cured later. They cut and separated the wheat, but it would have to wait until after the quarantine before they could take it to the mill.

They had just began harvesting the apples when Anne* returned, "It was bad but could have been worse. It was contained quickly. We had forty cases, three children and ten adults died as well as six Indians. They were all buried immediately to prevent further spread." Anne* Ardouin-Badeau was only fifty-two years old, but she looked older and thinner than she had only a few weeks ago.

The apple crop was glorious. François* had taken extra care to nurse the fruit along, and his efforts had brought great results. He looked at these wonderful red balls and realized they were the key to his own farm. Only the very best apples were stored and the rest pressed to give twice as much cider as the year before.

The grapes were equally as good, and Anne* predicted a vintage wine this year. As the maize was not dry enough to pick, they began the arduous task of stump removal. Needless to say, the horse earned her keep on this job. She would be harnessed to the stump as Henri, Philippe and François* began to dig and chop the roots. Eventually the stump would come free and be dragged to the side of the field. Three weeks later they were ready for the maize and once that was completed, Pierre* Tremblay and Gabriel arrived to began to help clear trees.

Chapter 31

Time flew by, and before he knew it, François* was preparing for the *rendez-vous*. He, Henri and Philippe loaded the canoe and headed west. They carried a list from Anne* and a number of tradable items. Even though the cider was not quite done, he and Henri had distilled some Calvados. François* realized it was not high quality, but he was certain he could find a market. He put it in smaller containers, realizing this group would be more interested in consumption than conservation.

The event was no disappointment. There were campfires, singing, dancing, and Indian women along with contests, fights, feats of strength, feats of daring, and feats of stupidity. François* was seated by the campfire of Henri's brother when a stranger approached him and stared intently at him. The man approached and asked, "Monsieur, are you François* Allard?"

Shocked at the question François* replied, "Yes I am."

The man extended his hand, "My name is Louis* Marier. I live in Montréal and came from the village of St. Symphoien near Tours in the Touraine region of France. I came with the military in 1665 but now farm in Montréal."

François* asked, "Should I know you?"

"No, but I recognized your necklace," referring to the wampum, "My dear wife wears an identical one."

With this François* froze.

"She told me that you gave it to her. She also said that were it not for you, she would not be alive today. I believe I owe you a debt of gratitude, Monsieur Allard."

François* blurted, "Mathurine*, is she well?"

"Well enough, she expects our first child soon. We were married in May. I fear sometimes she is a little in love with you, but I am in a position to be nothing but grateful."

Louis* Marier sat down and the men talked and drank into the night. Eventually he arose. "I must be getting along, I wish you well, monsieur. Mathurine* will be thrilled to hear of our meeting and how well you are doing." He left François* to his thoughts of joy, jealousy and a bit of lust.

As fall progressed into winter and the beautiful red and yellow countryside began to turn to green and white, the work preparing the farm for winter progressed. François*'s new dog, Violette, had grown to almost full size. She was intelligent, well-trained and rarely left François*'s side. Her heritage made her an odd looking dog with a shaggy black and white coat and the unmistakable face and eyes of a wolf but with floppy ears. She had all the farming instincts of the border collie and all the wilderness instincts of the Indian dogs.

François* had nicknamed the horse, Louise, the feminine form of Louis, as he felt this was a truly royal animal. She had become his good friend and most important asset. Anne* had obtained an old saddle. François* was able to ride the beast on occasion, although even he had difficulty mounting such a giant.

Christmas of 1667 came with all its gaiety, and Québec was soon again the great clean, white, frozen wilderness. As soon as the ice was passable to the city,

Anne said, "We will go to town to see Noel* Morin. Now that we have a horse, we should have a proper cart." François* hitched Louise to their old small cart to which he and Henri had already added the winter runners, and they proceeded to cross the ice to Québec.

In the short while François* had been in Québec, the area had expanded and improved. The population had grown by a few hundred, half new settlers and half births. More farms were being developed and along with that, more roads. There was a road along the north coast of the Saint-Laurent almost to the end of the *Ile d'Orleans.* There were some stretches of road along the coast of the *Ile* itself, and some on the less developed south coast of the Saint-Laurent. There was even a rudimentary road north to Charlesbourg. These were often not easily passable but improving. There was even talk of a road that would eventually go to Montréal. The Beauport area was now so populous a small chapel had been built close to the farm.

At the Place Royal in town, François* and Anne* could drive the cart into the square and up to the upper town, then all the way through the town to the carriage shop of Noel* Morin. They discussed their needs and decided on a cart large enough to handle many of their bigger chores in one load. When it was done, Morin would keep the old cart and convert it into a real carriage with a convertible top to keep out the rain. Anne* would be one of Québec's first carriage owners. Because it was the slow season, and in deference to Anne*, Morin said the cart would be finished in a few weeks.

Chapter 32

Beauport, Québec, February 17, 1668,
Dear Marie

I must start this letter early to make the first mail in the spring. I cannot tell you how your letter gladdened my heart. Give my love to father and to Jacques's family as well as your own. Express my regrets and love to Pierre and his family as well. I am proud that you have made your new son my namesake.

I hardly know how to begin. Québec is the most wonderful place. I have had the great fortune to find myself in the employ of the most wonderful woman, Anne* Ardouin, a widow who has treated me more as a son than a worker. It is she who is aiding me with this letter.

This country defies imagination. It is clean, grand and open. There are lakes, forests and streams without end. There are mountains that reach into the clouds. The people are beyond compare. I find myself being addressed in town by the most important men in the country. Here a man is truly judged for himself and not only his position.

I hope to have a farm of my own before long. Land is plentiful and awaits improvement. Land is not yet owned by the farmer, but word has it that this will someday no longer be the case due to its incredible abundance. I also hope to find a wife although eligible women are as rare as land is plentiful.

The winters are incredible, cold beyond belief with snow to the rooftops. The water freezes solid enough to support traffic. I have learned to hunt and fish as never before. Inform Pierre that I have in one day caught as many fish as he and I had caught during our entire youth.

The native population is not at all what I had expected. Indeed my closest companion is an Algonquin man named Henri. He lives with his family on Miss Anne*'s farm. He is a Christian, indeed the most Christian man I have ever met. He is skilled and knowledgeable not only in the ways of the wilderness, but in the ways of society in general.
I pray that this letter finds you well and that I shall hear from you again.

Your loving brother,
François*

Winter ended and the ice again broke, beginning the great celebration. The apple crop had been exceptional, and François* and Henri had made a large store of cider which they turned into Calvados. They judged this year a better product than last. Spring came with more births, the most important the birth of a new purebred Perchon stallion. The crops were planted and spring chores done. The boats and new immigrants began to appear in the harbor.

In June, Anne* came to François*. "I fear I must ask you to go to Montréal for me. I had hoped to send my son François Badeau, but he is too busy with marriage contracts for the new *filles du roi*. You must take some documents to the notary and return others to me. I will have Henri accompany you as he knows the town and the route."

Two days later Henri and François* took the smaller, faster canoe and began the journey west. Three days of hard paddling during the day and camping out at night brought them to *Trois Rivieres* where they had turned north for the *rendez-vous*. Beyond this the Saint-Laurent became completely wild with no signs of civilization, only the forests on the south bank and the mountains on the north. The next evening they turned up a smaller stream and one hour later arrived at an Indian camp.

"Village of Anuk," said Henri, referring to his brother. Anuk greeted them and took them into the camp. The Algonquin camps were more mobile than the Iroquois, using tents rather than long houses. This reflected their more mobile hunting society. Anuk explained they would soon move up into the mountains where the summer hunting and trapping were more favorable.

After dinner the men smoked at the campfire and had a discussion in French and Algonquin which François* could follow with some difficulty. One of Henri's cousins, a guide, had returned from the winter when he had guided a party of traders to the south and east. "We go to land of narrow lakes in the country of the Iroquois and *l'Anglais*. I fear these English. They treat the Indian poorly and have no regard for the Indian way. Their trade with the Iroquois is with guns and whiskey. It corrupts their society. Each year there are many more of these English. They clear the wilderness and push the Indian to the mountains. I hear them say they will soon want also the land of the Algonquin and the French. They are coming in numbers too many to count."

Eventually the discussion ended, and the men went to their beds. Henri and François* were greeted by two young Indian woman. Henri cautioned François* not to protest or they would insult their hosts, so François* spent his second night in the company of an Indian maiden. In the morning, Henri explained this was a test to make certain that Henri had not become "too French."

After three more days of paddling, they began to see civilization as farms began to appear on the banks. They reached the prominent fork in the river around the island of Montréal which was much larger than François* had imagined, larger than even *Ile d'Orleans*. They took the south fork of the river and after several miles came to the harbor and the foot of the town. Montréal was slightly larger than *Trois Rivieres*, but nothing like Québec. The buildings were small and all made of rough wood. The few streets were mud.

Landing their canoe, they proceeded to the town hall. François* made inquiries as to the notary and was told to return the following afternoon as the notary was out working on marriage contracts. Leaving the building, François* heard his name called and turned in surprise to see none other than Marguerite Bourgeoys. "Monsieur Allard, how wonderful to see you again. How have you fared with my friend, Anne* Ardouin?"

François* indicated that he had done very well and thanked the nun profusely for her intervention in his behalf in introducing him to Anne*. She in turn explained that she was busy with the *filles du roi*. "I did not make a voyage

176

this year. I fear next year may be my last trip to France. We are very occupied with a number of fine young ladies this year. I suspect that you may be in search of a bride in the next two years, Monsieur."

François* indicated that indeed he would be and reported his hopes of acquiring a farm after his service with Anne*. The nun replied, "I have no doubt that you will find a mate. I must be on my way, God bless you and grant you good fortune, François*." And she hastened off.

Henri indicated they might do well to go to see the southern part of the city, so they returned to the canoe and headed south. In an hour they came to a strong current and landed the canoe. They continued south on foot and saw the largest and most wild stretch of rapids imaginable. "Frenchmen call this 'Lachine,' takes one or two days to portage, biggest rapid this side of Niagara," Henri reported, indicating they should make camp there for the night. "Sometimes too many fights at night in Montréal."

The following morning the men made the easy downstream passage back to the harbor. As they were early, they sat in the square watching the activity. François* noticed a lady with an infant strapped to her back who turned, facing him, and his heart stopped. There was no doubt, it was Mathurine*.

When she recognized him, she came over, "I knew some day we would meet again. Jacques* told me of your meeting at the *rendez-vous*. How wonderful to see you, François*." They sat and began to trade histories. "When I arrived in Montréal, I was housed at Maison Saint-Ange. Each Saturday eligible men visited us. I considered a few until I met Jacques*. He was a soldier and very handsome. We were married last year and this is our first son Michel, born in April. Jacques* acquired a farm just north of town. At first I'm afraid I was of little use, as Parisienne girls know little of the country life. However I am learning. Whenever I was cold or afraid, I remembered how strong and brave you were. Sister Bourgeoys continues to be of assistance to all the girls."

François* told her of his life working for Anne* and his plans for the future. She replied, "I am certain that you will find a wonderful girl and have a wonderful life. I must confess I often dream of you, but Jacques* is a good man and I am content. Now I must say my goodbye." She pulled out her half of the wampum and showed it to him. She then gave François* a more than platonic kiss, and turned and walked away.

After completing Anne*'s business with the notary, the men set off on a much easier downstream ride, arriving at the farm in less than four days. Anne* met them with a large list of chores to make up for the almost two weeks absence.

Chapter 33

Summer had descended with the hot weather, chores and wonderful Sunday picnics along with it. Soon the ships began to arrive. François* always tried to attend the landings as did most Québécois. During one such landing, François* was gazing dreamily at the young *filles du roi* as they walked down the gangplank into the Place Royal. He was joined by his friend Guillaume* Renaud. From his army connections Renaud had taken a position as domestic for Louis Chartier, a rich gentleman from Paris who now served as Lieutenant General of Québec. The position was a paying one, so Renaud had just been able to purchase a farm in Charlesbourg.

The numbers of the young women were growing each year. In 1666 only 24 came with François* and Guillaume*, while the next year 91 women had come and possibly more this year. Renaud said, "There is a social gathering Saturday evening for single men to meet these young ladies. François*, why don't you accompany me?"

François* replied, "I will not be well placed to marry for at least two more years. None of these woman will be interested in an indentured man with no land."

Renaud countered, "None the less, all single men are invited. It would be fun and I would not have to go alone. Six o'clock at the great hall in the Ursuline convent, what do you say?"

"I will try, if Miss Anne* does not need me."

Renaud ended, "I will await you outside the convent at six o'clock sharp."

Having obtained Anne*'s blessing and use of the small canoe, François* bathed in the river. Donning his best clothes, he headed to town. He met Renaud pacing in front of the convent. Pacing along with him were at least sixty other anxious men. Renaud said, "I've heard there are thirty-eight women here tonight."

At six o'clock sharp, Madame de La Peltri, the famous benefactor of the convent, came out on the porch for an announcement. "Gentlemen, in a few moments we will invite you in to meet our new ladies. I expect nothing but perfect behavior and demeanor. You may move about and speak with whomever you please. There will be another meeting next week. If at any time you and a young lady feel you may have an interest in a marriage contract, you may contact the notary. Monsieur François Badeau is at your service this evening. Now if you would follow me in an orderly fashion," and she turned, walking through the doors followed by men trying to be as orderly as possible under the circumstances.

The great room was indeed large enough for the event. Young ladies sat on one side with a number of chaperones while men lined up on the other side. François* thought of a barn cat facing off with a rat. However, he was not certain who was the rat and who was the cat. The more experienced of the men made their moves. François* and Renaud held back with the younger men. François* recognized some of the chaperones and was pleased that Marguerite Bourgeoys came over to say hello. "I am leaving tomorrow for Montréal with some other girls. I am pleased to see you, Monsieur Allard. I believe this is our old shipmate, Corporal Renaud." François* and Guillaume* bowed shyly as she continued, "Are you now in the market for a wife?"

François* indicated he probably was not, but Guillaume* was. She then steered him over to the chaperones and introduced Madame de La Peltri, and Lady Anne Gasnier whom he had met with Anne* in Québec. Marguerite said, "Miss Gasnier is the widow of our former prosecutor, Jean Bourdon. As you may know, he passed on this winter. Miss Gasnier has agreed to help us with the *filles du roi* program."

Anne Gasnier added, "I have met Monsieur Allard with my good friend Anne* Ardouin. She speaks quite highly of you, sir." François* thanked her sheepishly. Marguerite then introduced him to Sister Marie de l'Incarnation, the Mother Superior of the convent, who appeared as though she could render a man useless with a mere glance. As the men took their leave, Marguerite whispered something to Anne Gasnier that would shape the course of François*'s life.

As Renaud and François* strolled across the room François* caught the glance of an attractive young woman. Both stared with the look of vague recognition. The young woman left the company of two older men who were obviously boring her and came over. "Monsieur, I believe I know you. You are a boy from the country who came occasionally with his mother to our church in Rouen. We referred to you as the tall boy with two different eyes."

François* said, "That could be me. My mother would occasionally go from our town in Blacqueville to Saint-Maclou as her mother had come from there. My name is

François* Allard, and this is my good friend Guillaume* Renaud."

She replied, "I am Marie* de la Mare; as you know I am just arrived. I begged my parents to let me come. We learned of Canada in school. This is the new world and the great adventure. How odd to meet someone one knows way over here. You know all the girls at Saint-Maclou were in love with you."

The three conversed and it became clear to Marie* in spite of her attraction to François*, Renaud held more promise and was much more appealing than the older prospects. As they became more interested in each other, François* wandered off. He spoke with a few young ladies and ran into his friend, Jean* Poitevin. François* said, "Laviolette, don't tell me that you are in the market."

Jean* replied, "One can always dream. I thought it would do no harm to come. However like you, I have one more year of service." He indicated that it would appear he would be able to acquire a farm near his current employer in Charlesbourg at the end of his service.

Later François* paddled back across the river to Beauport. It was a calm, warm night with a clear sky and a full moon. The haunting calls of the loon filled the air. François* thought, as he often did, what a wonderful life this was.

Chapter 34

Fall brought the harvest and with it another excellent apple crop. The Calvados-farm fund continued to grow. Anne* and François* had taken the habit of attending mass in the new chapel in Beauport, a short walk from the farm. Most of the Charlesbourg residents had also found this more convenient, and a society of the near north shore settlements of Beauport and Charlesbourg had begun.

Sunday after mass, Guillaume* Renaud ran to catch François*. "Well, my friend," he began, "thanks to you, I am to be married. My employer and his wife have graciously offered to serve as witness, but I would be honored if you could come and serve as well. I am certain Marie* would appreciate if the beau of Saint-Maclou could be there."

François* agreed happily, and on November 1, 1668, Marie* and Guillaume* were married in the Beauport Chapel with the small but growing community in attendance. Following the ceremony a celebration was held at their new farm in Charlesbourg. Warm weather prevailed, and beautiful Canadian fall colors still hung in the air. François* learned Marie* de la Mare was a trained *sage-femme* or mid-wife, as had been her mother. These women served as doctor, nurse, surgeon, and pharmacist to the wilderness community.

Marie* was not as demur and quiet as the other girls. She was filled with spirit, life and an undeniable thirst for adventure; exactly what Québec needed. François* could only hope he could do so well for a wife.

Winter of 1668-1669 descended with a vengeance a mere two weeks later. The temperature plummeted, and three feet of snow lay on the ground in the last days of November. The north wind was relentless, and the older residents began to reminisce of the terrible winter of 1641 when many residents died of the cold.

By Christmas there was almost no travel, and the holiday passed with little festivity. Anne* asked François* to move to the house, and in an unprecedented move, the Indians and their dogs moved into the barn. The snow soon covered all the windows. Henri, Philippe and François* spent much of each day clearing the doorways and beating paths, finally having to shovel down to the roof of the house to clear the chimney.

Fortunately the farm was organized for such a winter. Supplies, food and wood were readily accessible. Most of this was due to lessons the settlers had learned in that awful winter of 1641. François* worried about Guillaume* and Marie* in sparsely populated Charlesbourg. They lived in the small primitive house that he, Guillaume* and Henri had hastily built that fall. Travel to Charlesbourg or anywhere was out of the question. It took more than an hour to get to the barn to help care for the animals. The cows and horses had coats so thick they looked like bears.

Fortunately in February a brief thaw occurred, and the streams flooded. The snow was reduced to a mere three feet. Soon some travel became possible, and by March the sleigh could go as far as Québec. Then, as always, spring arrived suddenly. The snow melted, the ice began to clear and there was a festival of the ice breaking such as Québec had never seen. Indeed François* was able to sell all of his remaining Calvados in a single day.

Charlesbourg, Québec - Spring 1669:

After the roads had cleared, Anne* approached François*. "I believe you know Monsieur Jean Michaud in Charlesbourg. It seems that he has not found a wife and has prospects in France. He plans to return this season and sell his farm. I thought perhaps you, Henri and I could take a ride out there and see if it is of interest to you." François* could scarcely contain his excitement and soon Louise, the Perchon horse, was pulling the three of them north on the newly improved Charlesbourg road with Violette, the dog, following.

Unlike most towns in Québec which had long thin "ribbon farms" parallel to each other, the town of Charlesbourg was built around a town square where the town hall and soon to be constructed chapel were located. The farmhouses ringed the square, and the farms extended out like pieces of a pie. Around the centrally located farms were other farms in more conventional rows.

The Michaud farm faced the Town Square and extended north toward the Laurentian Mountains. There were only a few other farms in the area. Most was wilderness and virgin forest. A large pond on the property fed by a stream from the mountains continued east and south to join the Beauport Creek. A few acres were cleared, and there was a vineyard, orchard, vegetable garden and small fields in hay, wheat and maize.

The house, small but well located and sturdy, lent itself to expansion. There was a small barn with chickens, a pig, two goats, a sturdy cow and several barn cats who soon occupied Violette. They spoke to Michaud who was obviously ready to deal as he wished to leave as soon as possible, and a quick sale would suit him. Anne* had told François* she was planning to hire a new hand this fall, and they could work out an arrangement that would allow him to harvest the crop at the new farm this year.

François* would be able to meet the price with a small loan from Anne that he could soon pay it back with this year's Calvados profits. The deal was struck, and a few days later the men met at the office of François Badeau to sign the agreement. Of course, François* did not actually own the land and would pay annual dues to the Seigneur, but he would actually be in control of the farm.

So it was François* started the last few months of his indentured duty with his goal in hand. One morning, as he was preparing the cornfield for planting, Philippe appeared. After a short while he spoke, "My father says that you are to move to your own farm. I believe you could use an Indian, and I would like to offer my services." François* had not even hoped for such an opportunity and agreed immediately. With that Philippe smiled and said, "Good, now I go get woman." And he disappeared as only the Indians could.

Three days later Philippe again approached François*. This time he was accompanied by an Indian girl of no more than fourteen years. " François*," he said, "This is Marie, my woman. We are to be married at the mission church in three weeks. We would be honored for you to serve as witness." Three weeks later François* and Anne* walked to the mission church on the Jesuit grounds to the west of Anne*'s farm for the marriage.

Later the celebration at Henri's camp was culturally different but every bit as merry as that at Renaud's farm. That evening as they returned to the barn, François* scratched behind the floppy ears on Violette's wolf-like head, saying, "Well girl, it looks like we are already gathering a family."

The first immigrant boat arrived early due to an early departure and a quick crossing. As a result, François* found himself in June standing before the Ursuline convent with his old friend, Jean* Poitevin. Both would fulfill their obligation in early August. Poitevin had arranged for a farm at Charlesbourg less than a mile from both François* and Renaud through his employer, Mathurin Moreau, who was splitting land into smaller parcels. Jean would owe some of each year's crop to Moreau until he had paid his indebtedness. His lot would be more difficult than François*'s.

The men entered the room and stayed together. François* rather enjoyed the outing, but he was shy around women and found conversations painful. Like all the men, he would like a woman who was strong and intelligent. Attractive looks and a dowry other than the 50 livres from the king would also be nice. Such women, alas, were rare in these rooms.

Jean struck up a conversation with a thin, attractive girl whose name was Madeleine* Guillodeau. She was 18 years old and from the small town of LaFlotte, on *l'Ile de Ré* just off the coast of Larochelle. Her father, a farmer, had died a short time ago, so she was encouraged to go to Québec by her parish priest. Talkative and energetic, she had a wonderful smile. François* could see his old shipmate was smitten.

François* left the convent and paddled back to Beauport. He felt he was never going to find a woman this way.

PART TWO

JEANNE*

Chapter 1

<u>Artannes-sur-Indre, Touraine, France - 1456:</u>

Father André Anguille hurried down the hall of the abbey. Entering through a heavy door into a large book-lined room, he encountered a man in his thirties seated at a large desk. The man stopped his writing and looked up. "Ah, Father André, I have a list of documents I require. They are, I believe, all at the library of the Archbishop in Tours. You are to leave at once and bring them to me. Please make haste. I feel urgency in this work. This young girl saved France and if anything she is a saint rather than a witch."

André replied, "Of course, Monseigneur Héli." He took the list and left for the courtyard. Monsiegneur Héli de Bourdeilles was what today would be referred to as an up-and-comer. Having joined the Franciscan order as a young man, he was now the head of the Abbey at Artannes. A voracious reader and writer, he had been imprisoned a few years ago by the English for his works. Today he was working on the beginning of what would become the rehabilitation of Jeanne d'Arc, a young girl burned to death as a witch by the English in the city of Rouen twenty-five years before. That was the very day Father André Anguille was born.

André took the small horse-driven cart and started north on the five-mile trip to Tours, the capital of the region of Touraine. André was in his second year as a Franciscan priest and the assistant in the parish of Saint-Maurice in his hometown of Artannes-sur-Indre. His father, who managed a prosperous farm in the area, had the influence to get André into the priesthood. Artannes, a small town of about 800 people, was crossed by the River Indre as it wound its way to join the Loire River in Tours. The Franciscan Abbey was its largest enterprise, but there was also a picturesque mill and two warm springs said to have healing powers. The church of Saint-Maurice was adjacent to the Abbey.

Chapter 2

<u>Artannes-sur-Indre, Touraine, France - 213 years later, Spring 1669:</u>

Michel* Anguille sat with his wife finishing their midday meal. Michel* managed the largest farm in the area as had his ancestors. Now with businesses in the town of Artannes, he had become a prominent citizen with means, one of the emerging French class known as *bourgeois*. He could see his wife had something on her mind and was rather certain he knew what it was.

Etienette* Toucheraine-Anguilles had been born in Tours to a family with minor aristocratic ties. She had been a wonderful match for Michel*. She was well educated, and as a result, not afraid to speak her mind. "I simply do not know what is to become of the girl, Michel*. I fear she is to become the spinster caretaker of the Abbey."

Michel* replied, "She says she has no calling for the convent and rejected out of hand the three fine young men I have brought around. She claims she has another destiny but has not shared it with me. I doubt even she knows what it is. The girl is attractive, educated and strong, but she is now twenty-two, and both her younger sisters are married. I've asked André to talk with her as she always regards his counsel, but even he has had no effect."

Meanwhile, Jeanne* Anguille was helping to clear dishes in the dining room of the Abbey. She liked her work there, but since her brother André had been sent to Tours, it was not the same. She knew she had no calling for the sisterhood and could not have enthusiasm for any of the dull young men her father brought home. She felt she had a true destiny, but could not see what it was.

As she crossed the courtyard toward the church, Jeanne* paused at the small tomb of Artannes' most famous son, Cardinal Hélie de Bourdeilles, a Franciscan priest from Artannes who had risen to Archbishop and Cardinal of Tours. His writings on Jeanne d'Arc were now famous. In fact it was for the Maid of Orleans that Jeanne* had been named, as had all the oldest daughters in her family for more than one-hundred years, just as the oldest son had been Michel and the second André, and all the Andrés had been priests trained at the Abbey. Her second older brother André had always been her friend and confidant. She was always content working at the Abbey while he was there, but he had been promoted to the Archdiocese at Tours, and was likely to ascend to Bishop himself.

She had her dream again last night, always the same, a strange and wild place with deep woods, the sort of place that would be frightening, but she was never frightened, rather always calm. Her mother's younger sister, her Aunt Therese, told her dreams were just dreams, but Sister Sainte-Barbe at the convent had told her sometimes they were a sign from God, just as they had been for her name sake, Jeanne d'Arc, many years before.

She ascended the steps to the church office to do her daily cleaning where Father Pierre, The church pastor, was reading at his desk. He looked up and said, "Jeanne*, I have received a request from the Archbishop that originates from the King himself. There is a program to recruit young women of good character to immigrate to the colonies in North America to become brides for settlers. They are asking for recommendations from the parish priests. Do you know any young ladies with no prospects who may be interested?"

Jeanne reflected, "Not really. I've heard of colonies, but what are these like?"

"A savage and wild place, I believe, called Québec, an Indian word I think. I believe it is winter most of the year." Jeanne* replied she would give it some thought.

At dinner, Jeanne* endured the usual questions and lectures from her parents. She promised as usual to try to do better and meet a young man. She then left for bed. That night she again had her dream: thick woods and streams, not like the Touraine countryside but much more wild. She awoke bolt upright, suddenly realizing the meaning of her dream.

That morning at breakfast, she said, "Father, I would like to take the cart to Tours. It is important that I see André."

Her father replied, "I will see if Michel can take you on Saturday."

She objected, "I must go today. I am no child. I can drive better than Michel and fight off highwaymen better as well, and as you have pointed out, who would be interested in an old spinster such as me?"

Realizing that he was no match for her, Michel* shook his head and replied, "Very well, but it is imperative that you return well before nightfall."

Jeanne* bolted from the table, gave her father a brief kiss on the forehead, and headed for the barn. Michel* continued to shake his head as she left.

The ride to Tours was wonderful, especially on a spring morning. The road followed the Indre River, possibly the most beautiful in France. It ended as the Indre became part of the larger, slower Loire River. The Loire Valley had become a scene from a child's fairytale when King François I had begun building castles on it over one hundred years ago. It was now dotted with magnificent chateaux, built in the style of Italian architecture, made popular by the Medici family. Jeanne turned right into the city of Tours and soon was in front of the Cathedral.

Entering the office of the Archdiocese, she inquired about André who soon appeared and gave her a grand hug, "How wonderful to see you. What could have brought you?" André had entered the Abbey at a young age and was now in his fifth year of priesthood, already on his way up. He knew his sister had some mischief brewing. They shared more than the family, and what they shared was a reluctance to take the easy path.

Jeanne* replied, "Could we take a short walk?" They exited the office and headed to the park of the Cathedral. "André, what do you know of Québec?"

He replied, "It is a colony in the Americas, a long voyage away, a new and wild place I am told."

"And do you know of a program to recruit young women of marriageable age?"

195

He replied, "It is called the *filles du roi* program. A lady was here last year named Jeanne Mance. She had information. I still have it."

Jeanne continued, "I should like to see it as I believe I am interested."

The young priest startled, "You? Why it's a brutal voyage of a month or more with storms, pirates and disease. The country is primitive and savage, and winters are unbearable. What would you tell father?"

She returned, "That's what I need you for. André, this sounds wonderful to me, and I believe it is my destiny." Then she told him of her dream.

André sighed, "I will see if I can have permission to return with you. We shall discuss it with father and with Father Pierre. It seems preposterous, but knowing you, it could be the correct thing." Jeanne* grabbed his neck and gave him a kiss which raised the eyebrows of two old priests on a nearby bench. On the ride back, Jeanne* read the small book by Jeanne Mance. By the end she was certain of her decision.

That evening they broke the news to their parents. Etiennette* was nearly hysterical and left early for bed. Michel* was more thoughtful. It saddened his heart to think of his daughter crossing the ocean to God knows what, but he realized that she was not prospering as she was. He and André agreed if she were to go, a marriage should be arranged beforehand. Jeanne* objected but realized that this would be the only way to get permission.

The following morning Father Pierre was quite surprised at the news. He said there would be little difficulty if he would vouch for her character. André said he would discuss the possibility of finding a suitable man with the Archbishop. He returned to Tours and Jeanne* returned to the Abbey with a renewed vigor.

The following day the Archbishop told André he knew someone who he was certain could help. He would write a letter, and André should start Father Pierre on the paper work. He warned André this could take more than a year.

Tours, Touraine, France
June 15, 1669

Sister Marguerite Bourgeoys
Montréal, Canada

My Dear Sister,

How long it has been since the days of our youth. I have managed to keep track of your wonderful work with young women in Québec. I hear that Archbishop Laval believes you to be overly liberal and aggressive. I find that easy to believe and delight each time I hear it. I am certain our late father would delight at it as well.
The reason for this long overdue correspondence is the case of a young lady in my Archdiocese. Her name is Jeanne* Anguille who is 22 years of age. Her brother is a young priest in my service. Her father is a businessman of some means in the village of Artannes-sur-Indre, five miles from Tours. I have met the young lady and had dinner in the home of the family. I can vouch for their character without hesitation.

197

The family had hoped to have her marry or join the convent but she has shown no interest in either. She is intelligent and strong and feels her destiny lies in Québec. Of course, the family is concerned of the proposition without a suitable marriage in view. I hope you will help me find a man of good standing and character to this end.
I might add that the young lady seems to have little use for comforts and rather seeks the work and adventure of a true colonist. If such a match can be made, she would leave as soon as is feasible.

I thank you in advance and hope that God continues to bless your work.

Your loving brother,
Bishop Jean-François Bourgeoys
Archbishop of Tours

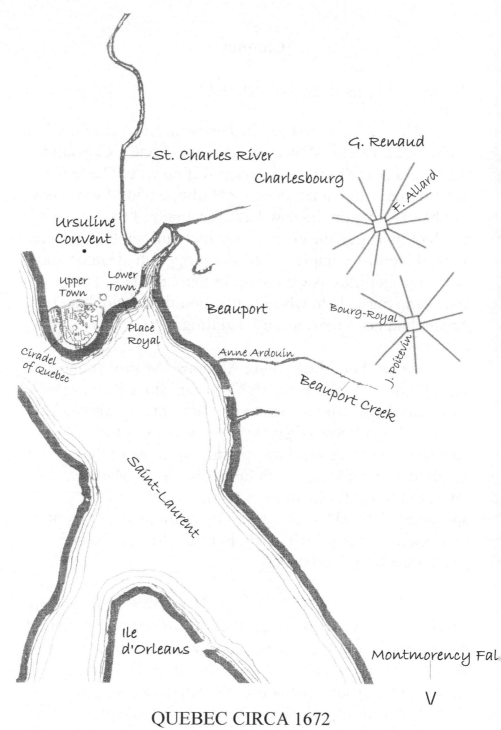

St. Charles River

G. Renaud

Charlesbourg

F. Allard

Ursuline
Convent

Upper
Town

Lower
Town

Beauport

Bourg-Royal

Place
Royal

J. Poitevin

Ciradel
of Quebec

Anne Ardouin

Beauport Creek

Saint-Laurent

Ile
d'Orleans

Montmorency Fal

V

QUEBEC CIRCA 1672

Chapter 3

<u>Beauport, Québec - November 1670:</u>

The long awaited day had arrived. In spite of his excitement, François* was sad to leave Anne*, Charlotte, Henri and Angélique. He wondered if he would have the heart to leave had it not been for Philippe and Marie. They had been living on the new farm for much of the summer and had managed the crops. They had built an Indian camp to rival Henri's complete with smoking, fish cleaning and distilling facilities as well as an Indian bath tent. François* had come out to help whenever he could be spared, and Anne* had been most accommodating.

Anne* had hired young Alphonse Morin, youngest son of Noel* to take François*'s place. Since he was not indentured, she would have to pay him, but he was seeking work and was knowledgeable in the ways of Québec farming. Anne* gave a large picnic, for most of the neighbors to come and wish François* well. Many gave him gifts of useful small tools, which were much appreciated. Noel* Morin gave him a grand gift of an old re-worked cart to which he could hitch the cow he had purchased from Michaud.

At the end of the festivities, François*, Philippe and Marie hitched the cow which Philippe, having been alerted by Henri of the gift of the cart, had walked down to Anne*'s farm, to the "new" cart and rode north on the Charlesbourg road. The house was small and simple. François* had only slept in a house during the two terrible months of the past winter. This first night he took his first meal as a truly free Québécois at the Indian camp with Marie and Philippe.

After dinner, they discussed their plans over a pipe of Indian tobacco. It was difficult to see who had the most excitement for the new adventure, François* or Philippe. Finally François* decided to spend the night under the stars in a deerskin. François* was not a deeply religious man, but like all good Frenchmen he prayed to thank God each night. This night he gave a special thanks for bringing him to this special place and wonderful life.

The next morning work began in earnest. The crops were not yet ready to harvest, so François* and Philippe worked on the house and barn. Once these were in order, the harvest began. The first Sunday François* attended mass at the new chapel in the Charlesbourg Square, only a short walk from home. Afterward there was a picnic at the home of Guillaume* Renaud. His old friend Jean* Poitevin had indeed married Madeleine* Guillodeau only four days after the end of his service, and the couple attended the picnic as their first social event as a family.

Of the pie-shaped areas of Charlesbourg proper and Boug-Royal next to it, only a few of the farms were occupied. Most like François*'s were large, with the thought of splitting them for their offspring. Among the ten or so houses around the square were his old friend Jean* Poitevin and Madeline* Guillodeau.

In a long large ribbon farm just to the north of the Charlesbourg pie-shaped farms was the farm of Guillaume*

Renaud and Marie* de la Mare. These and a few other families formed the society of early Charlesbourg.

François* and Philippe worked the farm like men possessed. With the help of the new cart and Michaud's old cow, they brought in the wheat and hay. They harvested their apples which they planned to add to Anne*s and continue the Calvados business. As they waited for the maize to dry, they began to clear land and were even able to contract Pierre* Tremblay and Gilbert for a few days to cut trees. Half the wood was turned into firewood, the rest into lumber used to start an addition on the house.

When the maize was ready, they brought it in. Between the various crop harvests, François* and Philippe made short jaunts to mountains behind them to collect game for the winter. As one of only two bachelors, and the only young one on the square, François* found he did not lack for invitations to dinner. Although there were no daughters of marriageable age in the families in the square, there was the occasional friend of the family, but François* could not see in these girls what he dreamed for and was too painfully shy to pursue it anyway.

One night in late autumn he was invited to the home of Isaac* Bedard, a man of fifty-three years. He not only farmed but was a highly respected carpenter and builder. He had three children. He told François*, "My wife and I were born Huguenot in Larochelle where we married in 1644 at the Calvinist Temple. During the early reign of Louis XIV, who was only five years old at the death of his father, the Cardinal Mazzarin ruled for him as regent. He had little use for the Protestants, and times were bad for us.

In 1660 Marie* and I converted along with the children. We objected, as many did, to some aspects of the Catholic Church. We heard things were better in New France. As a result we came in 1661. We had five other children in France but, alas, they were born weak and died young.

"Marie was born in 1664 in Québec, and soon after we moved to this farm in Charlesbourg. Now our son Jacques is married and lives next to us. A farmer and a carpenter, he will soon become a master carpenter." François* knew that tradesmen in Québec could become master tradesmen after three years service, a time much shorter than in France.

Isaac* continued, "Jacques is now twenty-five, Louis* fourteen, and Marie four. Life here suits us fine. The church in Québec is less severe and opportunities are boundless for those with energy. I would not return to France to be King," he said as he raised his glass, "*Au Québec!*" And everyone drank the wine including young Marie. He went on, "I foresee a day when communities such as Charlesbourg will have frequent marriages between young people born in Québec, and we will have our first generation of true Canadian Québécois."

At the end of the dinner, Isaac* and Jacques volunteered to give their services on Saturday afternoons to the addition on François*'s farmhouse. Later his neighbor Jean LeMarche, a master cabinet maker, came to help as well. By the onset of hard winter, the small home Jean Michaud had built had become almost as grand as Anne*'s and the barn almost as large.

Life in Charlesbourg was different than Beauport primarily due to the two-mile ride or walk to the Saint-Laurent where their canoes were kept. François* was fortunate he could take the cart with Michaud's old cow to haul loads, though he longed for a horse. The pie-shape arrangement of the farms made visiting easier and soon a bit of a town arose from the square with a small store and even a tavern.

Philippe had two Indian dogs from a litter of Henri's dogs and was able to construct a functional dog sled. In the spring Marie had found a mortally wounded wolf with two small cubs that she brought home and nursed. They grew into very domesticated animals and played readily with the other dogs. Philippe hoped to add them to the sled team next year.

Chapter 4

Charlesbourg, Québec - Spring 1670:

The cold winter passed quickly. Soon it was spring, and François* and Philippe were hard at plowing, planting and expanding into the newly cleared area. His neighbor Jean* Bergevin had been a master gardener in France and now maintained two beautiful flower gardens at the home of Lady Anne Gasnier of Québec in his spare time away from the farm. He was also able to help François* set up his vegetable garden and expand his grape vines and orchard. François* realized much of his Calvados would now go to repay his neighbors for their good will and support.

Charlesbourg, Québec, The Renaud Farm - Summer 1670:

On a Sunday in early summer, while François* and the others were having a picnic at the home of his old friend, Guillaume* Renaud, they were surprised to see a fine carriage with a driver and two ladies in the rear. As the carriage stopped at the house, the ladies, Sister Marguerite Bourgeoys and Lady Anne Gasnier stepped down. Marie* De La Mare-Renaud rushed to graciously greet them. Marguerite thanked her, saying she needed a word with Monsieur Allard.

She began, "François*, I have grand news. Yesterday I received a letter from my older brother in France. As it happens, he is Archbishop of Tours. It seems he knows of a young lady from a good family who wishes to come to Québec as a *fille du roi*. Her family is of some means, and her father is reluctant to allow it unless a match can be assured with a man of good character. He asked me to assist and I must confess I immediately thought of you."

François* was dumbstruck. He had not done well with the concept of meeting the girls off the boat and was not overwhelmed by any of the maidens suggested by the wives of his friends. It could be just the thing for him, but he was uncertain. Marguerite continued "I will leave my brother's letter, and you may let me know next week. I would need to write soon so he will receive it this season and plan for her to come next summer." The two ladies took their leave, and Marie* De la Mare helped François* read the letter.

That night François* contemplated the matter, certainly "a bird in the hand." She sounded to be of good character, would probably bring some dowry, may have some education, and was raised on a farm. On the other hand, she was 22 or now 23 years old, which would suggest there was something preventing the Touraine lads from marrying her. She was likely ugly as a stump. However, François* had noticed a strong farm girl with poor appearance was better on the farm than a pretty city girl.

Later that week, François* attended the meeting with the newly arrived *filles du roi* at the Ursuline convent. He met an attractive young lady who had not been outside the walls of Paris until the voyage, another who stated farm animals were filthy and not to be touched, and two ladies of 15 and 16 years old who could not stop giggling.

That evening he had a strange dream. He was at the port with Jean* Poitevin watching new girls come off the boat. Among the ladies was none other than his long departed mother who came directly to François* and said, "My son, you must have a young lady of character."

The following morning he went to the convent to see Sister Bourgeoys. "Sister, I am ready to accept your proposal."

She replied, "I will write to my brother at once. We should have ample time for him to receive word this year and have the young lady sail next summer. I know my brother François*. You will not regret this decision." With that, François* returned to the farm with renewed industry and attended no more meetings at the convent.

On a morning late in October, François* was surprised to find his old friend Henri sitting on the porch. He was further surprised to see that Henri's usual neutral face appeared very sad, in fact it appeared that he had been crying. "Miss Anne* has left to be with her ancestors," he said sadly. Apparently she had died suddenly the evening before. The funeral was to be at the Beauport Chapel the following day. The men sat reminiscing over their old friend and memories of those three exciting years on her farm. François* arose and stared out on the Charlesbourg Square in front of him. When he turned around, Henri, as only Indians could, had disappeared.

The following day François*, Philippe, and Marie rode into Beauport. The chapel was filled to overflowing. Along with the local residents, almost all of old Québec society was in attendance. Anne* Ardouin-Badeau was one of the early settlers and touched the lives of most everyone in the colony. Her children's old friend Germain Morin said the mass. She was then taken by canoe and buried with her husband Jacques* Badeau in the cemetery of the Cathedral in Québec.

Afterward there was a gathering at the home of Noel* Morin. News of François*'s impending bride had spread, and he was given advice by all of Québec society, male and female, but he was surprised that Henri and Angélique were not in attendance. When he asked Philippe, he was told, "My father and mother have left for the Indian country. Without Miss Anne* there is no reason to remain. My father has been missing the Indian ways and now is his time to return."

When François* asked when they would be likely to see him again, Philippe replied, "One does not know. He may return some day, or not." François* felt a pain of remorse wondering if he would ever forge another friendship as close as that which he had with Henri.

Chapter 5

Bishop Jean- François Bourgeoys
Archbishop of Tours

Québec City, Canada
July 14, 1670

Dear brother,

I rejoice in informing you I have found a willing suitor for your young lady. His name is François*Allard, a wonderful young man of 31 years. He is from a small village in Normandie near Rouen and the son of a tradesman. Although he arrived here as an indentured servant, he has served his three years well and is now the owner of a new and prospering farm.

He is industrious, honest and a Christian of the finest character. I believe he is exactly the sort that is to make this wonderful new land prosper. He anxiously awaits the arrival of the young lady who we shall expect next summer.

Your loving sister,
Sister Marguerite Bourgeoys

Artannes-sur-Indre, France - August 16, 1670:

Jeanne* Anguille was a changed woman. She had given up all but a few hours of work at the Abbey. She worked full time on her father's farm, at least as hard as any of the men. Her father claimed had he had known she was capable of such energy, he would have never agreed to the voyage and kept her on the farm forever. She had not discussed it with her father, but she was so determined in her new destiny that she was determined to sail for Québec in the summer even if no marriage arrangement could be made.

Cutting hay in late summer under the strong Touraine sun, Jeanne* saw her brother André's coach arrive. She ran to the house and greeted him.

"I have news, Jeanne*! The Archbishop has received a proposal of marriage for you." Filled with excitement, Jeanne* followed him up to the house.

Having convened the family after dinner, Michel* started, "Well, my dear, it seems a man of good character has been located. I wish he could have been from our part of the country, but I believe there have been some civilized Normands. I will be true to my word, and André will make arrangements for your voyage early next summer. I shall provide you with a dowry of 300 livres. I only hope you are secure in your decision to leave Artannes for this savage new world." And under his breath he murmured, "And I hope this young man also knows what he is in for." Jeanne* hugged her father and told him that she was certain that it was exactly what she and God wanted.

Her vigorous farm work continued through the rest of summer and fall. She studied everything she could in preparation for life in the wilderness. She even found a copy of Pierre Boucher's book about life in Québec, *Les Pioneers,* and stayed up nights reading. That winter she spent several nights in the garden under blankets to harden herself for Québec.

Winter turned to the spring of 1671 and plans began in earnest. The final details of the trip were made. Jeanne* would take a carriage to the port of Dieppe in Normandie at the end of June. Although she assured her father she was capable of the voyage, he disagreed, "It will be of no trouble for André to accompany you and wait until you are safely at sea with the others." Michel* had no idea how optimistic the term "safely" was.

Jeanne* also learned the Crown would provide her with an additional dowry of 50 livres and an assortment of practical items. In addition, on arrival in Québec, she would be provided with clothes appropriate for the country. Also upon her marriage to François* they would receive some items useful to farming.

Chapter 6

Artannes-sur-Indre - May 27, 1671:

At long last the day of departure had arrived. Michel*, Etiennette and Jeanne* rode their cart to Tours. Passing through the village, Jeanne* realized she would never see the Abbey, the mill or anyone in the town again, but the enthusiasm of her destiny overcame the sorrow. They followed the bank of the Indre River to Tours where they met André who had arranged dinner with the Archbishop and lodging in the rectory of the Cathedral for the night.

At dinner Archbishop Bourgeoys regaled them with tales of his sister Marguerite. "Our father insisted she pursue the religious life. She was a fine student but much too spirited for the convent. She heard of Sister Marie l'Incarnation's work at the Ursuline mission in Québec bringing the word of God to the savages. Marguerite knew this would be the life for her. She left for the colonies and began her work.

"Originally, the King believed if men would go to the colony, they would marry native women and raise good French families. However, the Indian women do not have large families, and many of the men preferred the Indian life. When the idea of sending young women as *filles de marier,* that is, girls ready for marriage appeared, Marguerite led the project. I believe she has crossed the Great Atlantic more than Champlain himself.

"She is a woman to contend with. I have heard she holds her own with both the Archbishop and the Governor in Québec. I believe she would have advice for the King and the Pope as well if the opportunity arose. My dear Jeanne*, I am certain you will be happy in this new world. You seem to have her sense of adventure, and she has nothing but wonderful things to say of life in the New World."

In the morning the Anguilles said their tearful farewell to their daughter, as she and André boarded the coach for Orleans. Traveling along the coast of the Loire, Jeanne* was spellbound by the series of magnificent chateaux, lining the coast along the entire route. André explained, "Beginning with King François I to the present, the royalty has seen fit to build these beautiful palaces along the Loire. Many are elaborate hunting lodges or summer homes for the King and the royalty. They make a splendid scene, though somehow I feel the money could be better used."

That afternoon, as they entered the gate of Orleans on a hill overlooking the city, André commented, "It was exactly on this spot in 1429 where your namesake broke the siege of Orleans. Indeed it was said it was on this bridge where Jeanne d'Arc was wounded by an arrow."

Jeanne* looked out with excitement at the busy squares filled with commerce. Orleans was the same size as Tours with a more earthy tone, Tours being more a university center. They stayed the night at the Abbey of the Cathedral of Sainte-Croix. Jeanne* and André visited the old gothic cathedral where Jeanne d'Arc was honored after the siege. It was hard to go anywhere in the city without seeing monuments to the great heroine of France.

The following morning they boarded the coach for Paris. Jeanne* had anticipated Paris would be the largest and most exciting place she had ever seen, but she had never anticipated how large and amazing it actually was. Large buildings, great construction, throngs of people, old carts, grand carriages, and commerce were everywhere.

They stopped at parish of Saint-Sulpice on the left bank of the Seine. A friend of André's from the seminary, Father Maurice Dubois, was assistant priest. He greeted them and showed them their rooms. He gave them a short tour of the large church, most of which was under reconstruction. "This is one of the oldest churches in Paris." He explained. "The renovation began twenty years ago and will continue throughout my lifetime."

At dinner he told Jeanne*, "You will be interested to know some girls from my parish have gone with the *filles du roi* program. We are a poor parish, and many of our orphaned girls have few prospects. I recall a young girl, newly orphaned when I arrived here five years ago, Mathurine* Gouard. In fact, two young ladies are going this year, although I believe they departed a few days ago, Catherine* Clerice, and a girl originally from Saint-Menard parish, Catherine* Gateau. Perhaps you shall meet."

He continued, "Tomorrow I shall give you a tour of Paris, and for the evening we have had the most extraordinary good fortune. The Bishop heard of your visit and has invited all three of us to attend a performance at the

Tuileries Palace, a play by Moliere. I fear they are a bit racy; however, the Bishop enjoys them. Who knows, perhaps we shall have a glimpse of the King."

Jeanne* was unable to shut her eyes that night for excitement. After mass in the morning, Father Maurice took them to the *Ile de la Cité,* an island in the Seine in the center of the city, explaining, "This was the site of the original city. It was called 'Lutecia', and the people were able to protect themselves by fortifying the island. Later the Romans came, and after them the Franks with King Clovis who brought Christianity to France. He set his capital here."

They walked along the Seine and saw the many palaces including the Palais Royal, the Louvre, the Concierge, and the Tuileries where they would go that night. They saw the magnificent Cathedral of Notre-Dame in some need of repair, but Jeanne*'s favorite was the smaller Chapel of Sainte-Chapelle with spectacular stained glass from floor to ceiling depicting the entire story of the Bible. Maurice explained, "This was constructed by King Louis IX, now Saint-Louis, before the third crusade. He hoped to bring the story of the Bible to the masses through pictures. He returned with the actual crown of thorns which is housed in the altar here."

They crossed the Pont Neuf at the end of the *Cité.* Looking west, Maurice pointed out an old gray building with the appearance of a prison. "That is the Salpetriere, previously a factory for the manufacture of gunpowder. The King has recently turned it into a hospital for the poor, more for removing undesirables from the street than anything. It houses the homeless, the mad, the orphaned and prostitutes no longer suited for the trade. I fear some of the young ladies you will meet on your voyage will have spent some time in that unfortunate place."

When they returned to Saint-Sulpice, Jeanne* was aided by the matron of the rectory, Madame Dubay, in dressing for the evening. As she had not brought a formal dress, nor had she expected to ever need one again, Madame Dubay had to acquire proper garments from a friend.

Chapter 7

That evening they were called for by a grand carriage, carrying the Bishop of Paris and his aide, a priest named François Lachaise. The Bishop, a portly jovial man who fawned over Jeanne*, gave opinions constantly about Paris, France, Québec, and the theater. Lachaise was a more serious type. They arrived in a line of grand carriages depositing elegantly dressed men and women at the palace. Before being seated they gathered in a great hall where refreshments were served. "Always good to have a taste before the show," said the Bishop as he had champagne brought for all. Jeanne* and André sipped theirs while the Bishop managed to "taste" three glasses.

When a bell sounded, they proceeded to their seats. The Bishop had a well-located box with a perfect view of the stage. Just before the curtain, a trumpet sounded and everyone stood in unison. Jeanne* noticed some commotion in a box near the stage as its occupants entered. The Bishop leaned over to Jeanne*, whispering, "The King," and Jeanne* watched the King of France enter to be seated not forty feet from her.

At the intermission, they returned to the great hall where they each had another champagne and the Bishop had three. At the end of the play, the audience applauded as the King stood, motioning to a man in front of him who stood and bowed to the crowd. "Moliere," said Lachaise, "a favorite of the King. Sometimes the King will play a part in his plays."

Afterward they attended a reception in a larger more ornate ballroom. Various grandly dressed people came to greet the Bishop, who in turn introduced them to André and Jeanne*. Everyone seemed to know Lachaisse. Jeanne* continued to wonder at the opulence before her. Becoming lost in her thoughts, she heard a booming voice, "Well, Bishop, how nice of you to come. I am happy to see that some of our clergy are not so prudish to ignore the genius of Monsieur Moliere."

Jeanne* looked up to see two grandly dressed men, the speaker in a black wig of long curls. The Bishop responded, "Your majesty, how gracious of you to visit us. May I introduce Father André Anguille from Tours and his sister Jeanne*. Of course, you know *Père* Lachaise."

The group all bowed and murmured responses while Louis XIV responded, "*Enchanté.*" Then he asked, "Mademoiselle Anguille, what brings a lovely Touraine girl such as you to Paris?"

Jeanne* regarded the King, who was younger looking than she had expected. Although he was only 33 years old, he was King before Jeanne* was born. She thought if she was to brave the savage new world, she could certainly answer a question. She summoned her courage and replied, "I am on my way to Québec to serve his majesty as *fille du roi.*"

Louis responded, "How wonderful to see such a young woman as yourself going to serve France in her colonies. I believe this is a wonderful venture to maintain our status as leader in the world. Allow me to present

Monsieur Jean-Baptist Colbert, my secretary of State and Finance." Jeanne* curtsied, and with that the King took the hand of young Jeanne* Anguille which was then kissed by the two most powerful men in the world.

Once Jeanne*, André, and Maurice had been returned to Saint-Sulpice, they began to discuss the evening. André said, "The Bishop must be a man of importance to draw the attention of the King himself."

Maurice answered, "It is not the Bishop, but Father Lachaise who is the attraction. It is said that King Louis has been summoning him to the palace for confession. A King seeks out someone he can trust for his confessor, and it appears Lachaise is to be that man. It is said it is a position almost as powerful as the King. In certain circumstances it can be even more so."

Chapter 8

<u>Normandie, France – The Next Day:</u>

The following morning, Jeanne* and her brother took the coach on the next leg of the journey to Rouen, following the Seine River the entire way. Jeanne* was impressed by beautiful rolling farms with large fields of wheat and apple orchards. She thought to herself, "If my new husband is from this region, he must be an energetic farmer."

They shared their coach with two elderly ladies. The more talkative of the two started pleasant conversation with André, who eventually explained he was accompanying his sister to Dieppe where she would sail to Québec. The old lady brightened at the mention of Québec. "Why my dear, my sister Agathe and I know everything of Québec. We have read every issue of "The Relations of the Jesuits" dating back to the first issue in 1607. Our father had great interest in the New World and always brought them home. Agathe and I still live in his house in Paris. We have a third sister who is married and lives in Rouen. She is the purpose for our voyage today."

Jeanne* had heard of this annual series of publications which were the daily journals of the Jesuit missionaries in Canada, published annually in French and Latin and sold in Paris. They were a big hit and always sold out. She had seen part of one issue at the abbey, but the total collection encompassed an entire wall of the library. She asked the ladies what they knew of Québec.

The talkative sister, the younger of the two, named Beatrix replied, "Simply everything, my dear. It is a wild and savage place with terribly cold winters. It is filled with wild animals and even worse wild men called Indians. The Jesuits have saved some but most remain heathen. They have been known to capture young woman, have their way with them and afterward cook and eat them. However, I must add that I am extremely excited for you, I have always dreamed of an adventure in the wild, savage land, much better than the dreary life in the city."

Her sister interrupted, "I can just see you in the wild. It would be wonderful until your tea was late. Tell me, child, what will you do there, who is to watch over you?"

Jeanne* replied, "I sail with the *filles du roi* program. My father has arranged a marriage."

Agatha replied, "Gracious child, be prudent. The men there are almost as savage as the land. There is no telling what liberties they may attempt. My advice is to go directly to the convent and join there."

Beatrix retorted, "My sister lives her life in fear of men's liberties. However, I believe she has little to fear at this point. My advice, child, you have but one life; seize it and drink of it full!"

The sparring of the sisters continued until the walls of Rouen. André was happy to hear that they were not continuing on to Dieppe.

In Rouen Jeanne* discovered a town much like Orleans, large and bustling with the common man. André

221

took her to the market square where he showed her the monument to Jeanne d'Arc. "It was here your namesake was executed." Later they stopped at the Saint-Maclou Cemetery and the monument to victims of the great plague. Little did Jeanne* know, but she stood in the exact place François* Allard had stood five years previously contemplating his voyage to the new world.

The following day they boarded the coach for their final journey to Dieppe. The coach had taken on two girls from Rouen, both younger than Jeanne*, who were also headed to Canada. Each had recently lost her father and had no dowry or prospects. The parish priest had recommended them to Sister Bourgeoys. Fifteen year-old Marie Arinat, actually from the town of Les Andelys near Rouen, had come to Saint-Maclou after her father's death and was now on her way to a place she had never heard of a few months ago. She was clearly frightened to death.

Her companion was Madeleine Auvray from the parish of Saint-Vivien in Rouen. At nineteen and orphaned with the recent death of her father, she left to find better prospects. She had taken on a mother role for the younger girl; however, she also showed a certain level of uncertainty. Both were overjoyed to be joined by an older girl and especially her *curé* brother. They showed little knowledge of the new colony, but Jeanne* filled them in with very enthusiastic and reassuring stories. Afterward both girls fell deeply asleep probably for the first time in weeks.

Chapter 9

Dieppe, Normandie, France - June 1, 1671:

Upon arrival in Dieppe, they proceeded to the church of Saint-Jacques where the girls were to stay in the convent until the voyage commenced. Greeted by the Mother Superior of the convent, all three girls were assigned quarters. They were instructed, "Madame Gasnier-Bourdon is out making arrangements. She will meet with the girls tomorrow afternoon. Try to rest well tonight." André excused himself to go to the rectory but told Jeanne* he would return to take her to dinner.

The girls were assigned to a six-bed dorm. One bed remained empty. They met their two roommates. Catherine* Gateau, twenty-one years old, was an orphan originally from the parish of Saint Menard in Paris but now from Saint-Sulpice. The other was Catherine* Clerice from Saint-Sulpice. Jeanne* excitedly explained she had been told of both girls by Father Maurice Dubois and fell into the entire story of her Parisian adventure. The five girls immediately formed a bond and were all visibly overjoyed by the prospects of such amiable travel companions.

When André appeared for dinner, Jeanne* was almost disappointed to leave her new friends. They went to a small inn across from Saint-Jacques which André had determined did more trade with the town's people rather than the rough trade from the port. After dinner André said, "Jeanne*, I pray you are secure in this decision. You know if you choose you could return with me to Artannes, and no one will be sad."

She responded, "André, I have always greatly regarded your counsel, and I still cannot imagine life without you. However, I am certain that this is my destiny, and not even you can convince me otherwise." With that they returned to the convent.

André said, "I am told you have a busy day tomorrow. I don't know if I will be able to see you, but I shall see you before your departure. Father has instructed me not to leave until your ship is beyond the horizon."

When Jeanne* returned to her room, the sixth bed had been filled. Madeline de Roybon D'Alonne, or more simply Madeleine de Roybon, was a girl of twenty-five. She was from the town of Sens between Paris and Orleans. Her father was in the King's guard which put him in high social standing. She was pleasant enough, but more mature, worldly and educated than even Jeanne* and with more than a subtle hint of superiority. As the evening progressed, Jeanne* guessed that rather than going to something, Madeleine was being sent away from something. Ignoring the advice of Mother Superior, the girls talked into the night. They all awoke slowly when they were alerted for mass in the morning.

After lunch the girls gathered with others for a meeting in the great hall. Between thirty and forty girls in all, they were of all shapes and sizes, some very young and a few rather old. Some like Marie Arinat quite frightened, and some like Madeleine De Roybon appeared to be waiting for their servants. There was a group of eight girls giggling loudly. Catherine* Clerice told Jeanne*, "Those girls are from Larochelle, and they are very active. There had already been talk of some of them sneaking out in the evening."

The Mother Superior entered with another mature lady who looked very prosperous and confidant but also had a wonderful air that reminded Jeanne* of her own mother. The Mother Superior spoke, "Ladies, allow me to again welcome you. I trust your stay so far has been pleasant. I will now introduce your sponsor and chaperone for your voyage, Lady Anne Gasnier-Bourdon. Madame and I, as it turns out, are girlhood friends from Paris.

Lady Gasnier-Bourdon took the floor, surveyed the group until everyone was quiet before beginning, "Good afternoon, ladies. My name is Anne Gasnier. I was born in the parish of Saint-Germain-l'Auxerrois in Paris and first married there. However, my husband died young. Like many of you here I felt I had a destiny for adventure. So in the early 1640s I sailed for Québec. After some time I married my second husband, Lord Bourdon who passed on now three years ago. Since that time I have worked with my dear friend Marguerite Bourgeoys in bringing young ladies to Canada.

"Sister Bourgeoys frequently accompanies the young ladies, but this year for reasons of health she has asked me to stand in. It is my third crossing and the first with you ladies, so we are all somewhat new. However, I was not born yesterday and will not stand for poor behavior. Today we will obtain and assemble your cargo. We shall sail in two days' time, weather permitting. You will be assigned accommodations aboard ship. We will go over the rules, and they are not to be broken. I may appoint certain young ladies for certain tasks who are not to be disobeyed when they work in my stead.

"As for my name, as is the custom in France you may call me Madame, Miss Gasnier, or Widow Bourdon. I would prefer Sister Anne although I am not a nun. Are there any questions?"

After a few routine procedural questions, Madeleine de Roybon asked, "Will we be allowed to speak to the sailors?" The girls from Larochelle stifled giggles.

"Only to report a fire. There will be no fraternizing with the crew or passengers outside of my personal presence. I can assure you that the young men have also been appropriately instructed and warned."

She continued, "In closing, allow me to say that I left a life of privilege in Paris for the life in the wilderness, and I would not change that for anything in the world. We are about to embark for the most wonderful, exciting and exhilarating place on earth. There will be hardships, but let me assure you they will be well outweighed by the rewards. We will meet in one hour to gather our things, that is all." As the girls arose she added, "Would Mademoiselle Anguille please stay and see me?"

As Jeanne* approached, Anne took her hands and said, "My dear, how wonderful to meet you. I have anxiously awaited this since Sister Bourgeoys first showed me the Archbishop's letter of introduction. As you can see we have a large group and I daresay a few free spirits. I will count on you to help me maintain order.

"When we arrive in Québec we will all lodge at the convent for the first few days. After that the others will stay and attend meetings with the eligible men. You will stay at my home. We will meet Monsieur Allard and I advise you and he to take a period of time to become acquainted and make certain that you also approve of this match. I realize that is not how things are done in France, but as you shall see, in Québec a woman's opinion is more highly regarded. If you both agree, we shall do the contracts, and a few weeks after, you shall be married. Now you may go and join the others."

As Jeanne* was leaving she stopped and turned, "Sister Anne?"
"Yes, my dear."
"What is Monsieur Allard's nature?"
The older lady thought for a second and smiled. "Well, he is young, tall, strong, intelligent and I daresay handsome. He has the most amazing eyes, as you shall see. He is industrious, and I would say that he has as fine a character as any man in Québec. Aside from that he is the basic Québécois. Let me assure you, Mademoiselle, you are a very fortunate young lady."

Later in the day, Sister Anne took the girls down to the port to pick up their new belongings. Jeanne was overwhelmed by the activity in the port. More than a few men whistled and made lewd comments to the girls. Sister Anne told them to look straight ahead, ignore them and keep close to her.

They noticed workers lowering huge colorful boulders down to build a new harbor wall. Anne said,

"Those are granite boulders from Québec. The ships require ballast which is the cargo and passengers on this voyage, but as there is little on the return, the holds are filled with these beautiful Canadian rocks. They are unloaded in France and used to build the harbor. Soon the entire harbors of Dieppe and Larochelle will be of these stones."

At the port, each girl was given a small chest. They then quickly followed sister Anne back to the convent. Once inside they inspected the contents that included a headdress or *coiffe,* a bonnet, a taffeta handkerchief, a pair of stockings, a pair of gloves, ribbon, four shoelaces, two knives, and two livres in coin which was more money than most of the girls had ever seen. In addition there was room for a few other items they may have brought. Jeanne had some spare clothing and a few domestic items which her mother had supplied, as well as Pierre Boucher's book, *Les Pioneers.*

A few girls had more than would fit and required a second box. Madeleine de Roybon had a great deal more and would require assistance in transporting it. Most girls had nothing at all of their own. At dinner the girls from Larochelle were giggling about some of the men they had seen at the harbor. When the girls returned to their room, Madeleine de Roybon said, "Those Larochelle twits, as if they knew what to do with such a man."

Catherine* Clerice challenged her, "And I suspect that you do."

De Roybon replied, "Why do you think I find myself on this wretched voyage? My father was weary of keeping the young men from Sens to Paris from between my legs."

The girls were struck speechless, and the conversation dwindled as they drifted off to sleep.

Chapter 10

<u>Dieppe, France - June 4, 1671:</u>

The big day arrived. The girls were awakened, fed and readied before dawn. As they were escorted to the docks by Sister Anne Gasnier, Jeanne* became alarmed. She had yet to see André. The docks were a madhouse of activity. Livestock, cannons, machinery and other large items were hoisted onto the ship with ropes as a crowd of passengers waited on the dock.

Their ship was the *Saint-Jean-Baptiste,* a slightly larger version of *l'Aigle d'Or.* The girls were allowed to board early among cheers and catcalls from the crowd. Each girl carried her chest, and two gardeners from the convent carried Madeleine de Roybon's extra gear. They went directly below via the spiral staircase to their quarters in the rear of the boat. The rear of the boat was more spacious and comfortable than the center and front where the other passengers would live. Sister Gasnier explained, "The sailors refer to this section as the *Sainte-Barbe* after the patron saint of cannon gunners. Most cannons are here, and that means more windows, light and air."

The area for the forty girls was cordoned off by canvas sheets. There were groups of small mattresses, and each girl was assigned a place to sleep and keep her possessions. After they had been organized, Sister Anne said, "We shall now go above decks to take in the air and the view of the departure. As always, we must stick strictly together." When Jeanne* arrived above here heart jumped as she saw André waiting with a slightly younger priest.

230

She rushed to embrace him. "Oh André! I was frightened that you had been delayed."

Her brother replied, "The captain gave me permission to come aboard until the departure. I waited for Father Mathieu who is a passenger as well."

Jeanne* curtsied to the *curé* and they exchanged pleasantries. Father Guillaume Mathieu was from the Champagne region of northeastern France. He was a Jesuit missionary working in the Indian mission of Québec. As Jeanne* and André walked to the rail to watch the activity, André said, "Well, here you are, little sister, off to the world's great adventure to fulfill your great destiny. I don't know if I am more afraid or jealous."

Jeanne* replied, "André, I believe you were more suited to the bishopric than Indian savior."

He laughed and continued, "Always remember who you are and from whence you have come. If you continue your life with the same zeal and love you have lived it to this point, you will have no difficulties. I find Father Mathieu a man of good character, and you may call on him if you have need."

At that point the first mate indicated it was time to sail, and André kissed his sister saying, "Write when you can, remember it will take two years for mail to be received and responded to. That is if the mail completes the voyage at all." He hastened down the gangplank, which was then drawn onto the ship. Jeanne rejoined the girls and watched the ropes taken up and large skiffs row the boat out of the harbor.

It was a magnificent June day with a clear sky and grand breeze. As the sails were unfurled, *Saint-Jean-Baptiste* gained speed and headed to sea. France faded into the distance, as Sister Anne told the girls to follow her below.

Jeanne*'s area of the *Sainte-Barbe* included the six girls from her room and five of the girls from Larochelle. When Anne appointed a leader for each of the four groups of girls, Jeanne* was given the responsibility for her group. Anne listed the rules, "We will be to bed at dusk and up at dawn. There will be three meals at the traditional times, weather permitting. Each group will assign a girl each day to empty and clean the toilet buckets. You are responsible for your own area and its orderliness and cleanliness.

"Captain Guillon is in charge of the ship, and his orders are to be immediately obeyed. I am next in charge and your leader is next. We will always move about the ship in groups. We have two hours a day for exercise above decks. We will have lessons below daily. We are fortunate to have a priest, Father Guillaume Mathieu, aboard. There will be a mass above deck for all each Sunday, and we will have a brief private service each morning before breakfast. Father Mathieu will hear confessions on Friday. I trust you girls will have little to confess. There will be no mingling with the other passengers without my permission. Is this all clear?" The girls murmured an agreement.

The girls settled in talking among themselves. Young Marie Arinat said, "I hope that we have no terrible storms. I greatly fear drowning."

Jeanne* comforted the girl fully eight years her junior, "I have read Pierre Boucher's book, and he says the ships are strong and never perish." At the same time she thought to herself she now had at least one lie to confess on Friday.

Dinner was surprisingly good, fresh bread, a good soup and an apple with a glass of reasonable wine. After dinner the conversation continued. Anne Gasnier was with the rest of the girls from Larochelle on the far side of the area. She had felt keeping these girls separated in two groups with Jeanne* at one end and Anne at the other would help keep order. However, this also placed Sister Anne out of earshot of Jeanne*s group.

Madeleine de Roybon having commandeered the best mattress and largest space said, "I only hope I can manage to pass these weeks in the company of you peasants."

Madeleine Auvray replied sarcastically, "We are not all peasants, 'Miss de Royalty'. In fact Jeanne* has been to the Tuilleries Palace where the King of France kissed her hand."

De Roybon retorted, "When I was 16 years old, my father took me to the palace where I met the King. That evening he invited me to his chambers and he kissed more than my hand."

The girls gasped.

She continued, "Then the randy young monarch showed me how to ride the royal stallion."

The silence was broken by one of the girls from Larochelle who asked what they all were dying to know, "What exactly do you mean?"

With that, Madeleine de Roybon embarked on a long and detailed discussion of her sexual exploits with the King of France, while her shipmates listened with their mouths gaping open. Jeanne* knew as leader she should probably stop the discussion, but she also realized this would make the time pass quickly. In addition, as she was embarking to get married without her mother to guide her, perhaps this information would be of some value.

Chapter 11

<u>The Atlantic Ocean - June 5, 1671 - First Morning at Sea:</u>

The girls were awakened at dawn. They washed and dressed, and Father Mathieu appeared for a very brief mass followed by a breakfast of a hard roll and weak coffee. Jeanne* assigned herself to the first toilet bucket duty. She could see this was not to be a job to Madeleine de Roybon's liking. Following morning chores, Sister Anne appeared for their first lesson. For the next week they would work at sewing. This was quite simple for the country girls. However, the city girls, particularly those who had been orphaned, found it a challenge, though a useful one. They would have a lesson each morning, and work on projects during the day, to improve their skills and pass the time. Sister Anne stressed the importance of the repair of clothing in the New World. Here new things were not necessarily available, even for the wealthy.

The lower deck was organized with the girls at the very back of the ship. Two families with a total of seven children came next. A few soldiers and the single men occupied the more crowded forward part along with the livestock. When the weather was good and the cannon windows remained open, the girls had enough light for their projects and worked diligently with the exception of Madeleine de Roybon whose sewing was quite awful.

The walk above deck was the highlight of the day. The girls had a two-hour break along with the families. Soldiers and single men had a different schedule. Every three days they had the opportunity to bathe. Whereas the men bathed above decks with buckets of icy water drawn straight from the sea, the girls bathed in their quarters with warmer water that was close to room temperature. They also had the luxury of a small amount of fresh water into which they could dunk a cloth for a minimal rinse of the salt.

Dinner was again bread and soup but still not bad, and at bedtime Madeleine de Roybon held her sex education class. The girls from Larochelle were filled with questions, and she was ready with explicit answers. She described things Jeanne* had never heard of and could scarcely imagine. The Larochelle girls had fits of uncontrollable giggles, and Jeanne* began to fear this could get out of hand.

As the days progressed, the sewing lesson filled the mornings, and the afternoons were lessons on various points of the culture, history and nature of Québec: social graces, duties of wives and the like. Among the most interesting were the talks on the Québec courting process. Anne described how they would be housed at the convent or in nearby homes. Weekly there would be meetings where the eligible men would come to call. It all sounded perfectly awful to Jeanne* who was now pleased she would avoid it, particularly in view of the glowing description Sister Anne had given her on the subject of Monsieur Allard.

Anne explained, "Unlike France, you ladies have a choice in this matter. Indeed in Québec you will discover that you have an influential voice in most matters for better or for worse. Regard these suitors carefully. In the New

World, character and industry are more important than age and appearance in a man. It is also true that you will fare better with a man of some property and means. Do not overlook these questions." Madeleine de Roybon later confided in the girls her idea of the ideal man was one who was rich and never home so that she could seek her own excitement.

As the days passed, the weather and winds remained favorable. The girls progressed with their lessons. Following two weeks of sewing, they began lessons on farming. Again the country girls were at an advantage. Evening sessions with Madeleine de Roybon became more animated and vivid. They also became better attended as many of the other girls began to sneak over to take part.

One evening Jeanne* awoke and realized Madeleine was not in her bed. Knowing if her absence was discovered, it would bode poorly for all the girls, she took the chance of getting up herself. Sneaking up the spiral stairs to the upper deck wearing only her nightclothes, she moved quietly onto the main deck aided by the moonlight. She listened carefully and heard groaning noises to her left. She discovered Madeleine and one of the seamen in a large coil of rope, coiled themselves and completely naked. She stood and engaged them saying, "I don't care what you do to yourself, but you are not going to cause difficulties for the other girls!" The young man grabbed his trousers and disappeared. Jeanne* threw Madeleine's nightshirt at her and told her to follow. The girls returned below and returned to bed.

The next day to Madeleine's amazement, she realized Jeanne* had told no one. Later in the day she spoke to Jeanne* privately, "I must thank you for your discretion. I realize I have been a poor companion. I apologize and hope we can be friends." Jeanne* smiled politely and declared she should like nothing more. After this the relations between the two girls improved immensely.

A few days later, Sister Anne summoned Jeanne* and Madeleine for a conversation in private. "It has come to my attention your group has been having nightly discussions on a rather delicate subject. I also understand Mademoiselle de Roybon is somewhat of an expert on that subject."

Jeanne* looked sheepish. She knew she should have come forward; however Anne continued, "As a nun, Sister Bourgeoys had little interest in teaching the topic of sex. I myself have been married twice and have some knowledge on the topic. I had planned a series of talks with the girls starting next week. I feel it would be invaluable to most, especially the orphans. Now that I realize I have an expert in my midst, I would like to have Mademoiselle de Roybon assist me in this task."

The girls were dumbfounded. In spite of a need to quell her feelings, Jeanne* let out a short laugh. Madeleine followed, and soon all three women were having a good laugh at the situation. This also served to form a bond among the three most mature of the ladies. And so it happened that Anne Gasnier taught the girls the facts of married life, and her assistant added color and comment somewhat less theatrical than before but no less useful and interesting to her audience.

Following the formal lessons, Anne suggested that the girls continue their discussions after dinner and invite the others. "However, keep it proper and consider occasionally including other more mundane topics."

Chapter 12

<u>Atlantic Ocean - July 7 1671 - Day 33 at Sea:</u>

With the exception of a few brief rainstorms and brisk winds, the weather had been good. However this day the sky turned a frightening dark yellow. There were a few strikes of lightning and the wind began to rise. Preparations were made and the *Saint-Jean-Baptiste* entered the first real storm of the voyage. Rain fell in sheets occasionally with hail. The wind became ferocious, and the inside hold and lower deck began to take water.

Night fell with no relief. Few of the girls had been troubled by seasickness during the voyage, but by midnight they were all affected. Marie Arinat crawled into Jeanne*s bed and cried that she felt she was to die. Jeanne* held the young girl and reassured her this was not a severe storm, and the boat would have no trouble. She then asked God not to disprove her.

Forty-eight hours later the storm began to abate. By evening the seas started to calm and the passengers rejoiced on deck. No passengers had been seriously injured, but one of the cows had broken its neck. The ship's cook came and saw to the animal announcing there would be an improvement in meals for the next few evenings.

Two days later, while taking their daily exercise, Jeanne* struck up a conversation with two younger girls from Paris who were in a different group. The older of the two related their story. "We are both poor girls from the poorest area of Paris. We were both orphaned in our early teens and obliged to fend for ourselves on the streets. It became necessary to steal and beg for food. I must confess that sometimes we were forced to sell ourselves.

"We were both apprehended as 'undesirables' and sent to the Hospital of the Salpetriere where we met. All the women were brought to the courtyard, stripped naked and washed by the guards. The younger more attractive would be taken by the head guards to their bed. We were both afforded that dubious honor and then sent to the wards.

"It is an unspeakable place, filled with the stench of death and cries of the mad and the dying. Many are completely mad and scream all day and night. We were made to work long hours in the laundry for a few scraps of food and suffer the abuse of the guards. Fortunately a priest made regular rounds and singled us out with some others for the *filles du roi* program. I fear we should soon have perished or worse had it not been for him. We both look with joy at our prospects. We know nothing can be worse than our past."

Chapter 13

<u>The Atlantic Ocean - July 15, 1671 - Day 41 at Sea:</u>

Believing they were on the last half of the voyage, passenger morale improved. The girls had settled into their routine, and even Madeleine de Roybon had become a model worker, student and friend to all. Father Guillaume Mathieu came this week for a series of talks on the church in Québec. He had originally gone to Québec in 1667 to work with the Indian Missions. In the fall he travelled to Paris to make the annual report to the Cardinal and was now returning.

"I am quite excited in my new situation. I will be taking the new parish in Beauport." Jeanne* was excited to hear this and asked him if he knew François Allard. He stated he did not as he had been occupied in the western province with the Algonquin missions. "The mission of the church is to convert these people to Christianity. Although it seems a laudable goal, it is quite difficult. Some years ago there was a plague of smallpox carried by the Jesuits. As a result we are not trusted by the more distant tribes.

"It is also of note that although these people are not true Christians, their society is in many ways very similar and embraces the same important tenets. They regard each other well, value life and have a moral standard different but in some ways more Christian than some of the French."

That afternoon, Anne summoned Jeanne* and Madeleine de Roybon. "It seems the Petit family of four has fallen ill. This late in the voyage I doubt it could be cholera but it looks suspicious. We are going to quarantine them above decks and I will require your assistance to care for them."

The Petit family was from the Perche region of France; there was the father, mother and two small children, a boy of four and a girl of six. Madame Petit had discovered she was pregnant at the beginning of the voyage. They were placed in a room with four beds. The girls were to wear special dressing gowns in the room and remove them and leave them in the room as they left.

They had to attempt to feed the patients and force them to drink water and a special concoction of Anne's. They were to bathe them twice a day. When the girls left the room, they were to douse their hands in alcohol and ignite it. The effect was impressive but it did not burn. They would shake the fire out. The girls were not to rejoin the others but were given a small room in which to sleep.

As the days progressed, the mother Jeanne-Louise Petit was, in spite of her pregnancy, clearly strongest. By day four she was able to give the girls some assistance. Monsieur Jean-Pierre Petit and six year old Marie-Therese stayed lethargic and dangerously ill. Little four-year-old Jean-Philippe did poorly, and on day six he died.

Father Mathieu gave a short service after which the boy was buried at sea in front of his sobbing mother. The following day Jeanne-Louise told the girls, "I will forever mourn his loss, but I must be strong for my husband and daughter and have hope in God for my unborn child."

That evening, Madeleine told Jeanne*, "This voyage and these people have not only changed my view of Québec, but of life itself. You are correct, my friend, this is to be a wonderful adventure."

Over the next two days, the others recovered and were allowed up for short times. That evening both the girls felt they could sleep at night rather than leave one on watch. In the middle of the night they were awakened by a noise. By the moonlight they could see two men entering the cabin. One said, "We thought we would keep you ladies company tonight. We have heard that one of you is a woman of action, why not both?"

Madeleine arose and whispered to Jeanne*, "Follow my lead." She walked toward the larger man and put her arms out. As he came forward she hit him with a knee in the groin virtually taking his feet off the floor. As he fell, she kicked him squarely in the face and again in the stomach. As he lay on the ground, Jeanne* made her move. Having been raised with two older brothers, she was no stranger to fighting. She repeated Madeleine's action. With both men on the deck, Madeleine produced a large knife Jeanne* had never seen and knelt with a knee in one of the men's back. Holding the knife to his throat she said, "We won't mention this, you're not worth the effort. However, if either of you comes near one of us or the other girls again, it will surely be your last act in this world."

She arose and the men ran off. Madeleine turned to Jeanne*, "As you can see, I'm not all talk." In spite of their recent fear, both girls laughed uproariously.

The following morning, Sister Anne declared the remaining Petits cured. She told the girls they could return below deck but they must first be decontaminated. She asked the captain to clear the men from the deck and had actual hot fresh water brought up. She had the girls undress and took their garments to boil. She then scrubbed each one of the girls with strong lye soap and large amounts of the precious fresh water.

Jeanne* realized that she was standing in full daylight stark naked. She found it exhilarating. She knew the decks had been cleared but, knowing Frenchmen, realized that there had to be a few prying eyes about. After her experiences of the last several weeks this no longer seemed important. The girls dressed in clean clothes and returned to their friends with many new stories.

Chapter 14

<u>The Atlantic Ocean - August 1, 1671 - Day 57 at Sea:</u>

The captain had predicted they were only a week from the mouth of the Saint-Laurent. The spirits of the passengers were high and the weather was grand. The girls were taking their daily exercise above decks. Captain Guillon noted something on the horizon that worried him more than a storm. A ship approached from the south. As it drew closer, he examined it with his glass, and called the officers and Sister Anne.

"I fear we are being followed by a much swifter craft. I have altered our course, and she has altered hers accordingly. It does not appear to be French. We should make ready the cannons and see to the women."

With that Sister Anne asked the girls and the families to make haste below where they were addressed by the first mate. "We are being approached by a ship which may be hostile. We must react as though it is pirates. We have an accommodation to hide the girls as well as the women and children of the families. We will begin immediately."

In the center of the back deck, against the wall of the ship, was a room which enclosed the rudder and steering mechanism. It was standard on all ships of this sort. However, on the *Saint-Jean-Baptiste* there was a second wall along the back of the boat that followed the room for the steering and provided space for up to sixty people in very cramped quarters. It was lined with canvas for soundproofing and was entered by a secret door not evident from outside or in.

All the belongings of the women were stowed inside and the group gathered around so that they could enter quickly when necessary. Some of the men would bring their belongings to the back of the boat so that there was no obviously vacated space.

As the boat approached, Captain Guillon realized that it was worse than he had feared. "They are neither French nor Privateer. Alas, these are renegade pirates," referring to the pirates who lived outside all law and answered to no country. "We can neither outrun them nor outfight them. Our only hope is to be boarded and pray they will take what cargo they desire and leave us on our way."

The crew waited anxiously for another hour as the boat drew closer. It was true it was a faster, better-armed craft flying the dreaded skull and crossbones. The pirates fired a canon shot. Guillon had the men raise a white flag and came about to be boarded. As the pirate skiff prepared to board, Guillon looked up as to be searching for inspiration. His face brightened, and he said to the mate, "I will invite the captain to my cabin for a drink and negotiations. If ordered take whom he chooses below and show them what they wish. Try not to betray the presence of the women. You other men offer anyone left on deck some of our best grog. I believe if we can stall there may be hope."

Twenty pirates boarded. Their ship stood close by with all guns and cannons trained on the *Saint-Jean-*

Baptiste. The captain, a fierce looking man with one eye, approached Guillon. "Captain Jack McSwine, master of the *Black Cloud*."

Guillon replied, "Jean Guillon of His Majesty's ship, *Saint-Jean-Baptiste*. If the captain would be so kind as to accompany me to my quarters, we may enjoy a refreshment and discuss your proposal."

McSwine replied, "My proposal is we take what we want. However, I'm glad to see you French are becoming more hospitable and I must admit to a sudden thirst."

Guillon motioned to one of the men, "Laporte, see to Captain McSwine's men."

And McSwine countered with, "Mr. Whipple, see what they have below."

In his cabin, Guillon poured a generous glass of his strongest Calvados. He took a smaller glass and raised it, "To men of the sea," and he sipped it. McSwine killed his with one gulp and looked as if smoke was about to come out of his ears. He slammed the glass down and requested another which Guillon promptly provided. They made small talk until three of McSwine's men burst in.

The tallest stated, "They have the cannons, some machinery, a small amount of food and some livestock. There are sixty passengers apart from the crew, all men."

McSwine looked around, "We'll take as much of the livestock as we can slaughter and eat, all the weapons and powder, we could use two more cannon and we shall check the machinery." He rose and followed his men out and then down below decks. He checked the farming and other industrial equipment including two looms. Then he surveyed the rear of the boat.

He walked by the men's new quarters in the rear and spied something of interest. He bent and picked up what was clearly a woman's comb. "I've heard of Frenchmen with strange habits, but this seems too queer." Then he began to examine the walls with interest. Guillon realized he was knowledgeable enough a seaman that the ruse was not likely to hold. McSwine tapped the walls and examined the boards until he discovered the door.

He forced it open, at first nothing was evident but the steering gear; but he was now convinced and probed far enough to find the women. He brought them out and leered at each and every one. He said to his mate, "Tell the helmsman to bring the ship abeam, we'll load this cargo directly. We can have our way with them as we head south and still have enough life in them to fetch a fair price when we reach the islands. Follow me, ladies. You are about to see real adventure."

Jeanne* was in the front and Guillon whispered, "Stall and take as much time as is possible." Jeanne* was frightened beyond belief but this new task gave her something to focus on. She whispered to Madeleine, "Tell the others to follow my lead." She swooned and almost fainted with every step. Suddenly McSwine had a sorority of hysterical woman on his hands. Progress became very slow.

As they finally reached the spiral stairs, Jeanne* ascended with theatrical slowness. As her head came into the light all eyes on deck were on her. She, however, was looking in back of them and suddenly realized why the captain had asked her to stall. With one last effort she swooned and fell, or rather threw herself, on Madeleine and the girls behind her. The domino effect was wonderful. Everyone including the pirates crashed back down. Jeanne* was worried she or someone may have broken something, but as they all stood up, she realized it was nothing but bad bruises. They regrouped and slowly re-ascended. They were all gathered together and McSwine gave the order, "Transfer the cargo."

At this point, Captain Jean Guillon shouted, "Captain McSwine, I beg you to reconsider our negotiations. I feel if you would only turn around you may see things my way."

McSwine looked over his shoulder and his jaw virtually dropped to the deck. He saw what Guillon and a few of his men had noticed over an hour ago. It was an enormous boat traveling at high speed and less half an hour away. It flew a large blue flag with three unmistakable gold *fleur de lys*. Both captains realized that this could be only one ship, the *Bon Roi Henri IV,* the flagship of the French Navy, and the undisputed fastest and best-armed warship in the world. Guillon had no idea what it was doing in these waters, and did not care.

He continued, "Because you have acted in somewhat a civilized fashion, I will make you one offer. Leave immediately, and I will delay his majesty's navy for one hour. That may give you enough time to make yourself unworthy of pursuit."

Without a word, McSwine and his men jumped to the skiff and raised their sails.

Guillon called out, "Make haste directly to the *Bon Roi Henri IV.*"

Within an hour the skiff of the warship had landed the captain on the deck of the *Saint-Jean-Baptiste*. The Captain was none other than Admiral Louis Phélypeaux, comte de Pontchartain, at scarcely thirty years of age, the most powerful man in the French Navy and destined to become one of the most powerful men in France. He greeted Guillon, "We have been here some weeks sweeping the area of just such vermin. We will let them run for an hour to keep your word. They will not be difficult to find."

Guillon told the story of the raid and said, "Were it not for the heroic theatrics of Mademoiselle Anguille, I fear we should have perished."

Pontchartrain turned to Jeanne* and said, "I am pleased to see that Québec is acquiring young women who can even stand up to pirates," and another great man kissed her hand. As he turned to leave he noticed Madeleine de Roybon and said, "Excuse me, Mademoiselle, have we met?"

Madeleine returned a sly smile and replied, "Yes, *Monsieur le comte*, I believe it was in the gardens of Luxembourg after a royal ball." Pontchartrain blushed, and the girls from Larochelle giggled. Jeanne* realized things were already returning to normal.

The *Bon Roi Henri IV* left in pursuit of McSwine, and Guillon called out, "Full speed ahead to Québec!" The girls sat up late into the night singing songs.

Two days later, two sails appeared on the horizon. As the day progressed it became clear it was the *Bon Roi Henri IV* leading with McSwine and crew in chains. The French sailors were following with the *Black Cloud.* Like *l'Aigle d'Or* five years before, the *Saint-Jean-Baptiste* would have an escort to the Saint-Laurent.

Chapter 15

<u>The Flueve Saint-Laurent - August 8, 1671 - Day 65 at Sea:</u>
"La Terre Voila!" The shout went out, and passengers rushed to the rail. All those below were granted permission to come above for the duration. The thin line on the horizon began to grow, becoming green and hilly, and Jeanne* could feel her destiny pulling her in.

<u>Iles de la Madeliene</u>, <u>Canada - August 9, 1671</u>:

The passengers were taken by skiff to the shore where tent areas were constructed. Since the conclusion of the pirate attack, the mood had been jubilant. Now the mood was almost giddy. Even the most serious of the girls were in a playful mood. They were taken to bathe in the freshwater lake. Even the prospect of public nudity could not lower their enthusiasm. They splashed, pushed each other and sang songs. Even the most prudish of girls joined in. Madeline noticed that Jeanne* had an enormous bruise on left buttock which was also quite swollen from her fall down the stairs. She gave Jeanne* a playful swat on the tender area saying, "I hope that fades before you meet your Monsieur Allard."

The following day was a feast of rest, fresh air and exercise. Two men had gone to the woods for game, and dinner that evening and for evenings to come was a wonderful roast of deer and pheasant. The plan was to load and set sail for Québec the following morning. However in mid-afternoon two strange men and several Indians appeared. They seemed to know the crew, and a discussion ensued. Jeanne* and some of the girls crept close to get a better look.

The two men were rough sorts in fringed deerskin clothes and carried long rifles. The Indians were as exotic as Jeanne* had imagined, dark skinned with long hair tied back with a leather strap that held one or two large feathers. Some wore deerskin garb such as the white men, some were naked from the waist up. All carried bows with large knives and a hatchet in their leather strap belts. They looked quite wild yet not as ferocious as Jeanne* had imagined.

Jeanne* started to step back when she felt someone behind her. Turning, she was shocked to be looking directly into the black eyes of an Indian. She was further shocked when he said in passable French, "*Bonjour Mademoiselle.*"

The Captain spoke with Sister Anne who in turn summoned the girls, "Ladies, it seems as though we must set sail immediately. These men have brought word of Iroquois raiding parties in the vicinity and fear the island will not be safe tonight." Passengers and crew made haste to assemble and begin to load the ship. They completed their tasks and set sail about dinnertime.

The captain had told them, "We will sail until dusk to a wide part of the river where we will anchor for the night. It is not possible to sail the river after dark. We shall post guards to protect us against raids by canoe." That night as they went to bed, Jeanne realized this was the first time they had slept on the ship without motion. Later that night they could hear loud noises, gunshots and screaming. They could see large fires burning to the west.

The following morning, they weighed anchor at dawn. As the sailing was relatively calm, the passengers were allowed on deck at will. Jeanne* marveled at the shore, alternating sand beaches and granite cliffs, dense forests of pine and hardwood. The smell of pine was almost overwhelming. Occasionally they would see a small building on the shore and occasional clusters of three or four farms.

Later in the day they passed a large island called *Ile d'Anticosti.* On the south shore a wide peninsula jutted out. Sister Anne called it the *Gaspé* Peninsula. On the peninsula they could see two farms whose buildings were burned and still smoldering. Much worse they saw people hanging from the trees.

The captain brought the ship about and dropped the anchor. Sister Anne summoned Jeanne* and Madeleine de Roybon. "We are sending a party ashore with Father Mathieu to give these people a proper burial. I shall require your help to make shrouds." The long boat was lowered and the priest and the three women accompanied eight armed men to shore.

Once ashore, the women and the priest cut down the bodies while the others inspected and secured the area. There were two men, one woman, and four children of about four to ten years. Their hair had been scalped off and the bodies appeared to have been beaten and mutilated. All were missing an ear and some fingers. All four of the burial party vomited their breakfast early in the task. They laid the bodies out and began to sew them in sacks brought from the ship.

Father Mathieu said, "I have seen this twice before, each time it is more difficult." Four of the men returned. They had found a woman and two small children hiding in a hidden cave. The woman was sobbing hysterically, and the children, a boy of three and a girl of five, were as silent as death. A large brown dog followed them down to the beach. The women stopped and went to comfort the three. The other men appeared and began to quickly dig shallow graves while two others stood guard.

They buried the bodies quickly. Father Mathieu gave a hurried blessing, and they made haste to return to the ship. Back on board, the lead man told the ladies, "Apparently last night the Iroquois descended on the farms. The noise at the first farm alerted the second family who took refuge in a cave built for such a purpose. The father of the second farm went to fight, hoping the Iroquois would think he was alone at the second farm. They massacred the first family and the second man, but did not find the others. Before morning they burned the houses and left." Eventually the woman gained enough composure to tell them her name was Marie-Laure Rimbaud. She and her husband had been farming there for two years. The family next door was her brother and his family.

That evening the ship anchored by the mouth of a river entering the Saint-Laurent, where there was a small trading post called *Tadoussac* that looked to be unoccupied. The captain thought it prudent not to investigate and said the guard would have to be more secure tonight as the river was narrower. After the girls made space for the Rimbaud family, the children started to react and talk and played with the girls and the large dog who they called *Loupé*.

That night they were suddenly awakened by a great deal of noise, shouting, rifle shots and occasional great splashes in the water. A few of the men came below and guarded the stairway. At one point Jeanne* noticed one of the cannon doors being forced open, and a man began to crawl through. He was Indian complete with feathers, but his face was painted and he was the most ferocious looking creature Jeanne* had ever seen. He seemed to embody all that is evil. Jeanne* screamed, but before anyone else could react, Marie-Laure Rimbaud jumped up and produced a small hatchet from under her dress. She hit the man squarely in the face, and blood filled the area. She began shrieking and swinging, virtually shredding the man before their eyes. By the time she was subdued, she had removed his head, an arm and sliced his torso into pieces.

Marie-Laure collapsed into a sobbing heap. Later she told the girls her husband had given her the hatchet when he left her and the children in the cave. She had carried inside her bodice since then. Jeanne* began to wonder if the adventure might be more than for which she had bargained. That morning the men had already removed most of the evidence of the attack. Fortunately no one from the ship had been harmed. A few Iroquois had however apparently been shot.

The riverside became more populated as the day progressed. Canoes and other small craft became common.

257

Marie-Laure seemed to have again recovered, and she and the children with *Loupé* the dog strolled along the deck. Later Sister Anne told Jeanne* that Marie-Laure had asked to stay with the girls and look for a new husband in Québec. Jeanne* was shocked at the apparent boldness of this act, but Anne explained, "In this country there is no time for the luxury of extended grief. An intact family is necessary to survival. Remarriage soon after the death of a spouse is the rule rather than the exception."

Jeanne* asked if the children would present a problem. Anne answered, "Quite the contrary, a woman with farming and family experience and two children almost ready to work in the fields is a big plus. She will be much sought after. She is also young. In spite of six years of marriage and two children, she is one year younger than you."

That evening they anchored off the *Ile d'Orleans*. The captain said they would post a guard but expected no trouble this close to Québec. Tomorrow morning they would land in Québec.

Chapter 16

<u>Québec City - August 15, 1671</u>:

François* had come to town to see the ship. There had been six other ships this year, and each time he had come, hoping to see his bride. Because of the distance and slow travel, there was no way to know who would arrive on any particular boat. This may be the last one of the year, and perhaps he would have to spend another winter alone. Maybe she had changed her mind, or died, or run off with a sailor.

He had convinced himself she would have to be too homely for anyone in Touraine and had accepted that fate. As the girls came down, he watched and wondered. Anne Gasnier led them. There were two beautiful girls with her, a tall girl with dark hair and a shorter one with lighter hair. They both carried themselves well. He figured they would be here to marry someone with money. There was one particularly wretched looking girl, short and quite heavy. He sighed, "I suspect that is her." After the boat was emptied, he did a few errands and returned home. Now he would wait. Sister Bourgeoys said she would send him word when his girl had arrived. There was no way to hurry the process.

That evening he had been invited to have dinner at the home of Guillaume* and Marie* Renaud. After dinner he sat on the floor and played with their son, Louis, who was to turn one year at the end of the month. François* told them the story of the ship and his concern that he was waiting for an ugly bride who was never coming. Marie* reassured him, "Why François* I am certain she was on this ship, and I am further certain she will be lovely."

Guillaume* added, "Actually you should better wish she is strong enough to pull stumps," alluding to their upcoming fall project. "At any rate I hope she comes soon so I can finally come to dinner at your house." They all had a good laugh and François* left. Violette the dog was waiting for him on the Renaud porch. They walked the half-mile back to the farm, passing in front of the newest addition to the neighborhood, the new home of Pierre* Parent. He and his wife Jeanne* Beadeau (oldest daughter of Anne* Ardouin) along with their now eight children had leased their old farm near Anne*'s in Beauport and bought a larger one here in Charlesbourg. François* was certain they would be a wonderful addition to the town.

In the evening, two days later, his neighbor, Jean* Bergevin, stopped by. "I was at Lady Anne Gasnier's today, working her flower beds. She asked I tell you that you are expected for dinner tomorrow evening."

François* almost grabbed him and asked, "Did she give a reason?"

Bergevin replied, "Not exactly, but she did suggest you take a bath beforehand." And with a laugh, Bergevin walked to his home next door.

The next day François* could hardly contain himself. As he and Philippe began to bring in the hay, Philippe said, "François*, have you been testing the Calvados early? I swear you are worthless today."

Unable to contain himself any longer, François* told him of the invitation. Philippe replied, "I suspect we should quit for today and let you prepare."

François* said, "I will be down in a while to take an Indian bath." Philippe told him he would have Marie get it ready.

That afternoon François*, Philippe and Marie sat in the steam bath, discussing plans for the farm now their new partner was to arrive. They had discussed this regularly ever since the letter from Marguerite Bourgeoys, but tonight it had new meaning. Marie arose, went out, and came back with a small pottery jar. Marie was now pregnant with their first child and it had begun to show, particularly in the steam bath. She went behind François* and rubbed an oil on his shoulders, "This is an ancient Algonquin 'courting oil'. It is said to bring one luck in finding true love."

François* returned and dressed in his best clothes. He carefully combed his curly hair and picked a handful of mint from the garden to chew on his way to Québec. He started down the path to the river, and Violette joined him, seeming to sense he would need support tonight. They boarded François*'s small canoe at the river and paddled to the port.

Québec City - August 18, 1671:

Time had passed more quickly for Jeanne* than for François*. After two nights in the convent, she said goodbye to her friends and returned home with Anne Gasnier. Anne's home was on the main square of the upper town in the most fashionable area of Québec. The house was large, and grander than the Anguille home in Artannes. Almost all the windows had glass. The front looked over the public green, and in back there were two magnificent flower gardens managed by François*'s neighbor, the master gardener, Jean* Bergevin.

The house was furnished with objects from Paris. If one did not look outside, one might think it was in Paris itself. The house had many lamps lit at night, and the walls were lined with books. Jeanne* had slept in a wonderful bed the night before but had not sleep well as a result of the excitement concerning dinner tonight. There was a knock at the door and Anne's maid answered. It was not Monsieur Allard but her friend Madeleine de Roybon on the arm of a young military officer.

Anne explained, "I thought you could use some support in conversation so I took the liberty of asking Lieutenant Rivard to bring Madeleine tonight." Soon another knock came, and this time it was indeed François*. Anne came to greet him, *"Bonsoir, Monsieur, entrez si vous plait."* She showed him into the main room where he saw the others. He knew Rivard, but there were only the two rich girls from the boat, where was his girl?

Anne took him by the arm and said, "Monsieur Allard, I believe you know Lieutenant Rivard from the fort."

François* indicated he did, and the men shook hands. Anne continued, "He has escorted Mademoiselle Madeleine de Roybon."

François* bowed slightly and replied, *"Enchanté."*

Then Anne continued, "And this is Mademoiselle Jeanne* Anguille, your young lady from Touraine."

François* was speechless. He was thunderstruck. He felt his legs would fail him. He was totally unprepared for this. Having spent so much time getting ready for an ugly girl, he would have been pleasantly surprised by a mere plain one. But here in front of him was, in his eyes, the most beautiful girl in Québec. He managed to croak out a weak, "*Enchanté.*"

The group was seated. Fortunately for François*, Rivard took the conversation. He was from Tourouvre in the Perche region of Normandie. He and François* had met through Guillaume* Renaud and had been hunting, and fishing together over the past two years. Rivard regaled the group with stories of their hunting expeditions while François* again found his tongue.

At dinner Anne said, "Monsieur Allard is developing one of the finest farms in Québec, located in Charlesbourg just north of the city. Jeanne* my dear, perhaps if Monsieur Allard would invite us, we could ride out there after mass on Sunday."

François* decided he must speak, "Lady Anne is too kind in her description of my small farm, but I would most welcome the visit." Now that he had spit out a complete sentence, he hoped he would be all right.

Jeanne* said, "I certainly look forward to it. What crops do you raise, Monsieur?"

Finally a topic on which François* could be at ease. He launched in to a description of the farm and his plans: crops, animals, Indians; then realizing he was rambling, he cut himself short.

Jeanne* said, "We started maize on my father's farm in Artannes-sur-Indres two years ago. I find it quite fascinating but do not have a full understanding of it."

François* thought, "Not only is she beautiful, she is interested and knowledgeable about farming. I only hope this is not a dream, and I am to wake up in the hold of *l'Aigle d'Or.*"

The evening flew by and soon it was time for François* to take his leave. On the way home he told Violette about the evening in excruciating detail. She sat at the front of the canoe and listened intently as only collies can do.

When they were alone, Jeanne* said to Anne, "How nice of Lieutenant Rivard to come tonight; I think it was a wonderful idea. I wonder how to thank him."

Anne looked at her and replied, "I wouldn't worry. I suspect he is being rewarded even as we speak."

Jeanne* looked shocked and then both women broke into a grand laugh. Anne continued, "And what do you think of Monsieur Allard, my dear?"

Jeanne* thought for a second and replied, "Perfect."

Chapter 17

François* returned to Charlesbourg filled with excitement. Jeanne* seemed to be everything he could ask and more. What had he done to again gain such good fortune? Needing someone to talk to, he headed directly for Philippe's camp. He rambled, "She is charming, intelligent, interested in farming, she looks quite strong. I think we should sign a marriage contract right away." Then a thought hit him, "What if she doesn't want me?"
Marie assured him that no Frenchwoman could resist him, but he continued, "She is coming to visit Sunday. We must make the farm appealing to a woman. We shall began tomorrow."

He continued listing strings of ideas until Philippe said, "We still have to have a working farm, and if we don't get sleep, we will be of little use tomorrow." So François* went back to the farmhouse and planned his future.
The following morning he arose early and went directly to Renaud's. Guillaume* and Marie* were just rising when he knocked. Marie* welcomed him and included him at breakfast. François* launched his plan. "She is truly a remarkable woman. I will need feminine assistance in making my farmhouse appealing. I hope you can help." Marie* assured him that they could and that she would be over tomorrow with help.
François* returned home where Philippe was beginning the wheat harvest. He said, "François*, I hope this courtship does not remain all consuming. We do have a farm to run."

The following morning Marie* Renaud came with Marie* Guillodeau-Poitevin and Jeanne* Badeau-Parent. They ordered François* to go harvest the wheat and they would attend to the house. When François* returned from the field, he felt he was back at Anne*'s. The house was clean and orderly, the kitchen in perfect order, and his few pieces of furniture arranged. There were even two books on the table, a French prayer book and *Les Pioneers* by Pierre Boucher.

Marie* Renaud ordered François* to leave everything in order. "I have asked Jean LeMarche to make you a proper wedding bed and dining table. He will have them in two days. I hope you will have a good supply of Calvados to repay him. We will have two quilts for you by Sunday." They all looked at François* like a prize bull at market. Then Marie* gave him a sisterly peck on the cheek and they departed.

François* and Philippe finished the wheat and on Saturday they went to the mill. At the Montmorency Falls mill, word had spread of François*'s elegant woman who stayed with Lady Anne. François* found himself the butt of much of the good natured joking that married men give to their soon-to-fall brethren.

Sunday morning François* was up well before the sun. In fact he had hardly slept. He planned to go to Québec for mass and had persuaded Guillaume*, Marie* and young Louis Renaud to go along for support. They walked to the river and took Renaud's larger canoe. As they entered the cathedral, François* saw Anne Gasnier and Jeanne* sitting in the front of the transept where he could easily see them.

He was somewhat surprised to see Madeleine de Roybon with them. During the mass he could not take his eyes off Jeanne*, she behave perfectly and piously. Madeleine, on the other hand, squirmed like a schoolboy.

After mass they met in the square. François* did introductions and everyone fawned over young Louis Renaud. Jeanne* indicated Madeleine had also moved in with Sister Anne. Madeleine reported, "I simply could not endure the 'meat market' at the convent." Marie* Renaud indicated somewhat coldly the "meat market" had worked well for her.

Attempting to maintain civility, François* interrupted, "Guillaume*, you and Mademoiselle de Roybon have a mutual acquaintance in Lieutenant Rivard." This seemed to avert a crisis, and Anne indicated they hoped to call on François* in the early afternoon. As François* and the Renauds departed, François* felt his stomach in knots.

As scheduled, Lady Anne's carriage arrived in the early afternoon. François* who had been pacing nervously sat down on a porch chair to try to look relaxed. He arose as if he had just noticed the carriage, although he had seen it much earlier. He and Violette went down to greet Anne and Jeanne*. After Anne complimented François* on his farm and Jeanne* fawned over Violette, he invited them up to the house.

The Allard farmhouse was typical of the period. It sat high off the ground for protection from snow and floods which also allowed farmers such as LeMarche who were also tradesmen to have a shop under the house on the ground floor. Also in this ground area was a shallow cellar for storage with a deeper portion to store roots and vegetables. The steps to the front porch rose almost one story. The porch ran the length of the house and faced the Charlesbourg Square only a few hundred feet away. Neighboring houses were relatively close to provide protection and sociability.

Two shuttered windows with no glass flanked the center door. François* explained he hoped to obtain a glass pane at this year's *rendez-vous*. The door led to a large front room also running the entire front of the house. One wall held a large stone fireplace. There were four chairs and a dining table recently completed by Jean LeMarche. In the back was a bedroom complete with the new bed and a new quilt. Beside it was the kitchen. The proximity of the fireplace to the kitchen allowed it to serve for heat and cooking. A ladder led to a loft divided into two parts. "One for boys and one for girls," François* explained hopefully.

The back door led to a smaller porch with a view of the farm. There was a vegetable garden, a grape arbor and an apple orchard between the house and the barn. As they exited to the back porch, François* noticed visitors approaching, the Bedard and Bergevin families were making a call as they had planned on Saturday. Introductions were made and Madame Bedard suggested they could go in for tea. She told François* she would prepare it if he would show her where to find the necessary implements. Actually François* was not sure where they were as Madame Bedard herself had brought them and arranged them for him yesterday, but he played along.

Marie* Piton-Bergevin said, "Mademoiselle, you may be interested to know I came from Paris as a *fille du roi* in 1668. I met and married Monsieur Bergevin who is from Angers in the Touraine region of France."

Jeanne* replied, "What a coincidence, I am from Artannes-sur-Indres near Tours." Marie* of course knew this as they had rehearsed Saturday afternoon to give confidence to the shy and terrified François*. Anne also indicated Jean* Bergevin was the master gardener who tended her fabulous flower gardens in his "spare time".

After carefully extolling the wonderful features of François* and his farm, the neighbors took their leave. At that point, François* recommended a tour of the farm. "I should like nothing better," Jeanne* replied politely. They again exited the back. At the barn Jeanne* was enthralled with the animals. She seemed to be knowledgeable about each one and was certainly not afraid to touch them. She told François* if they were to marry, among the gifts from the King would be a second cow and an ox. François* looked upon this as a hopeful sign of her eventual acceptance of the match.

As they surveyed the fields, she showed great interest and know-how. She was surprised at the size of the apple orchard. François* told her he made cider and then Calvados which had helped to finance the purchase of the farm. Jeanne* was especially interested in the maize as it was a relatively new concept to her. François* realized she had showed as much interest in the farm as he had when he first toured it with Michaud.

Eventually they made it back to the Indian camp of Philippe and Marie. Jeanne* was fascinated with the smoke house and the steam bath and had questions on every detail. She and Marie toured the camp. Suddenly Jeanne* looked up and screamed. She had seen the two wolves, now fully grown along the edge of the woods. Philippe laughed and whistled, the two came quietly and allowed Jeanne* to scratch their ears. They explained how they came to live as pets. Jeanne exclaimed, "This place is as amazing and wonderful as it is wild." Jeanne* and Marie had a long animated conversation out of earshot of François*. As they left Jeanne* said to Marie, "I know we shall be the best of friends."

When they arrived back at the farmhouse, Madeleine* Guillodeau-Poitevin was on the porch. Lady Anne excused herself and went to speak with Madeleine*, putting Jeanne* and François* out of earshot but not out of sight. François* took the opportunity to ask, "Mademoiselle, may I ask what you think of my poor farm so far?"

Jeanne* replied, "Monsieur Allard, I must say that I find it simply wonderful." And gathering boldness she did not know she had, she added, "And what is more, Monsieur, I believe I find you to be equally as wonderful. Sister Anne told me to wait some time for a decision. However, between the two of us alone, I am in agreement with the match."

Dumbstruck again, François* was barely able to make his enthusiastic affirmative reply. Jeanne* continued, "Sister Anne tells me that it is considered unusual to hold a marriage until the end of the harvest."

François* agreed it was rare to have a wedding before November. Jeanne* asked, "What do you suppose would be a tasteful date?"

François* replied, "What do you say to the first?"

She laughed and gave a sly smile that would delight him daily for the remainder of his life and replied, "Perfect." She then added, "We should, however, wait some time to tell Sister Anne. If she believes the decision is made, she may not allow me to visit often."

She looked squarely at François* and began to stare. He asked, "Do I have two noses?"

She replied, "No, you have two eyes, that is two different eyes. Sister Anne told me you had wonderful eyes, and now I see it is true." She turned and headed back to the farmhouse, and François* followed behind her just as Violette followed behind him.

When they rejoined the two ladies, François* made the introduction, "This is Madeleine* Guillodeau-Poitevin, my neighbor, She came as a *fille du roi* from an island off Larochelle. She is married to my friend Jean* Poitevin who was my shipmate in 1666. He is also called 'Laviolette' but that is a different story."

The ladies exchanged pleasantries and Madeleine* said, "I came to invite you and Lady Anne to our farm after mass next Sunday. It is our fashion to have a picnic at one of the farms after mass when the weather is fair. If it would be convenient, perhaps you could come to mass at our new chapel here on the Charlesbourg square. We currently share a priest with Beauport, a new curé, Father Mathieu. It will be his first mass here."

Jeanne* excitedly told of her relationship with Father Guillaume Mathieu and they all agreed on the plan. They said their goodbyes and headed back to Québec in the carriage. Madeleine* looked at François* saying, "I do believe love has found François* Allard."

He replied, "Madeleine*, you could not be more correct." When they returned to the house, Philippe was waiting and said, "If Monsieur is not too taken with romance tomorrow, perhaps he could meet me in the fields. I believe we have apples and grapes to harvest and winter wheat to sow." François* assured him he would be most ready and went in to bed.

The following week François* and Philippe attacked the harvest with renewed vigor. Soon it was Sunday. As the new Charlesbourg chapel was only a short walk away, it was not difficult for François* to be early to mass. He was surprised to see that Lady Anne, Madeleine de Roybon and Jeanne* were already in attendance in the front of the new chapel speaking with its even newer priest. François* approached the group and was greeted by Lady Anne. She introduced him to Father Mathieu and indicated he already knew Madeleine and Jeanne*. They all smiled, and Jeanne* gave him a quick smile and a wink. He continued to be impressed with the boldness of this wonderful woman.

Father Mathieu was explaining the chapel was to be named the church of Saint-Charles de Brommée, and the two small squares of Bourg-Royal and Charlesbourg would henceforth together be the village of Charlesbourg. There would be a formal ceremony at the chapel on November 4, the feast day of Saint-Charles. During mass, François*'s thoughts were only of a day 3 days before feast of Saint-Charles when he hoped to marry his bride.

Following mass, most of the congregation moved to the nearby farm of Jean* Poitevin. Jean* and Madeline* greeted the guests. Madeleine* held their first child, François* Poitevin. Although he was merely three weeks old, his mother, a true Québécois pioneer, had been back to her normal chores for more than two weeks. They greeted Jeanne* warmly, and the ladies settled in with the baby. As a young girl, Jeanne* had helped with her two younger sisters and later with many of the young children in Artannes through her work at the Abbey. As a result she was quite at home with babies. She and baby François* Poitevin got along wonderfully.

The ladies of the neighborhood filed by to see the Charlesbourg's newest citizen, and the lady they expected to be its next new member. Each extolled the virtues of François* and his farm as well as the community. Later, as lunch was served, Jeanne* was pleasantly surprised she and François* managed to be seated together on the ground by themselves.

She started, "The food here is so wonderful. I wonder why all the ladies are not as fat as a lord."

François* returned, "The nature of our work allows us to eat well and remain thin, you will see."

She replied, "Oh François*", breaking etiquette by using his first name and later using the French familiar *tu* instead of the formal *vous* which would be appropriate in the pre-married state, "I yearn to begin that work. Will we really clear these giant trees?"

"Indeed we shall, it is incredible work, but I now believe you will truly enjoy it."

She looked over the dense forest bordering the fields. Autumn was coming to its peak and the colors were now beyond comprehension to any one from the Old World. She continued, "Heaven can be no more beautiful than this. I am now certain God has sent me to this exact place to fulfill my destiny with you."

As they rose François* added, "I hope you feel the same in January."

She assured him she would, and noticing they were suddenly out of sight of the others she said, "François*, quickly, kiss me."

As he took this bold woman in his arms, she looked up. At 5' 6" Jeanne* was quite tall for a French girl and taller than many of the men. But at six feet, François* was much taller. He kissed her. François*'s only other passionate kiss had been Mathurine* on the *Iles de la Madeleine,* and it paled compared to this. As they returned to the picnic, he wondered how he would survive the next six weeks.

Chapter 18

The best way for a Frenchman to forget romance and sex is a trip to the back country. As François* and Philippe were now ahead on their fall chores, they headed north to shoot game for the winter. They had a marvelous time. The woods were filled with game, and the weather was good. At night they made their plans for the future and talked of the earlier hunts with Henri.

As he had before, François* asked if they would ever see his old friend again. Philippe answered, "I believe we will someday, but I cannot be certain. My father felt the French way was the way of the future, and he felt the mission at balance was good for the Indian. However, he was raised on Indian ways and after you left, he talked more and more of them. When Miss Anne* died, he felt his place was no longer here.

"Myself, I have grown up with the French ways. I speak French as well as Algonquin and better than Huron (referring to the Iroquois dialect of the Huron Nation). I suspect my children will be more French than Indian, and I see intermarriage is becoming common. They say the wilderness is disappearing in the land of the Dutch and English. Who can say?"

Later, on a more practical subject, François* said, "I should like to get a glass for a front window this fall. I have not been to the *Rendez-vous* since Henri departed. The problem is that all I have to trade is some Calvados."

Philippe thought for a while and replied, "We will go. Give me the Calvados, and I believe I can trade for your glass."

The following Sunday, François* was again invited to dinner at Lady Anne's. To his surprise, along with Jeanne* and Madeleine, Sister Marguerite Bourgeoys was in attendance. She greeted François* and started, "Monsieur Allard, how wonderful to see you. I am so pleased with your young lady. I told you, you could trust my brother."

François* was surprised she spoke as though they had completed their marriage contract. Later she told him. "Next week I would like you and Mademoiselle Anguille to come to the convent for the meeting of the men and the young ladies. Not as participants, but I should think it will be good for you to mingle with the other new couples. Perhaps you could consider a contract yourselves. The good Lord knows you've had enough time."

François* turned bright red, but he did not miss the chance, "As a matter of fact Sister, I do wish to ask for Jean… that is Mademoiselle Anguille. I must confess that we have discussed it briefly, and I believe she is in agreement."

The nun looked at Jeanne*, "Is this true child?"

With her best convent modesty, Jeanne* replied softly, "Yes, Sister."

Sister Bourgeoys returned, "I see you have taken this liberty. I suppose you are addressing one another as *tu et toi* and using surnames?" They both murmured in agreement.

Sister Marguerite Bourgeoys stood slowly to her full height in her imposing severe black habit and looked at them both. They were all shocked when she shouted out, "Well good for you! This is what we need. This is a new land and a new country. Women will no longer be regarded with the farm animals! This is New France, not Old France; here we shall have liberty and opportunity. Men and woman will live without everything directed by the King, not even by the Church!" Then remembering herself she quickly crossed herself but continued. "Lady Anne, this calls for a toast. Get the wine, no wait, Madeleine, you know wine. You go get it. Bring the good stuff, three bottles."

At this point Lady Anne could control herself no longer and burst into laughter. The others followed suit. Madeleine poured the wine, beginning to pour small glasses. The nun took the bottle and filled each glass. She held hers up and said, "To Jeanne* Anguille of Touraine, and François* Allard of Normandie, now both of Québec. To your new life and the New World." And she downed a glass of fine burgundy in one swallow.

She continued, "We shall get to work on the contract. I fear your friend François Badeau is away on business. Paul Vachon will be doing the contracts this week. I shall alert him. We will read your three banns and have the ceremony as soon as possible and respectable. I suggest November first!"

Jeanne* and François* looked at the nun and each other and said in unison, "Yes, Sister."

Jeanne* had not seen so much wine consumed since her night at the Tuilleries Palace with the Bishop of Paris. When François* went to leave, Sister Bourgeoys asked, "Are you not going to kiss your fiancé, Monsieur?"

Again red in the face, François* went over and bent to give Jeanne* a modest kiss. She, however, returned with one at least as passionate as the kiss at the picnic. The nun again raised her glass and shouted, "*Bravo enfants et Bravo Québec!*" The next morning, François* could barely recall the canoe trip home.

The following week, François* prepared for what he hoped would be his final trip to the convent. He was accompanied by one of his new neighbors, Vivien* Jean. Vivien* had come in 1669 from Larochelle and had a farm just a bit south of François*. Unlike François*, he was very much in the market for a wife.

As they entered the great hall, François* saw the group of eligible girls standing along the wall, each dressed in the gray dress of the *filles du roi*. Jeanne* was off to the side with Lady Anne and Madeleine de Roybon. Jeanne* wore a white dress and Madeleine red. He greeted the ladies and gallantly kissed each hand. Marguerite Bourgeoys appeared and greeted the group. She appeared to have recovered nicely from the previous Sunday dinner.

As the evening progressed, an elegantly dressed young man entered the room and made a quick tour exchanging pleasantries. Sister Bourgeoys whispered to Lady Anne, "LaSalle." He quickly settled on Madeleine in her provocative red gown. They spoke for a while, and he moved on. She came over to François* and Jeanne* and said, "René-Robert Cavelier Sieur de LaSalle, my kind of man, very rich and he plans to spend most of his time chasing Indians and rabbits in the search of new land." They all laughed. Later to Lady Anne's dismay, Madeleine managed to disappear with LaSalle. She knew this reflected poorly on her as the girl was in her charge, but she also realized she was no match for Madeleine.

She sighed to Jeanne*, "At least these new ladies are unlikely to have unhappy wedding nights, thanks to the tutelage of Mademoiselle de Roybon."

Later Vivien* Jean came to them very excited, "François* and Jeanne* I have met a wonderful girl, would you come and visit with us?" The threesome threaded their way through the crowd and Jeanne* gave a short cry when she saw the young lady was her good friend Catherine* Gateau. Catherine* and Jeanne* regaled the men with tales of the voyage and as the evening wore to a close, it seemed as another *fille du roi* would be moving to Charlesbourg.

The following day François* had two visitors. The first was Noel* Langlois. François* was surprised and honored to be visited by one of Québec's richest and most notable citizens. Noel* toured the farm and congratulated François* on his success. "I told you some years ago great things can be had here by men with strength and ambition. Lady Anne has asked I witness your marriage contract, and I have come to offer my services."

François* replied, "I would be most honored, Monsieur."

The older man replied, "Then it is set, and please call me Noel*. This is **New** France."

Later in the day the notary, Paul Vachon, visited him. Vachon was the most prominent notary in Québec and had done hundreds of marriage contracts. He surveyed and listed François*'s possessions and explained the document. It would list both parties and the particulars of their families, also the possessions of both including the dowry from Jeanne*'s father as well as from the King. It explained what would happen to the property in the event of death or dissolution, although dissolution was almost unheard of at this time. It also swore allegiance to the Church and the State.

Both parties and several witnesses would sign it. Afterward a "Bann of marriage" would be read on each of three successive Sundays in church. After that they could be wed. The date of November first had been set. Because Father Mathieu had two churches, to have that date the ceremony must take place at the Beauport chapel. François* would have rather had it in Charlesbourg, but he was not interested in waiting any additional days.

The ceremony of signing took place, and the document was signed by Lady Anne, Noel* Langlois, Paul Vachon and Father Mathieu. Several other friends and notable citizens came to sign it as a sign of the community's support of the marriage. François* and Philippe continued to finish the harvest except for the maize and the days dragged on, but the day did arrive.

V

Chapter 19

Beauport Chapel - November 1, 1671:

Guillaume* and Marie* Renaud stopped to get François*. They would drive their cart to the Beauport Chapel and return with the couple. There was to be a party at the Renaud farm following the service. The weather had turned quite cold in the past two weeks, but fortunately, today was sunny and unseasonably warm. Marie* announced they would be able to have the last picnic of the year today in honor of the marriage.

The small chapel was filled with François*'s friends as well as several notable citizens who had come to support the marriage. Philippe and Marie made a rare visit to the French chapel, and even Madeleine de Roybon came on the arm of René-Robert Cavelier de LaSalle. Father Mathieu was in top form. This was the first marriage of the autumn in his parish. In fact, apart from a few ceremonies in the Indian missions, it would be the first he had performed in Québec. He spoke of the role of the Church in marriage, but also the importance of new families in the new world and looked to the future when marriages would occur between native Québécois.

The men in the congregation began to become restless with thirst to be quenched at the Renaud Farm. At the end of the ceremony, as was the custom, Father Mathieu asked the participants to sign the marriage document. As François* could not read or write, he declined as was the custom, but he was surprised when Jeanne* also declined.

Another first was the bell. Jean Badeau had fashioned a bell for the new chapel in the forge at his gun shop. He gave it to the church in honor of his late mother, and today was the first, but certainly not the last, time it signaled a new marriage in the young colony.

Following the ceremony, the congregation followed on foot or by cart to the Renaud farm in Charlesbourg. It was a typical Québécois wedding party with good food and plenty to drink. François*'s old shipmates Dery and Deschamps came and played music, and François* and Jeanne* were pleased to find Normand and Touraine folk dances were similar. Traditional games were played, stories told, songs sung and a few discussions ended in a friendly brawl.

With the sinking of the afternoon sun, the newlyweds took their leave. Several well-wishers offered a ride home, but Jeanne* declined, "I believe I would enjoy a walk through my new country." They headed east on the lane to the village hand in hand. It was as spectacular a late fall day as one could wish. The sky was blue and the temperature unseasonably warm with only a light breeze. A few trees held their autumn splendor, but the lane was carpeted with the fallen leaves.

As they kicked their way playfully through the leaves, François* asked why Jeanne* had declined to sign the marriage document. She replied, "I did not wish to seem more educated than my husband."

François* interrupted, "But you are, and I think it is fine. I have always wished I could read and write like Guillaume* and some of the others."

Jeanne* paused and looked up at François*, "I hear the winters are long and cold. I taught the school children of the village at the abbey. I should consider it an honor to help you learn."

François* replied, "And I should find it an honor to be your student." He put his strong calloused hand on her shoulder as they proceeded on. Walking though the wilderness, Jeanne*Anguille-Allard had never felt so safe.

At the farmhouse François* kept with the tradition of carrying his bride across the threshold. Lady Anne had already delivered Jeanne*'s things, and they had eaten dinner at Renaud's. All that remained was to go to bed. Sensing François*'s discomfort, Jeanne* said, "I shall go first and get ready." She disappeared into the bedroom, and soon called for François*.

He entered the room expecting her in bedclothes under the covers, but he was shocked that she stood in front of the bed stark naked. She came to her stunned husband, embraced him and helped him undress and get into bed. François* had the experience with the two Indian maidens, but he was surprised when he found Jeanne* seemed to know exactly what to do and better than the two Indian ladies. In fact, François* experienced things he had never heard of nor considered. After this amazing consummation of the marriage, they fell fast asleep.

François* was further surprised when his new bride awakened him twice during the night for repeat performances. The next thing he heard was the rooster. Looking over in the dark, he saw the bed was empty. He panicked, thinking it was all a dream, but he smelled food cooking. He quickly dressed and went out to the kitchen where he found Jeanne* dressed for work and making his favorite breakfast items.

"I hope these eggs are to your satisfaction," she started, "Marie showed me where things were and Marie* Renaud told me what you liked for breakfast." She walked over and gave him a great kiss, "Good morning, my new husband." Unable to reply, he sat down and began to eat; she did the same. She continued, "Philippe indicated that the maize would be ready to harvest today, I am anxious to learn how it is done."

François* finally found his tongue, "My dear, I must say that I was surprised, although pleasantly, that a girl from the abbey would be so skilled in the making of love."

Jeanne* laughed, "I assure you, sir, this was not learned at the abbey. Rather I learned traveling two months in the company of Mademoiselle de Roybon who regaled the girls each night on shipboard with tales about the art of love and, yes, the art of sex. I have been anxiously awaiting the opportunity to try them."

Digesting this along with his eggs, François* continued, "I must say that I was also surprised, though again pleasantly, at your enthusiasm for repetition."

Jeanne* stared directly into the wonderful eyes of her new husband and replied, "Monsieur Allard, I have been sent to you and this place by the King of France and by God himself to help you raise a family. I plan to put all the energy I have into this endeavor." And she gave him her sly smile that would always gladden his heart. François* Allard, the poor boy from the Normand countryside, again wondered what he had done that God should favor him thusly.

So François* and his new bride went out to another beautiful fall day, and Philippe, Marie and François* taught her how to harvest corn. By the end of the day, they could scarcely keep up with her. Dinner was exceptional, and the night activity was as intense and varied as the previous night. François* began to worry if he would have enough energy for the maize.

The following morning, the reality of Québec had returned. The sky was cloudy, the north wind blew, the temperature had plummeted and there was a small coating of snow on the ground. Breakfast was again ready when François* arose. Jeanne indicated that she had already been out to feed the animals. "The farm is spectacular in the snow!" she exclaimed. As they were going out, Marie and Philippe were at the door. Marie had brought deerskin clothing and boots for Jeanne*. She invited them inside, inspected the garments and thanked them profusely, adding, "Now I am a true pioneer wife."

Then to her husband's amazement, she undressed and put them on. As she took his hand to go out, she said, "Marie explained to me that Indians are not so prudish about the human body. I think it is a very practical view."

That afternoon, having returned from the fields, there was a knock on the door. François* answered. It was the notary, François Badeau. François* welcomed him in, introduced him to Jeanne* and asked him to be seated. Badeau began, "I came to congratulate you on your marriage. As you know, I have been in Montréal on business for two months. My business concerns my mother's will. As you know, she, as we all do, thought quite highly of you. She had planned two gifts for your marriage, and I have been instructed to bring them."

"The first is this rifle I carried in. She had my brother, Jean, make it, and felt you could give the old one to your new bride." François* was overwhelmed at such a fine present and thanked Badeau profusely. The notary continued, "The second gift is outside, I thought it better to leave it there," so they went out on the porch. François* was overwhelmed, tied to the rail of the porch was the Perchon stallion he had helped deliver four years ago. Badeau continued, "She said of all men in Canada, you could clear half of Québec with this horse. She insisted it be given to you. She named it Henri, I think she saw a subtle humor in it."

As Badeau departed, François* said to Jeanne*, "I wish you could have known Anne* Ardouin. She was a wonderful woman in all regards. I am certain you would have been wonderful friends."
    Jeanne* said, "It's a wonderful animal. I will put him away." Bringing the horse by the reins to the porch, she climbed a few steps and hopped on bareback and rode the horse off to the barn like any cavalry officer.

After dinner, Jeanne* announced Marie had invited them for an Indian bath. Surprised and not knowing what to expect, François* went along with her to the Indian camp. They undressed, sat in the bath and discussed plans for the future. François* was somewhat perplexed as he sat naked

286

with his wife in company. It was at this point that he realized she was becoming Québécoise even more quickly than he had.

Charlesbourg, Québec - November 4, 1671:

On the Feast day of Saint-Charles de Brommée, the congregation gathered to christen their new church. Although François* was not an overly religious man, like all the other residents he took great pride in this church and community he had helped to build. Father Mathieu gave a sermon on the life of their new patron saint, a saint no one actually knew.

He told how Charles was a devout man, the Cardinal of Milan over one hundred years earlier. He was always depicted, as he would be in the new chapel, as a man in beggar's clothes and sandals with a rope around his neck. It is said he walked about dressed thusly to atone for the sins of man. Mathieu did not dwell on the fact he was a strong influence in the Counter Reformation of the time, as he felt many of his parishioners such as the Badeaus and Bedards, who were former Huguenots and perhaps Catholic more by force than choice, would not see this as an admirable quality. After the mass, Jeanne* and François* stayed and greeted the other parishioners as their first appearance at mass as a married couple.

Chapter 20

During the next several days the weather grew colder, and they finished the harvest of the maize. It was now time for the *rendez-vous*. François* tried to explain it to Jeanne*, but the concept was a little too foreign for her to comprehend. However, she did like the idea of a glass window. She and Marie would maintain the animals, and it would give her some time to give the farm a few personal touches.

When the day came, François* and Philippe took the two Indian dogs, a few miscellaneous items and a load of Calvados and began to canoe toward *Trois Rivieres*. François* had not been to the event for three years, but little had changed. The usual sorts were there and feats of strength, daring, skill and stupidity abounded. They met Anuk and stayed in his camp.

François* asked if he had seen Henri. Anuk said he had seen him in the far north two summers ago but not since. He had sad news in that Angélique had been attacked by a bear and died. Philippe took the news with some sadness, but he said, quoting his father, "Killed by bear is greatest honor for an Indian." François*, however, saw a distinctly French tear in the corner of Philippe's eye.

In the morning Philippe said, "You make the rounds and trade what you can and visit whom you wish. I will take the Calvados and meet you back in Anuk's camp tonight."

288

That night when François* returned, Philippe was sitting with not one but two windows. He told François*, "We shall leave in the morning. I will tell you the story on the way home."

During the homeward voyage the story came forth, "In Anuk's camp there are two Indian woman who sell themselves to the traders at night. I asked them to be especially pleasing and to confess they had been drinking my brew and it gave them an insatiable need for sex. By noon the story had spread. Had I enough Calvados, we could have had glass in all the windows."

The men laughed, and François* said, "I am glad we departed early. The men may not be happy when they discover the truth."

Philippe returned, "François*, I am surprised at you. When it comes to French trappers and sex, there is no truth, only perception. I suspect we will have a larger market for the drink next season."

When they returned home, Jeanne* was overjoyed with the windows. The men used the lumber left from last year's tree clearing to frame them in and then sealed them with pine tar. Jeanne* said, "With a horse, windows, and the most wonderful man in Canada, I must be one of the great ladies of Québec."

François* replied, "Indeed you are, Madame, indeed you are."

Jeanne* had obtained some books from the convent school and put them on a shelf near the table. She had also obtained an oil lamp to aid in the education this winter.

That night at dinner she finally asked François* about the wampum that he wore around his neck. He explained the story including Mathurine* and the second half of the piece. He was worried of her reaction, but she said, "Everyday I find you are even more wonderful", and she pulled him from his chair, and to his surprise, made love to him in front of the fire.

During the following two days, François* devoted himself to teaching his wife to shoot. She started with a target on the barn, much as he had started. He did not know Jeanne* had been taught to shoot by her oldest brother, Michel, at an early age, and he was surprised at how rapidly she progressed. Later he suggested she also learn to use the bow. This proved much more difficult, and she only attained a basic level of skill. François* felt that this would be adequate, but Jeanne*, being more determined to excel, went to Marie who showed her the woman's touch to the Indian weapon. François* would not know until some years later how adept his wife had become with the weapon.

The next day Pierre* Tremblay and Gilbert arrived to began tree clearing. Jeanne was amazed at the process. Pierre* and Gilbert adeptly felled the trees in an exact spot. François* and Philippe would cut the branches and the logs into sections. Marie showed Jeanne how to haul the trees with the horse. As Jeanne had grown up with horses, she had mastered it by the end of the day. They were all thrilled by the strength of the magnificent Perchon, now known as *Henri le cheval,* or Henri the horse. That evening Pierre* Tremblay told François*, "That horse is the strongest in all of Québec, and I believe your new wife is one of the strongest women," adding with a sly grin, "and one of the most beautiful as well." François* believed that Pierre* was correct on all three counts.

At the end of the week they had cleared two acres, stored the firewood, and collected the logs, which would be hauled down to the Saint-Laurent and on to the mill at Montmorency. Then their attention turned to the dreaded task of pulling the stumps from last year's tree harvest. As François* had suspected, Henri the horse made the job much easier. Sometimes he could completely uproot a tree by himself.

Most of the time people would cut the roots as they became exposed. Jeanne*'s skill with the ax was impressive. Marie whispered to François*, "If I were you, I would not make this woman mad," and gave a laugh that somehow reminded François* of that wonderful laugh of his missing friend, the other Henri.

Chapter 21
<u>Charlesbourg, Québec - Winter 1672:</u>

At the end of November, François* and Jeanne* took the horse and cart to the Beauport chapel to witness the marriage of their neighbor, Vivien* Jean to Jeanne*'s old shipmate, Catherine* Gateau. Their little town was growing, and as winter fell, the neighbors became more social rather than less. The arrangement of the farmhouses around the Square made travel from house to house or to the chapel of Saint-Charles de Brommée simple even in bad weather. As hard working as the Québécois were, they were in the end French and valued fun and socialization even more than hard work.

The tradition of a picnic after mass on Sunday continued through the winter. Although the new chapel was used as an indoor banquet hall, the hearty Québécois spent a good part of the day outside. There seemed to be no end to the winter pastimes they had developed. There were races on "Indian slippers" or snowshoes, lacrosse on the snow, and occasionally *ah-kee* on the pond behind the Allard farmhouse.

One day Pierre* Parent came with a pair of long boards strapped to his boots, "I was given these some years ago by Pierre* Miville. He was born in Switzerland and these are from the Swiss Alps. They are called skis and allow you to glide on the snow." Everyone tried the devices. By the end of the winter everyone had their own homemade pair and had a race around the Square.

The best event of the winter was conceived by Isaac* Bedard, "A dog sled race down the Indian road north to the Laurentians and back. Each family will enter their sled, and to make it interesting, we will have the woman as drivers." The Allard sled had been built by Philippe and François*. It used four dogs, the two Indian dogs and the two young wolves who seemed even better suited for the work than the Indian dogs.

The women decorated their sleds with a feminine touch. The Sunday of the race was perfect. A clear sky was with a new layer of snow. The sleds started from the Square. As the women had little experience with the sleds, the start was comical. A few of the men had gone ahead to the turning point about two miles up in the foothills and cheered them on at the turn. When they returned, most were covered with small pine branches from unplanned detours through the trees. Everyone had a grand time and the party continued until well past dark.

Because the weather was good on Christmas, everyone went to Québec for Christmas mass at the Cathedral. Jeanne* and François* hitched Henri to the cart to travel in style. A sudden cold spell had caused the ice to freeze early, and they had been able to cross the Saint-Laurent for over a week. After mass they encountered Madeleine de Roybon on the arm of LaSalle. Whereas most women wore deer or other functional skins for warmth, Madeleine sported a white ermine fur. She told Jeanne* she had "moved in" with LaSalle and provided the colony with a much-needed scandal.

Later they saw Lady Anne Gasnier who confirmed that Madeleine had moved out. "I was sorry as it reflected poorly on my oversight. However, I believe the arrangement has saved two other people," and they had a good laugh.

After mass they had been invited to Christmas dinner at the home of Pierre* Parent and Jeanne* Badeau-Parent. The large family gathering was like French Christmases of Jeanne*'s youth. The Parent family now had eight children, and the oldest, Marie*, was there with her new husband, David Corbin, a butcher from the Languedoc region of France. After they returned home, Jeanne* and François* exchanged gifts. He gave her an Indian knife such as the one Philippe used. He told her she should carry it under her clothes when she went out. Always the pioneer spirit, Jeanne* would not have been as happy with a diamond.

Her gift to François* was a child's reading primer, and that night by the light of the oil lamp, they began his lessons. François* showed himself to be a capable student and advanced quickly. Jeanne* was also a fine teacher and, understanding Frenchmen, rewarded him each night he did well with extra-special marital exuberance.

One morning at the end of December, Philippe came to the barn for chores without Marie, "She was busy last night and will not be here until later," he said. Jeanne* realized what this meant and raced to the Indian camp where she found Marie nursing the newest member of the family.

Marie, now a mother at just seventeen, said, "Although it is not the Indian custom to repeat names, we have decided to call him Henri. I hope he will be as fine and strong a man as his grandfather." Laughing, she added, "I also hope he won't be confused with the horse."

True to Philippe's word, in the early afternoon Marie presented herself for chores. She had young Henri in a swaddled garment and harness that attached him to her front where he would remain warm and could be nursed without greatly interfering with her chores. Jeanne* realized this would be a difficult feat to follow.

But follow it she would. In the beginning of February, Jeanne* began to fall ill each morning. When she asked her mid-wife friend, Marie* Renaud, what she should do, her friend laughed, "Wait a while, silly. This means you are pregnant." Realizing her nightly activities had been rewarded, Jeanne* rushed home to tell François*.

Chapter 22

Charlesbourg, Québec - Spring 1672:

Winter passed, and before Jeanne* began to show her pregnancy, spring arrived with a vengeance. The ice broke melting faster than anyone could remember. Although this did not affect Charlesbourg, the lower areas close to the rivers flooded. As most of the houses were built high off the ground, there was not a great deal of damage, but many food stores were lost and some animals drowned.

As always, the colonists banded together to help those in need. It was during this time that François* had his best idea since Calvados. After mass in early spring, he asked Father Mathieu to ask the congregation to stay for a short meeting. The usually shy François* arose to speak, "I have been thinking as we join together for various activities such as house and barn building and the slaughter of the hogs, perhaps we could begin to do this during the busy periods of crop farming.

"In the periods of planting and harvesting, instead of working alone for weeks on each task, we could pool our efforts and do one farm at a time. The arrangement of the farms in Charlesbourg is ideal for this." There was a good deal of agreement and the farmers decided to give it a try. It was here that the concept of co-operative farming, which would last for the next two centuries, was born.

There were some difficulties at first, but by the end of the planting season, things ran rather smoothly. Each farmer would bring what was required. Henri the horse became a fixture each day. The men would divide the labor so things moved very quickly. Some of the women and older children helped, but the older women and those very pregnant or with very young children remained by the house where they would prepare meals and care for the young children. The best part was the socialization, which was now almost daily instead of weekly.

As the first boat of summer arrived in the harbors of France and Québec, two letters crossed in the Allard household.

Charlesbourg, Québec
June 1, 1672
Cher André,

It would take an entire year to tell you all the exciting things that have happened to me since we parted in Dieppe. I must begin by telling you that this is indeed my old and recurring dream of the woods; and that there can be no doubt that this is my true destiny, ordained by God.

The voyage from France was filled with excitement and also some danger. Sister Anne and the filles du roi formed great bonds and we learned a great deal from one another. Many of the girls are now married and are now my neighbors, including Catherine* Gateau from Saint-Sulpice.

Québec is the most marvelous and wonderful place on Earth. I cannot see how heaven could be better. It is a savage land, but clean and grand and without bounds. The winters are indeed harsh, but the people have learned how to abide in them, and both the people and the winters are more marvelous than I could ever have conceived.

I am married to the most wonderful man. François* Allard is sensitive, strong and intelligent. His presence alone makes me secure in this wonderful land. He loves me as I love him. I could never have found a more suitable mate. We expect our first child in the autumn. I rather wish for a son; however women have a place here not found in France. We are valued and respected, and our opinions carry as much weight as those of the men. So a daughter would also be welcomed.

We have a grand farm which grows every day. The taxes are small and our independence is great. It is no different than if we were the lords of the manor. Our town of Charlesbourg is constructed like a pie with all the homes at the center. This insures security and a level of socialization not found in France. Our chapel of Saint-Charles de Brommée is in the square directly across from the house and your friend Father Mathieu is our priest. The neighbors are as charitable as one could imagine and everyone here is treated as an equal regardless of class or station. The finest people in the colony attended our wedding.

We have an Indian family that lives on our farm. We work side by side as if we were indeed family. They are fine Christian people but nothing like I had anticipated. Their ways are different but also wonderful. We have learned much from them as how to survive in this grand new land.

Tell mother and father and the rest of the family that I am well and happier than I could have ever expected. I think of you all daily and send you all my affection.

Love, Your Pioneer Sister,
Jeanne* Anguille-Allard

When Jeanne* brought her letter to be sent on the boat to France she was surprised to be presented with another in return.

Blacqueville, Normandie, France
March 25, 1672

Cher François*,

The curé is aiding me with this sad letter. I regret to tell you that our dear sister, Marie, died in childbirth this winter. Her family, my family and father all share your grief. Her young son, your namesake, is prospering and we hope that his father can find another mother for him. The village remains unchanged, and crops have been favorable. Your boyhood friend Pierre sends his greetings and condolences.

Your loving brother,
Jacques Allard

A long hot summer set in on Québec and Jeanne quickly learned the ways of the Québécois farm. The crops were planted and the community continued to grow with births and marriages. In addition to the births of livestock, the Allard farm grew with the arrival of two pigs, chickens, a cow and a bull as part of the King's gift to Jeanne* in reward for her marriage.

The Sunday picnics continued as always. Jeanne* began to show her pregnancy but continued to work along with the others as a good pioneer wife. At the height of the harvest, as the community worked at the Bergevin farm, she announced she believed her time had come. Fortunately her mid-wife neighbor, Marie* Renaud, was present and accompanied Jeanne* home.

Later in the day, some of the neighbors gathered in the Allard yard to await news. Marie* Renaud appeared from inside the house and informed François* the first native Québécois Allard, a healthy son, had been born without difficulty. As the neighbors congratulated the excited new father, they inquired about a name. The French tradition was to give the name of the father or one of the grandfathers, but François* said, "I will ask my wife, but I believe I know what it will be and not François, Jacques or Michel."

Two days later on September 12, 1672, André Allard was baptized in the Cathedral of Québec. Pierre* Parent and Jeanne* Badeau-Parent served as Godparents. The following day, André's mother appeared for duty at the harvest at the Bedard farm with young André swaddled and attached to Jeanne* with an Indian harness.

Jeanne* and François* continued with their energy to produce a family and Jean- François Allard, named for his two parents, was born July 31, 1674. This event was overshadowed by the incredible birth in the Parent household, Jeanne* Badeau-Parent gave birth to triplets which was rare enough but for the first time in anyone's memory they all were born healthy; and the identical brothers, Joseph, Jean, and Etienne Parent prospered.

The community continued to grow as Thomas* Pageot, a tailor from the Perche region of France, began a farm next to the Allards. He had worked for some years for the Jesuits but now wished to try his hand at farming, while maintaining a shop below the farmhouse. He soon found a wife in Catherine* Roy, a 16 year old Québec native born to parents who had come from Larochelle in 1650. The Allard and Pageot families were destined to form a long and close relationship.

After attending a mass in Québec that summer, Jeanne* and François* encountered Madeleine de Roybon again dressed in elegance with just the correct touch of scandal. She informed them she continued to live with LaSalle in a grand house he had built in the upper town. "He is now gone for the season. Talon has been recalled to France and replaced by a new Governor named Frontenac. He has sent LaSalle to build a fort on the great lake of the Ontario. I shall have the entire season to provide the ladies with gossip."

Madeleine continued, "I am told Talon had decided the colony has enough women to sustain itself and had asked the King to end the *Filles du Roi* program. It would appear we are now a disappearing group, Jeanne*. In addition I am told we may expect great things from Comte de Frontenac as he favors a more independent colony.

LaSalle says he believes more exploration and new frontier towns are in the future."

Charlesbourg, Québec - Winter 1676:

The extended family was to grow this winter. Soon after Christmas, Marie gave birth to a second son whom she named Joseph, and on February 22, 1676 Jeanne* gave birth to her third son. This time a name was chosen to remember the voyage from France and he was baptized Jean-Baptiste* Allard. This lad seemed larger and stronger than his two older brothers had been at birth. He reminded Jeanne* a great deal of his father. Little did she know as she sat and rocked her newborn son as one of the worst blizzards of the century raged outside the farmhouse, he would some day save the future of her family as well as the town of Charlesbourg.

TO BE CONTINUED

EPILOGUE

This story is and will continue to be based on the lives of my mother's Allard ancestors. The dates and places of birth, marriage, death, immigration, residency and occupation are as found in the wonderfully complete archives of Québec, as well as the archives of France and many other respected references. With few exceptions each person noted by first and last name, ancestors and others were real people. The time and place of events is probable, although some events, such as some Indian encounters, have been added. For example, every detail about Guillaume* Renaud: immigration, military duty and his subsequent life are accurately documented in the archives, etc.

The story is written to fit the facts as known. The facts have not been altered for the story unless noted specifically. Most events, the voyages to Canada, the Indian encounters, the Indian raids, the markets, *rendez-vous,* etc. are from historical depictions and occurred to pioneers of the time. Many of them have been documented as happening to one of our various ancestors although not always necessarily the Allards.

This being said, it is primarily a story, not an academic work. Do not quote it in your term paper without checking the facts.

<u>Life in Québec and France:</u> My primary goal was and will continue to be to give an accurate history to the lives and times of our ancestors.

Jeanne d'Arc: It is difficult not to use the heroine and now Patron Saint of France as a thread of the story. All references to her are accurate. Rouen, Artannes-sur Indres, and St. Clair Shores all have strong associations with her.

Jean* Allard from 1431: I have no documentation of him. However the Allards did live around Rouen at the time of the execution of Jeanne d'Arc, and François*'s father, Jacques*, as well as his grandfather, another François* born about 1550, were both shoemakers in Blacqueville.

André Anguille: Although not a documented person, the Abbey in Artannes was a large enterprise, so it is quite possible the second son of a local bourgeois family would have been a priest.

Jeanne* and François*: The description of François*'s life before immigration is probable. He would have likely been recruited in Rouen as no other person ever immigrated from Blacqueville. He did work his entire three years with the Widow Anne* Ardouin-Badeau who had one of the best farms of the time. The details of her and her entire family are accurate. She also remained a supporter of François* until her death. The fact that Pierre* Parent and Jeanne* Badeau-Parent were the godparents of André Allard indicates a close relationship and a high regard for Jeanne* and François*.

François* was able to buy Michaud's farm soon after his three indentured years, indicating a source of funds and support that he probably could not have brought from France (possibly from Calvados?). His relationship with some of the Québec notables is documented. The very influential early settler, Noel* Langlois and his wife

Helene* Desportes, played an influential part in François*'s early days in Québec.

The marriage would seem to have been arranged. Jeanne* came from a family wealthy enough to supply a sizable dowry, and she did stay under the protection of Lady Anne Gasnier until the wedding which was attended by a number of Québec notables. Jean* Bergevin was an Allard neighbor and the gardener of the famous flower gardens of Lady Anne. Lady Anne did escort girls from France after the death of her husband.

The Indians: All stories now and into the future of the Indians are adapted from historical accounts. The good relationship and the nature of the Algonquin, Christian or not, the Iroquois raids, hunting, fishing and *rendez-vous* are taken from actual accounts. Many farms had Indian families such as Henri's. The relationship was often as described. As these were poorly documented in terms of identity, I was forced to be liberal in my invention of Henri.

Marguerite Bourgeoys: Canonized in 1982, she was a very real person. She devoted her life to the women of Canada and was a principle force behind the *Fille du Roi* program. It is said that she was a force to be reckoned with and backed down from no one. I have exaggerated her relationship with the Allards, but there is nothing here that may not have possibly occurred.

Madeleine de Roybon: This wonderful character is also accurate. A child of privilege she was sent to the colonies and did come at the same time as Jeanne*. She provided scandal to the colonies and did become the longtime mistress of LaSalle. Although I exaggerated her relation with Jeanne*, everything here could have occurred.

Jeanne* meets the King of France: French-Canadian history is filled with episodes of various *fille du Roi* meeting Louis XIV. There are even paintings of such events. One hangs in Versailles. Whether or not this meeting actually occurred is not truly known.

Les Filles du Roi: Translated as "the Kings girls" the term is anachronistic. It actually referred to orphaned girls in the care of the state at this time. It has, however, become the common term used in the last century or so. The girls were actually called *Filles de Marier:* meaning girls ready for marriage. However, this is rarely used in current writing and it would be a shame not to use the wonderful term *Filles du Roi.*

The documentation of these girls is meticulous and complete. It remains the best record of any segment of western civilization existing intact from the seventeenth century. I have tried to be entirely faithful to these records.

The voyages from France: These events are accurately depicted from actual records. The ships and captains are real. The passengers are accurate to the time of their immigration, i.e. François*, Renaud, Poitevin, Mathurine* Gouard, and Marguerite Bourgeoys all crossed at about the same time, very possibly on the same boat.

The description of the accommodations is accurate; and diseases, storms, pirates, and the stop at the islands of the Saint-Laurent were all common and occurred on many voyages. The privateer, François Guyon, was real and the son of our ancestor, the early immigrant Jean* Guyon.

The wampum and the medallion: These are my invention and a vehicle for the story. Such items were relatively common.

Calvados: Distilling spirits was very popular, and the government tried very hard to control it with little success. François*'s contribution has been exaggerated.

Feudal System: A seignurial system did exist, and the settlers, with few exceptions, did not outright own the land. However, unlike France, the control was weak and often non-existent. Total ownership did not occur until after the British takeover in 1760, but at that time the seignurial system was so minimal it changed little.

Towns of France and Québec: Depictions of all are accurate. Today Blacqueville and Artannes-sur-Indres have changed little. The mill, church and abbey stand in Artannes just as they did the day Jeanne* departed. Old Rouen has been accurately restored after WWII. The view from the cemetery at Saint-Maclou where both Jeanne* and François* stood is exactly the same today. The only things visible even today are the cemetery, charnel house and the towers of the Cathedral and Saint-Maclou on opposing sides.

Today Montréal and Québec are modern cities, but the old sections have been preserved. Beauport is a suburb with some industry, but the center old Charlesbourg is preserved. The church of Saint-Charles de Brommée and the cemetery remain, and some of the old houses on the square including that of Isaac*Bedard and George Allard, son of Jeanne* and François*, remain today.

Farming is no longer active, and the fields remain meadows up to the Laurentian Mountains.

The Harbors of Dieppe and Larochelle: Today these are still built with granite stones from seventeenth century Québec.

The Festival of the Ice-breaking: This is still held annually in Québec.

Made in the USA
Columbia, SC
01 December 2018